Lee Crompton was born in B
1973 but has lived the majority
of England in Dorset.

In his mid-teens, Lee worked
Chinese restaurants, moulded sausage meat around scotch eggs in a local factory and wrote depressing poetry. He left school in 1992 and worked as a quantity surveyor whilst studying part-time for his degree. In 1997 he became a Bachelor of Science and took up a full-time position as a surveyor in Salisbury working on various projects throughout the South of England.

Lee quit his job in 2003 to go travelling around the world. Starting in India, he journeyed through Asia, Australasia and the United States before eventually returning to the UK in 2004. Whilst in Wellington Lee was involved in the writing and production of a short film for the New Zealand 48-hour film festival. After publishing his first book, *12 Months*, his travels inspired his second novel, *Worlds Apart.*

Lee now lives in Scotland. In complete contrast to his previous work, he has recently released a thriller entitled *Digging Deeper*. He is currently working on a screenplay.

For further information visit:
www.leecrompton.com

Also by Lee Crompton

WORLDS APART

DIGGING DEEPER

12 MONTHS

Lee Crompton

LAUREN

MY FIRST NOVEL.

HOPE YOU ENJOY

L Crompton

This edition is published in the UK by Ascendere.

First published in the United States in 2005 by Lulu.

A catalogue record for this book is available from the British library.

Printed and bound in Great Britain.

To Whom It May Concern:

This book would have been much harder to complete if it wasn't for the support and encouragement of my family and friends. In particular, I'd like to thank those of you who believed in me even when I didn't believe in myself. You know who you are. My gratitude goes to the creative genius that is Enrique for designing the cover image even if ultimately ruining the book by taking the executive decision to use a picture of himself. Last but by no means least, I'd especially like to thank Gemma with a 'G' and Jemma with a 'J' for keeping their respective promises …

Chapter 1

'Atmosphere' – Russ Abbot.

I've always hated New Year's Eve. Even on the rare occasions when I've pulled, I just despise it. There's something overbearingly depressing about the whole thing. Maybe it's because you have to queue for an age to get a beer; possibly because I usually opt to 'celebrate' in the neighbouring town of Swanage involving standing around in the town square scantily clad in fancy dress freezing my bollocks off. Maybe it's because everyone is so annoyingly happy. Me? I'm never happy at this time of year. I torment myself, reflecting on the past, worrying about the future and becoming utterly, some might say inconsolably, miserable.

1999 was no exception. I was resigned to spending the night on my own having split from my long-term girlfriend the previous day. It would have been the ideal opportunity to catch up with old friends if they hadn't all but fallen by the wayside whilst I'd been going out with Rebecca. She couldn't stand the majority of my mates; our social life therefore revolved around *her* friends. With recent events fresh in their minds I guessed the majority of *them* were unlikely to welcome me with open arms. Looking back, I realise I should have kept my own acquaintances. I'd been spineless. By neglecting them, I avoided confrontation with Rebecca. Whatever, these were still *my* friends. They'd be there for me in desperate times. When the chips were down I could count on them.

'What the fuck do you want?' grumbled Alan down the phone. Unfortunately for me, Alan was one of my more subtle mates. 'That silly cow finally seen sense and kicked you into touch?' he griped. Technically, she hadn't but this wasn't the time to discuss the matter, particularly not with him.

As the months had gone by I guess I'd become increasingly pissed off with towing the line. Being spineless, I hadn't said anything. For her part, she was unaware I'd become disgruntled with everything revolving around what she, or more precisely, what her mother wanted. Scorn was poured on the idea I might actually want to see my own parents on Christmas Day. Christmas Eve was spent at her parents. Christmas morning was spent at her parents. The afternoon involved dinner at her grandparents, and the evening consisted of a buffet at her Aunt's. It didn't stop there. An all day affair had been organised at her other grandparents' house for Boxing Day followed by various soirées with *her* friends leading up to New Year. I realised I was losing control of my life. No, I had lost control a long time ago. I decided enough was enough. I quit. It was over. It took Rebecca rather longer to appreciate I was being deadly serious.

After my brief and fruitless discussion with Alan, I decided against contacting the less delicate character of Jimmy. My ego was fragile enough without taking an earbashing from him. I was sure however, that Ellie, my long-term friend from school, would be more sympathetic. I hadn't seen her for ages either, but we had always managed to pick up where we'd left off. It didn't matter how long the period of isolation had been, we'd end up meeting for a drink as if we'd only seen each other yesterday. It had proven more difficult to meet on a regular basis since she'd moved to London to further her nursing career in any case, especially now she was dating my friend and ex-work colleague, Bob. Bob and I had worked together in Bournemouth and having been introduced to Ellie via yours truly he'd decided to move to London to be with her. They lived in separate pads. Bob lived alone whilst Ellie shared an all female house with four other nurses and a journalist. When I tried to ring Ellie, it was the lovely Mel, the journalist, who answered.

'Oh, hi Connor,' she purred, 'you after Ellie?' If the creamy froth on top of a perfectly poured pint of Guinness could be transposed into a sound, Mel's voice would be it.

'Yes, is she there?' I asked.

'No, 'fraid not, she's gone up to Edinburgh for the New Year with Bob. You got any party plans?'

'Errm,' I stuttered, desperately trying to think of something to say which might save me looking a complete arse.

'Connor, you're terrible,' she laughed. 'It's New Year's Eve for heaven's sake.' I kept the rest of the conversation as brief as possible. Hopefully without appearing rude, I hung up. I comforted myself by concluding that in my fragile emotional state, it was best I spend the night on my own. I didn't fancy having to give a blow-by-blow account of what had happened to anyone or try and explain where it had all gone wrong. No, tonight I was resigned to the company of me, myself and I. Just then my Dad rang,

'You don't want to be sat indoors feeling sorry for yourself son. Get out there and enjoy life. Get your arse down to *The Empire*,' he told me. 'There's bound to be someone there you know.'

I'm not sure whether it's just me but I always feel my parents, particularly my father, know best. Against my better judgement I went, hoping to bump into someone I could latch on to.

I felt awkward from the moment I stepped into the club. Although I had made the effort and was wearing my best clobber, I just didn't feel comfortable. I couldn't even settle myself down with a drink as I was driving. Self conscious at the best of times, I assumed everyone would look at me if I danced on my own, so I paced around the club for what seemed like hours. Intermittently, I'd hang over a balcony or lean against a pillar, pretending to be waiting for someone. The hiss of the dry ice machine caught my attention and I turned to see a familiar face. A very familiar face in fact. It was mine. I'd caught a glimpse of myself in one of the mirrored panels on the wall. I wondered if I *did* actually look as completely and utterly bored as the mirror suggested. In my defence, I could see no reason to be happy. There is only a certain length of time anyone can listen to a succession of party songs before wrist slitting is the only feasible option. *Agadoo?* I felt distinctly more *Agadon't.* I was neither in the mood to shake any trees or grind coffee. I was losing the will to live.

To cheer myself up I resolved to do something crazy, wild and reckless. I marched to the bar and after much pushing and shoving I emerged from the scrum clutching a pint of lager shandy. Was this what my life had come to? Before I could depress myself too much by concluding that the answer was actually 'yes', I was tapped on the shoulder.

'Hello me ol' mate, how's tricks?' It was Jason Withers, a guy I'd known from my student days. We'd worked together on the bakery counter at the local supermarket. Our attempts to entice potential customers with our cheeky banter and boyish charm had hidden the angst between us. I had tried my best to be accepted. He just took the piss. The evening shift was a much better prospect. The supermarket shut its doors to the public and I'd quite often abandon my cleaning duties to sneak into the cream room, where all the cake decorations were kept. It was always a good skive and I enjoyed helping myself to the chocolate chips and glacé cherries (although I was never overly keen on the latter), away from the prying eyes of the management and Rachel Summers. Rachel worked on the deli counter, adjacent to the bakery and although quite a bit older than me (she was 26 to my mere 18 years) she seemed to have a fascination for younger lads, especially when they were on their own. I'd got wise to this though, always alert for the sound of her high heels clicking on the tiled floor. Whenever I was in the cream room and heard her footsteps I'd duck behind the preparation table to avoid detection. Occasionally however, when I'd been too busy stuffing my face, she'd caught me off guard. The room itself was very small with only one door. She'd forced me back against the boxes of marzipan on more than one occasion. It's debatable whether I'd count this as a perk of the job. She wasn't unattractive, far from it. At that stage in my life however, simply the fact she was very forward and a fair bit older was enough to scare the crap out of me. It was probably my fear that made me so appealing to her. Following one of these close encounters, Jason had given me my first cigarette, suggesting it would help me 'chill out'. I remember the cheery yet sneering look on the others' faces as I proceeded to be sick in the cardboard skip in the backyard. After a few weeks of determined perseverance however, I got used to it and have smoked from that day to this. I could argue that all the phlegm, the coughing, the wheezing when I play football and the fact I've spent thousands of pounds on something which is inevitably going to kill me is all thanks to Jason. What price we pay, striving to be accepted into the 'in' crowd, free from isolation and ridicule. In reality, I got the piss ripped out of me even more.

Seeing Jason again brought it all flooding back. He hadn't changed one bit. He hardly looked any older, probably through lack of stress. He'd never given a fuck about anything whilst I'd turned worrying into an art form. Being in his presence still made me feel about two feet tall. I knew it was only going to be a matter of time before he said something to put me on the back foot.

'Bloody hell Connie.' He thought 'Connie' sounded much more effeminate than 'Connor' and was therefore his attempt at a putdown. 'You've put some weight on me ol' son,' he scoffed.

'Well, umm, thank you.' I realised my experience of life since my student days hadn't made me any better at quipping back at him.

'So,' he retorted. He looked suspiciously to his left and right before leaning towards me as if to confide his deepest, darkest secret. 'Who you knobbin' tonight then?' Why I didn't respond with some laddish remark, making me sound like some raging Casanova on Viagra, I don't know. It was as if someone had spiked my shandy with a truth drug.

'Errm, I'm not actually knobbing anyone at present. I've, umm, just split up with my girlfriend.'

It was no surprise that instead of lending me a comforting ear, he flashed me a look of absolute disgust. I was pathetic.

'So who you up here with then?' he said, in an attempt to move the conversation on as quickly as possible.

'Well, you know, the usual.' I was aware my face was not conveying the same message as my mouth. 'Actually, no one, I'm here on my own.'

It was at this point he realised talking to me for a moment longer might dent his impeccable street cred. His nose scrunched up as though I'd just given off a nasty smell and he began to shake his head with dismay. 'Yeah well, you … just …' and that was that. He turned and vanished into the crowd.

I didn't see anyone else I knew all night. I waited until *Auld Lang Syne* was played and wished myself the best of luck for the forthcoming year. Sick to the back teeth of seeing people enjoying themselves, I slipped unnoticed out of the club. Oh yes, when times are hard it's much better to go out and enjoy yourself than wallow in self-pity and depress yourself further. Thanks for the advice Dad.

I drove home, at least thankful I didn't have to wait around in the pouring rain for a taxi. I began to wonder what Rebecca was doing. Had she gone out? Maybe she'd stayed in, crying into her pillow. No, she'd have definitely gone out, probably with her brother and all his friends. Was she still dancing the night away? I peered down at the clock in the car. It was only 12.30am. I decided to go to the all-night burger van for a bag of chips. I mean, I was young free and single now. I didn't want to be outdone in the 'staying out all night stakes' by my ex-girlfriend. I drove down by the pier and proceeded to eat my chips very slowly, checking my watch to see how late it was getting. A mixture of boredom and cold and the novelty soon wore off. Who really cared who stayed out later than whom? She wouldn't know what time I'd retired to bed in any case. The car windows had steamed up with the heat from the chips. I wiped the inside to look out over the sea. Instead, I noticed the car park seemed remarkably full for the time of morning. Couples intent on testing their suspension were obviously enjoying chips too, their windows equally steamed up. Maybe Becci was one of the shadowy figures, bobbing up and down behind the veil of condensation. The thought made me feel queasy. It was time to leave.

The flashing green light on the answering machine alerted me to my messages as I walked in the door. This was it; she'd had a shit time too. I pressed play, a smug grin on my face, and waited in anticipation.

'Errm, hi Con, it's Mum. Just thought I'd ring and wish you a happy New Year.'

'Who's she talking to?' I could faintly hear my Nan say in the background.

'Hope you had a good night,' Mum continued, 'and errm, we'll speak to you when we get back, bye.'

The following beep signalled the end of my messages. My

heart sank. Just one? I dialled 1471 and recognised the number as my Mum's mobile. She'd rung at just gone twelve.

My mind began to race again. What could Rebecca be doing? Maybe she was still out? I had visions of her with somebody else and felt my greasy chips heave in my stomach. I headed for bed wondering if I would ever see or hear from her again. I was being ridiculous. I mean it had been me doing the dumping. I should be happy. Young free and single once again. I'd been the one to kick her into touch. So why did I feel like shit? I felt guilty I guess. There had been nothing fundamentally wrong with the relationship. It wasn't even as if either of us had cheated on the other. I'd got fed up being brain washed by the whole long-term relationship thing. It just seemed such a waste but I'd come this far, I couldn't give it one last go and risk going through all this again, could I? As I flicked the bedside lamp off my senses intensified. There was a faint aroma of perfume from the pillow next to me. I slung it out of the bedroom door, turned over and went to sleep.

Chapter 2

During the 'break up' process I reinforced my resolve by imagining the freedom that would prevail once the dust had finally settled. I would be a law unto myself, answerable to nobody. I could sleep, eat and fart when I liked and play *my* music when *I* wanted at whatever volume I saw fit. Most importantly, I could play video games for as long as I liked without having to break concentration to sound interested in Rebecca's day at work. There would be nobody else in the house demanding to watch *Coronation Street* when I was on the verge of beating Germany 2-1. It would be absolute heaven.

Three nights of solid PlayStation and the novelty had worn off. My perceived freedom rapidly transformed into the reality of boredom. The envisaged perks of single life were no longer so attractive. Nothing appealed to me. Although I'd made my decision and didn't want Rebecca to phone, there was something upsetting about the fact she hadn't. This just depressed me further. On a good day I could just about manage to switch on the TV, lie on the sofa and eat something unhealthy. Otherwise just lying on the sofa was pretty much as good as it got, watching the sun's rays creep slowly across the carpet until they eventually disappeared, leaving the room in darkness.

It's strange how having too much time on your hands can flip your mind into overdrive. True enough, even at the best of times I've always been one to think about things in too much detail but when your life is seemingly one big fuck up, it becomes worse still. Tinges of guilt occasionally intermingled with my deluge of maudlin thoughts as I contemplated all the things I should have been doing instead of sitting on my arse feeling sorry for myself. On rare occasions, I would conjure up enough will power to do 'something' but whatever it was ended up being shoddily done or left incomplete as I continued to daydream my life away. Anything I attempted was affected by my constant faffing about, whether it be washing up, hoovering or even driving the car which I happened to be doing on the morning I picked my parents up on the way to my graduation. I'd had my degree results the previous summer but for some reason the university always held the graduation ceremonies the following January. It was during this particularly boring car journey I found myself asking some fundamental questions. Do we make our own destiny or has fate already chartered our lives for us? Would Rebecca and I get back together? Did I want us to get back together? Would I meet someone else? Would she meet someone else? Where would my life be in twelve months' time? Did the fact the tarot cards Rebecca read for me just before we split up (I'd bought her a deck for Christmas) stating a long-term relationship was about to blow up in my face, subconsciously act as a catalyst to our demise? We had tried to ensure it didn't. When the cards had forecast an unsettled future, we poo-pooed the hocus-pocus and dealt the cards again. Once more the cards suggested the shit was going to hit the fan. A week later it did.

Other questions clearly needed to be answered. Where would I go now that I had no girlfriend and unreceptive mates? How the hell was I going to survive on my own cooking for the foreseeable future? Why was my car radio tuned to a local tin pot radio station I never normally listened to? Once again, fate had dealt me a crappy hand.

'This is a message for Connor McGrath from Rebecca Harvey.'

The shock of hearing my name on the radio made me swerve across a lane of traffic and clip two road cones on the hard shoulder. My mind went fuzzy. I vaguely remember the DJ saying something along the lines that she loved me lots, wanted us to get back together and was sorry for everything that had happened. He cheekily remarked on the situation and proceeded to have a bloody good laugh about it. I hated him for a full two minutes. How dare he treat our misfortune with such frivolity in the name of entertainment. The finger of blame soon pointed at Rebecca. It was all her bloody fault. If she hadn't rung the stupid station in the first place this poor excuse for a DJ wouldn't have had the opportunity to joke about it. My mobile phone rang.

'Hello?' I answered cautiously. Having originally bought it as a Christmas present for Rebecca, I'd never taken a call on it before. I'd intended paying her line rental. Once we'd split up she'd asked if I was still going to honour the direct debits whilst she kept the phone. I said something along the lines of 'you must be fucking joking' and she therefore decided she didn't want it. Having signed the twelve-month agreement with the phone company, I was lumbered.

'Hi sweetie, it's only me.' It was Rebecca. She sounded in a particularly good mood.

'Hello,' I repeated. I thought duplicating my initial greeting might give me time to think of something else to say.

'What radio station are you listening to?'

'Errm, Seashore FM or whatever it's …'

'Cool.' Cool? She never used the word 'cool'. I didn't have the heart to tell her 'cool' had gone out of fashion quite some time ago. At least I thought it had. Not having ever described myself as 'down with the kids', what the hell did I know. I'd thought I looked 'cool' at school because my Mum had said so.

Looking back now my mates must have been pissing themselves as I lumbered out to games lessons in my Hi-Tec trainers and bright red towelling tracksuit. I might therefore have been doing Rebecca an injustice with the 'cool' thing, but I was sure I was right. 'Well keep it on … you should hopefully get a little message soon, sweetie.'

'Is that in addition to the one a couple of minutes ago?' Silence.

'What … you mean they've already played it?'

'Well unless another Rebecca Harvey and Connor McGrath are having relationship problems, I would imagine the answer is yes.'

'Oh.' She sounded disappointed I'd heard the message before she'd had the chance to tell me to listen out for it. 'Well what did they say?'

'Errm, I don't really know.'

'You don't … what do you mean you don't really know? I take the trouble of ringing in and asking them to play you a dedication …' her tone had altered radically.

'Well,' I interrupted, 'it was all a bit of a shock really.'

'…telling you how much I love you and you can't even remember what they said.'

'Hang on, if it wasn't for the sheer fluke I happened to be listening to the crappy station in the first place I'd have missed it anyway.' My mind backtracked 'Dedication? What dedication?'

'I asked them to play a song for you and wish you all the best for your graduation.'

'Well I didn't hear any dedication. What was it supposed to be?' The line went crackly. 'Hello?' A constant dull tone signalled we'd been cut off. I was left wondering what song Rebecca had requested. Something puke inducingly sentimental I expect.

My bemused mood continued until I reached my parents' house. They were clearly brimming with pride as we began our two-hour journey to the capital or more precisely, the church opposite my old university where the ceremony was being held.

We arrived in plenty of time, which was unlike me but lucky all the same. I hadn't appreciated the time required to queue, pick up robes, join more queues, have photos taken, interspersed with making polite conversation to people I really couldn't stand. That, I hasten to say wasn't the case when I met Bob. Bob and I had started to study together on a part-time day release basis when we'd worked for the same firm. When he moved to London and changed jobs to be closer to Ellie, it was pretty much the only opportunity we got to see each other. Ellie occasionally popped in to see us both, depending on her shifts. Again, this was the only time I got to see her. Rebecca hadn't encouraged me to see Ellie much. When we had been invited, Rebecca had never wanted to come with me (I think she was jealous of our close relationship) and going on my own to spend a weekend in a house packed with nubile young nurses, was, in her opinion, out of the question. On a handful of occasions I'd chanced my arm, gone up alone and stayed with Bob for the weekend. The grilling I'd received on my return just made it easier not to go. Bob was obviously besotted with Ellie and didn't come home much, so university was the only time I got to see either of them. Nonetheless, we made the most of what time we had. For some reason though, this occasion felt unnaturally awkward.

'So how have you been?' Bob asked.

'Not so bad.' I said, looking at my shoes. I glanced up to see him squinting at me, his head cocked to one side.

'Rebecca all right?'

I hesitated, only slightly, 'Yes, she's doing just fine.' Under normal circumstances I would have poured my heart out to poor Bob, but this didn't seem the time or the place to regurgitate recent shitty events. He looked as though he was going to say something and then stopped. The pause seemed to last an age.

'That's not strictly true is it?'

I blushed. 'What do you mean?'

'My parents heard the radio message this morning in the car. Nearly didn't get here in one piece.'

So the cat was well and truly out of the bag. Who else had overheard the circus that was my ex-love life? Fortunately I didn't have too long to worry about it at that stage. The majority of the graduation pre-requisites out of the way, my mind turned to the ceremony itself. My main concerns were whether I'd trip over my gown or fall off the stage when it was my turn to be called up. The radio episode paled into insignificance.

In reality I needn't have worried. The event went off without a hitch. Nobody fell off the stage although one girl cried. The whole thing was a long drawn out anti-climax if the truth be known. A couple of people made complete pricks of themselves by attempting some kind of post goal scoring celebration, sliding as far as they could on their knees or pulling their gowns over their heads and punching the air. I always see those sorts of people as arrogant tossers. Always blokes, and nearly always short arses. I expect they left the proceedings in their ridiculously souped-up Ford Escorts complete with spoilers, beeping their horns as they sped off. Whatever, I was officially a Bachelor of Science with honours, for what it was worth. After attending the buffet that followed, stuffing my face with numerous minuscule canapés (I was starving, I hadn't eaten all day) and posing for a few more of my parents' photos, I made our excuses, bid farewell to Bob and began the journey to my grandparents' house.

Chapter 3

'How soon is now?' - The Smiths.

My Nan and Grandad had been unable to attend the ceremony - the 'cup final' style ticket allocation only allowing two guest tickets - so we'd agreed to visit them after the proceedings. The afternoon consisted of drinking lots of tea while my Mother re-enacted every moment of the graduation. Her enthusiasm wasn't matched by that of my Grandparents. They seemed more intent on dwelling on the fact they'd known all along Rebecca and I were never going to last. This infuriated me for three reasons. Firstly, our relationship had lasted. I considered four years to be pretty good by anyone's standard. Secondly, they'd only met the girl once, which was hardly a firm basis for their conclusion. Lastly, if they'd been so cock sure we were doomed to failure, why didn't they mention it sooner? I mean it's all very well in hindsight, shaking your head knowingly and tutting. Mum could see my agitation and tried to change the subject. It didn't work.

Five cups of tea and a couple of trips to the toilet later and it was time to head home. The farewell was reassuringly familiar. An awkward kiss from Nan followed by a firm, manly handshake from Grandad.

'See ya kid,' he whispered, slipping twenty quid into my hand. 'Take care of yourself.' Not only was I grateful for the money I was also aware he'd remembered to omit the normally obligatory 'and give our love to Rebecca.' I now realised it would have been hypocritical in any case. It appeared they'd hated her guts.

Mum, Dad and I got into the car to make our way back to the South coast. I wound down the window to give the traditional final wave to Nan and Grandad who were now stood on the grassy bank in front on their bungalow. The smell of sugar beet I remembered as a kid wafted into the car. Mum asked me wind the window back up. I pretended I didn't hear. I was the only person who liked the smell, but then it reminded me of years gone by when my grandparents were more active and youthful. Playing football in the park, jumpers for goalposts, play fighting on the rec, sledging in the winter. I used to stay with them in the summer holidays and was allowed up well past my bedtime, playing cards for pennies. The drinking of alcohol was also tolerated. (I was particularly keen on sherry at that age I seem to recall). Everything took place on the firm understanding that word of our crazy rock and roll evenings never got back to my parents. I obliged of course.

Looking at them standing on the bank I realised that this, for me was a proper farewell. Quiet and understated, it was in stark contrast to the bollocks I'd had to put up with from Rebecca and her 'lah-di-dah' family. Hugs and kisses by the bucket load and the patronising waves from the doorstep of the Harvey residence were never my cup of tea. I could have lived with it every once in a while but we were subjected to this ingratiating treatment all the time, even if we were only popping to

Bournemouth to do a spot of shopping. 'Bye darlings, bye' her mother would shout, melodramatically waving. She knew full well we'd be back within a couple of hours for some lunch. Leaving and returning from holiday was even worse. I always needed the holiday just to get over the exhaustion of the farewell. Then when we returned there used to be cards and banners lining our entrance route. 'WELCOME HOME BECCI' (my name never seemed to figure) would be strung across the porch with ribbons and balloons in the hallway, not the mention the bombardment of more hugs and kisses. It was all more than slightly embarrassing. Well it was for me anyway. The Harveys seemed to lap it up. I'd have been OK with it if I'd thought it was genuine, but it wasn't. It was bollocks. They'd have big rows, occasionally involving physical fighting, always involving ample amounts of crying before making up again within a couple of hours. This involved more hugging and kissing (and usually more crying) before the next onslaught of theatrical crap. I'd never had, or indeed never wanted anything like that when I got home to my parents from holiday. Dad would always ask me the same questions.

'Did you have a good time?' … 'Did you have good weather?' … 'Did you get my fags and booze?' The answers were always pretty predictable too.

'Yes', 'Not bad,' and, 'Have I ever forgotten yet?' (Although I realise the last one is technically a question answering another question, you get the general idea). Apart from one year, on a crackly line from Greece when I'd misinterpreted my Dad's request for 'Bells' as 'Bols', the annual question and answer round worked very well. The bottle of Crème de Menthe in question still stands unopened in my parents' drinks cabinet to this day.

As we turned the corner at the bottom of the hill I lowered my hand from the window. The conversation on the way home was subdued until, having discussed the ironing Mum had to do when she got back and Saturday's football results, it took an ugly turn for the worse.

'Brenda asked how you were,' she stated.

'Did you tell her I was OK?' Dad chuckled, knowing very

well Mum had been talking to me. She just glared at him, you know, like women do.

'I bet she did, the nosey cow,' I whinged. I had never been keen on Mum's next-door neighbour.

'Don't be like that.' Mum snapped, her glare now aimed in my direction.

'So what did you tell her? Everything is fine except Rebecca has gone and I'm living on my own?' I broke into patronising laughter 'Oh yeah, oh, ho, I bet she loved that.'

'No, I said nothing of the sort.' Mum was on the defensive. 'I just told her you were fine and the house was coming together.'

'Oh,' I replied. It seemed a strange thing to say. I'd been living there 12 months. I would have hoped it was coming together by now.

'You must have said more than just that. You were out there for over half an hour.' Dad planted his tongue firmly in his cheek in case anyone was in any doubt he was trying to stir things up. He looked at me in the rear view mirror. 'I had to make out there was someone on the telephone for your Mum just to get her to come inside.'

'Well,' said Mum folding her arms, 'she was telling me about Stacey.'

'What about Stacey?'

'She's split up with Alex.'

Suddenly things were relatively interesting. Stacey, Brenda's daughter, had been – quite literally - the girl next door. She was three years younger than me and we'd had various comings together in the past. She'd sent me an anonymous valentine's card some years ago. When she eventually owned up to sending it, I told her I didn't think it was very funny, assuming the whole thing was a joke. She, to my delight, being a very attractive girl, confessed it hadn't been a joke. It never, however, got very much further than snogging in the bedroom. This was mainly because my 'helping Stacey with her homework' ploy was pretty transparent and her Mum put a stop to it. In her eyes there was an age gap. I was 18, Stacey was only 15 and although neither of us saw it as a problem, everybody else did. In hindsight I have no idea why we didn't tell her parents to stick it up their arse.

There were various brief liaisons afterwards but they had been unprompted and infrequent. We'd each had various relationships with other people and our 'single spells' had never coincided, until now.

Stacey was now twenty-one and from the glimpses I'd caught of her whilst visiting Mum and Dad, she was as attractive as she'd always been. The age gap was now immaterial. Mum's off-the-cuff remark made me wonder what would happen if we become reacquainted. I felt gentle stirrings of excitement in the pit of my stomach.

Chapter 4

By the time I'd dropped my parents off and got home it was late. The air was crisp and still. As I turned the key in the door and stepped inside, I shuddered, realising my lounge was no warmer than outside. I could see my breath. The flashing lights from the answer machine attempted to create a more welcoming atmosphere, the walls reflecting the intermittent green and red glow. I wasn't fooled. Closing the door behind me, I turned to flick the heating on. The sound of cracking plastic came from underfoot as I did so. I picked up whatever it was I had trodden on, along with a couple of items of post and made my way to the phone.

BEEEEP! 'Hi sweetie, it's only me. Just wanted you to know I've been thinking of you all day today and hoping all went well with your graduation. I'm so proud of you. Oh, and I hope you like the tape . . . give me a ring when you get it.'

As I looked down at my hand I realised the tape was the plastic thing I'd trodden on. I was mildly excited for a second or two. There were a few indie tracks around she knew I liked. I switched the light on. An elastic band attached a scrap of paper to the tape which simply read, 'I love you, yours always, Rebecca.' I removed the note to reveal the song title. I dropped the tape and stepped back as if it had been electrically charged. It was *My Heart Will Go On* by Celine Dion. Had this girl learnt nothing from our years together? It went straight in the bin. I decided not to ring her back, took the phone off the hook and went to bed.

I stared long and hard at the ceiling. What the hell was I doing? Not so long ago the demise of my relationship with Rebecca had consumed me with guilt and worry. Tonight, for some reason, I felt ready to move on. This immediately produced pangs of guilt. Was I ready to move on? Wasn't it normal to have a period of isolation or soul-searching? Even though I was officially the 'dumper', I wasn't a bastard. Look at the pain, anguish and guilt I was contending with. But I was sick of it. I had to stop feeling sorry for myself. It *was* time to move on.

A week later I decided, for better or worse, to call Stacey rather than Rebecca. The phone rang a couple of times. I bottled out and replaced the handset. I gave it a couple of minutes, mulled over what the hell I was going to say and then tried again. Brenda answered. Not a good start. Before I had time to gather my thoughts however, there was a rustling of the handset as Brenda passed Stacey the phone.

'Hello?'

'Stacey, it's Connor.'

'Oh hi! I was hoping you'd ring.'

This sounded promising. I embarked however on my usual trick of analysing every word in meticulous detail. 'Hoping' I would ring eh? Hmmm, intriguing. The inevitable small talk ensued. The longer the conversation lasted, the more pressured I felt to suggest we met up. I needn't have worried.

'We should go out some time, have a proper catch-up.'

'Yeah, that'd be nice.' I wasn't convinced she actually meant it, like those people you sometimes meet on holiday and swear you'll 'have to stay in touch'. You never do. No, she was probably just humouring me or being kind. Best I play this cool just on the off chance though. Nice and cool.

'Well, you know, just give me a ring if you're free some time.' My tone was unnaturally flippant. 'I'm sure you're very busy.' I banged the palm of my hand against my forehead. Busy? How the hell should I know whether she was busy? I was, as is traditional in these situations, making excuses before I even started. On the rare occasions I've plucked up the courage, my dreadful attempts to ask someone out are immediately followed by a string of reasons why it's probably not such a good idea. I reckon they're probably going to feel embarrassed and want to find an excuse anyway, so by giving them a list of suggestions any prolonged awkwardness as they fumble for one of their own is wholly eradicated.

'What are you doing tonight?' she asked.

Hang on. This isn't supposed to happen. Maybe things are better than I thought. Still, play it nice and cool, gently does it.

'Errm, nothing really. Why are you errm, free? Errm, not sort of doing …'

Note to self. Must brush up on my chatting up technique.

When talking to women for the first time, my confidence is so low, it makes me wonder how I've ever had a girlfriend. My half-arsed attempts to chat someone up, only then to offer a list of excuses as to why they're not interested, is hardly endearing. The (rare) alternative, as with Rachel in the supermarket, is that the initiative is taken by the other person. This only succeeds in putting me on the back foot, increasing my nervousness. I 'm fucked either way.

'We could go out for a drink if you like?' she said. Again, the rulebook appeared to have been thrown out of the window.

'Yeah, yeah, that's fine. Um, what time shall I pick you up?'

'Make it about 7.30. I've got to have a bath.' I felt those gentle stirrings in my stomach again.

'OK, I'll see you then.'

I attempted to tidy the house. My football socks and festering shirt from Sunday night finally made their way from the floor into the laundry basket. Tidying never has been my strong point. All I ever seem to do is move items from one place to another resulting in a mess in another part of the house. The more I looked around, the more I realised the enormity of the task ahead. I might only have been single for a short while but I had easily mastered the bachelor pad look. I must admit I had been genuinely surprised at the short time it had taken for mould to appear in the dregs of coffee. What was I bothering for, anyway? Firstly, the chances of Stacey wanting to come in for a coffee were very remote. Equally unlikely was the chance of me plucking up the courage to ask her back for a nightcap to start with. Compounding both these remote chances made for very long odds indeed.

I looked at my watch. Time was getting on. I drove down the road towards where I once lived, my parents' house now home to just my Mum, Dad and Nan. I had visions of one of them spotting me from the window. I panicked at the thought I might have to get out of the car to ring Stacey's doorbell only to find my Mum coming out of the house with a casserole dish filled with left over lamb hot pot for me to take home. Stacey, God love her, had however cottoned onto the fact this operation needed to be completed in one swift manoeuvre and had made her way down the front path even before I'd come to a complete stop. Eyes belonging to Stacey's younger sister popped up over the sill of an upstairs window. Realising I'd spotted her she crouched back down but I could still see the top of her head bobbing about. Stacey got into the car. I checked my mirrors and drove off. There was no sign of parental activity.

The smell of expensive perfume, Stacey's bright red lipstick and the low cut cream top she was wearing, thoroughly confused me, so much so I took a wrong turning to the pub. My lapse of concentration didn't seem to be a problem however. We had plenty to talk about and eventually came to another on the outskirts of town. I hadn't been in this particular bar for a while but the atmosphere was as relaxed as ever and there was plenty of room between the tables which is always a bonus. I'm always paranoid about people on the next table listening in on conversations. I'm really not that interesting. I'm sure people have much better things to do than listen to me wittering on about utter crap. No, my paranoia stems from the fact I can't help ear wigging on other people's natterings and then ripping the piss. If I am doing it to them I am positive there must be someone else doing it to me.

The only change since my last visit was the addition of a games' table. Here, you could help yourself to a crappy board game to play whilst having a pint. Curiously enough, loads of people were playing snakes and ladders and draughts and stuff. Stacey made some comment about how sad it was so I guessed a quick dabble at *Connect 4* was probably not on the evening's agenda. Instead, I did the decent thing and got the drinks in (Stacey was on the Vodka as usual) and we continued where we'd left off. We reminisced about the past, and she talked for a while about her disastrous relationship with Alex. Mum was right. It was all over. She knew nothing of my current situation of course as Mum hadn't said a word to Brenda. I was holding all the cards.

'So you've split up with Rebecca I hear.'

I spat my Kronenbourg back in the glass. 'Excuse me?' I wiped up the bits that had missed the glass with a nearby napkin. 'How, how do you know that?' She began to laugh.

'Well, I was in the kitchen with Mum early one morning, getting ready for work and she was making Dad's sandwiches and I heard this announcement …'

'On the radio,' we said in unison.

'We couldn't believe it.' Her laughter level increased as she continued with her story. 'We thought it couldn't have been you, but they mentioned your full name …we pissed ourselves laughing.'

Great! It appeared I'd been the source of everybody's amusement. How many more people had heard that early morning plea? Just as I thought the evening was taking a turn for the worse, Stacey calmed down.

'There is something good to come out of all this you know,' she said.

'And what's that?' I asked sheepishly.

She lowered her head and looked at me as though she was peering over a pair of imaginary glasses.

'We *are* both single,' she whispered.

'And that's …a good thing?'

'Well I think so, don't you?' she said. I raised my eyebrows and nodded, urging her to continue. 'I mean, we're not tied to anybody any more. We get on well together … well, we always used to. Why don't we just have a laugh? It could be just the two of us, messing about, doing what we want. Nothing serious. What do you say?' I must admit she sounded very positive about the whole thing and it seemed perfectly acceptable to me. The last thing I wanted was another relationship. This way I could hang out and go places with a beautiful woman, no strings attached.

By the time we'd left the pub we'd organised a trip to a football match as well as a cinema visit at the weekend. I liked the principle of what we were doing. It was almost like a demon-banishing exercise for both of us. Stacey was really excited about going to the football. Her ex-boyfriend Alex had never taken her. His argument was that girls shouldn't watch football because they didn't appreciate it. I was just as pleased to be going to a match with a girl. Rebecca hated football with a passion and because she didn't want to watch it, nobody else was allowed to watch it either. I always lost the arguments we had on the subject, the bottom line being that her Mum thought football was a 'silly game', so that was that. I could count on one hand the number of times I'd got away with watching *Match of the Day* during our four years together and when I demanded to watch the World Cup draw, she'd locked herself in the bedroom, sobbing uncontrollably, refusing to come out. It was the draw for Christ's sakes. Not one ball was due to be kicked.
As for my trip with Stacey to the cinema, we agreed to see *Titanic*. Strange choice you might think, but it turned out we'd both refused to watch such a load of unadulterated mainstream claptrap with our respective partners. Now we'd gone our separate ways there was a warped sense of rebellion about seeing it together.

So my weekend was sorted. I was to pick Stacey up from work at lunchtime on Saturday in time for the footy and then on Sunday we were off to the cinema. Just for the record, she did come back to mine for a coffee. Once again she took the initiative and invited herself back to see my house. We had a coffee, she commented on how tidy the place was (I think she was being sarcastic), and watched a bit of TV. After riffling through my CD rack and bookcase she helped herself to a couple of novels and asked to be dropped home. Apart from reading far too much into the fact she hadn't wanted to borrow any of my music, the evening had been a roaring success. Much more so than I had ever imagined. The only thing I had to do now was keep myself occupied the following Friday night, before seeing Stacey on Saturday. Once again, my answer machine's green flashing light had the errm, … answers.

'Connor, it's Bob. Sorry we didn't have much time to talk at the graduation. It was all a bit hectic really wasn't it? Look, me and the lads are going to a club opening tomorrow night down the town. Nothing too hectic, just a few jars and then watching the footy on Saturday. Just thought you could do with a bit of a session to catch up on the goss. Give us a call if you can make it, cheers.'

Chapter 5

'Elephant man' – Suede

Before receiving the message I'd have been more than happy, sad individual that I am, to wile away the time sat on my own playing on the PlayStation. I didn't feel in the mood to party and make small talk but Bob always had a knack of talking me into things I really wasn't that keen on, making me feel so guilty about not participating, I was obliged to join in.

Bournemouth had an away game against Brentford on the Saturday. Jimmy and Alan were trundling up for a Friday night out in London before watching the match the following day. They'd both actually been *my* friends from school but had got to know Bob during our various nights out together. More recently, whilst I'd been too busy concentrating on my blinkered relationship with Rebecca, Bob had stayed in touch with the pair of them. Following my less than friendly exchange with Alan on New Year's Eve, I was concerned as to how they were going to react. It was like I was crawling back after having cut them out of my life. Still, I had to start regenerating old friendships sooner or later.

Alan was a complete football anorak. He could tell who scored the winning goal for Arsenal to prevent Liverpool doing the double in 1989 or who the European player of the year was for, well, any year you care to think of. Other than that he pretty much kept himself to himself. If anything, he was usually on the end of the put downs, put downs normally fired by Jimmy. I was expecting a barrage of criticism and insults from Jimmy myself, now. I don't think he ever meant anything by what he said but it always seemed to come out as offensive, rude and arrogant. He was blunt and to the point and liked nothing more than when Alan got one of his football statistic stories ever so slightly wrong. Now I was back on the scene, I was sure his malicious digs would be firmly aimed in my direction. But I couldn't hide forever. I was sure I'd get into the swing of the 'lads' thing again and they'd soon forgive me for snubbing them for the last few years.

'Fuck me.' Jimmy opened Bob's front door and stared me up and down. 'Look who's crawled out the fucking woodwork.'

'Hello,' I said nervously.

Alan popped his head over Jimmy's shoulder. 'What the fuck do you want?' Maybe this wasn't such a good idea. I stood on the stone step beneath them not really knowing what to say, for what seemed an age. Bob eventually saved me from their sneering faces by calling us all inside. We made our way down the hall and into the lounge where the onslaught of verbal abuse from Alan and Jimmy continued.

'What the fuck have you done to your hair man?' This was clearly a rhetorical question but I nonetheless made an effort to answer.

'I've had …'

'You look like Arthur fucking Scargill,' Jimmy continued.

'No, he looks like Mrs Scargill. You look like a girl' Alan sniggered behind his hand like a small child. 'He does, doesn't he Jimmy?' It never took long for Alan to jump on the bandwagon if he thought it might deflect some of the piss taking from himself. He always seemed to be trying to gain acceptance. Some things never changed. Unfortunately Alan was missing the point on two counts. Firstly, to the rest of us his reactions just made him appear very insecure and secondly Jimmy couldn't give a monkey's uncle if Alan stripped naked and covered himself blue. He still wouldn't have thought any more of him. I don't believe Jimmy actually thought a lot of anybody. He continued his assault.

'Yeah, where did you get yer shirt, Dorothy Perkins?'

'Dorothy Perkins, yeah, nice one,' Alan echoed. Jimmy gave him a glance. Alan lowered his head as if bowing to a higher being. Normally I could handle the piss taking but on this occasion it was making me feel like a total outsider. I hadn't really wanted to come in the first place. It was going to be a long night.

'Oh give the man a beer and shut up for fuck's sake,' said Bob, passing Jimmy a can of Kronenbourg. Jimmy didn't even look at me as he swung the beer in my general direction. He and Alan continued to chat amongst themselves, taking the piss out of various people on the telly. I got the feeling neither of them would have noticed if I'd got up, walked out and driven home. Bob sat on the arm of the chair.

'Don't take any notice mate. They're not staying here tonight. Jimmy's arranged to go out with a couple of his mates in Camden and Alan is tagging along for good measure, obviously.' The beers suddenly seemed to go down more easily and before long Jimmy and Alan made a move for their evening appointment.

'You girls have a good night, yeah?' Jimmy said to Bob, 'and I'll see you tomorrow.' Bob nodded. Jimmy's attentions then turned to me. 'Not you, you homosexual. I hear you're doing a runner so we won't see you in the morning you big gay boy.' Alan laughed unconvincingly as they made their way to the door. I didn't say a word, considering it best I just bided my time until they'd actually left.

'Oh and one more thing before we go,' said Jimmy wagging his finger at me, 'Wherever you guys end up tonight, make sure you don't wear that fucking blouse. It makes you look like a nonce.' Bob bundled them out of the door, Alan now chuckling like a hyena.

'Yes thanks very much, do call again,' he said, shutting the door on both of them. He gave an exasperated sigh, 'Don't worry, they've been getting on my tits all night too.'

He returned to the sofa and cracked open a couple more beers. The lounge was an eclectic mix of tidiness and clutter. I sensed a conflict between Bob's bachelor lifestyle and Ellie's influences. The silver picture frames, the vase of flowers and wicker basket filled with pot pouri on the coffee table hadn't been of Bob's doing I guessed. I knew from experience Ellie was a stickler for neatness and order. Personally it would have done my head in but then I wasn't the one who had to put up with it.

'Where's Ellie tonight?' I asked.

'Funnily enough I think she's gone to Camden with some of the girls from the house. If they're really unlucky they should bump into Jimmy and Co.'

'Any new additions to the girly house?'

'Hundreds,' Bob replied. I looked at him curiously. 'Well no, none. It's just the same as normal but it always seems like hundreds. Everywhere you look, there they are.'

'Spend a lot of time there do you?' I asked.

'Huh,' Bob scoffed, 'what do you think? As much time as possible, wouldn't you? Wall to wall totty morning noon and night.' I knew he was building up his part. Bob was strictly a one-woman man but I was grateful for the mental picture he'd helped to create in my sordid little mind.

'So where we off to tonight?' I asked.

Poison must have been the tackiest nightclub I've ever had the pleasure to come across. It was great. The fact it was their opening night made it even better. I'd never been to the premier of anything before. In reality it just meant we had to queue longer to get in and stand for longer waiting to get served. When we eventually reached the bar, they'd run out of the majority of drinks. Luckily I was oblivious to these minor inconveniences, as I was three-sheets to the wind by the time we arrived. It's hard to describe the theme of the club. The dance floor looked like a scene from Indiana Jones. It was smoky, atmospheric and had a multitude of what could only be described as plastic snake lady statuettes everywhere, which in my book is a good thing. Judging by the scene from *Raiders of the Lost Ark* where Indy gets lowered into a snake pit surrounded with gargoyles and things, it would have been Indy's idea of hell.

'Snakes. Why did it have to be snakes?' Yeah, a bit like that but with dry ice and dodgy cocktails.

The atmosphere in the club was tremendous although the novelty would probably have worn off fairly quickly if I hadn't been pissed. Bob wasn't interested in making a move on any unsuspecting young female because of Ellie. I was well out of practice and lacked enthusiasm, or rather, confidence to approach anybody. Don't get me wrong, if you had plonked me in a room full of nurses at Ellie's house to circulate at my own speed I'd have been fine, but I really couldn't go through the motions of asking questions and pretending I was hearing the answers in a noisy nightclub. I dunno, what is it you do? Laugh every now and then? Smile in what you suspect are the right places, their voice inaudible above the thumping base? It suddenly occurred to me I'd never actually chatted anybody up. I usually got talking to someone in these sorts of situations because I'd trodden on their foot of or spilt something over them.

That night, however, I had no desire to go round deliberately treading on people purely as a conversation starter. As the evening wore on, drinks became increasingly thin on the ground. The thought of wasting what little we had by spilling it over other people didn't appeal. They'd run out of draft, bottles were ridiculously priced so we moved onto shorts only to find they'd run out of both coke and lemonade. We decided to turn this otherwise negative situation on its head by inventing the Worst Drinks in the World competition. Basically, this involved ordering the vilest drinks imaginable when it was your round and then watching the disgust on the other person's face when they attempted to drink it. I won with Tia Maria and bitter lemon. We left the club shortly after.

Anxious for a decent drink, we headed for a rather tacky snooker hall on the way back to Bob's. He warned me not to make eye contact with anyone once we'd gone in. We thought it best to just sit at the bar in complete silence and look at the floor. It's funny how sobering a feeling of anxiety and intimidation can be. Unfortunately it hadn't sobered me up quite enough to remember to turn my mobile off. The snooker hall came to a standstill as the muffled tone of the William Tell overture emanated from my jacket pocket. Feeling a sense of impending doom, I made a quick exit from the club. My disposition was only partly because I was hot footing it from an establishment where the majority of punters were armed with snooker cues, looking for any excuse to give someone a right good battering. It was more to do with my ring tone. I've never been someone to go in for weird and wonderful tunes on my phone. A phone is a phone. I don't wish to change the cover three times a day or have it smile at me each time I switch it on. I never really wanted the damn thing in the first place but now I was lumbered, I thought I'd make use of it, in case of an emergency or suchlike. The only good thing about a choice of ringtones is being able to programme different tunes for different callers, friend or foe. Without looking at the phone I could therefore tell whether it was someone I wanted to speak to. Unfortunately the William Tell overture signalled 'bad caller'. This normally meant it was someone from work but it was too late for them to call now. There was only one other possibility.

Chapter 6

'Hi sweetie, how are you getting on with my phone?' It was Rebecca.

'Umm, great, yeah, just great.'

'I just wondered if it was OK to pick some of my stuff up on Sunday morning.'

'I guess so, yeah I'll be in, that's fine.' Surely it wasn't going to be that simple?

'Well, I was thinking I could come round and we could have a bit of a chat about things.' No, this didn't sound like a full-scale decant operation at all. What exactly did a 'bit of a chat' entail? I had to think on my feet. The problem with meeting people on home turf is it marginalises the capacity to get rid of them.

I remember telling an ex once that I didn't think things were working between us. When you're blowing someone out, there are two golden rules (I'm discounting cowardly acts such as doing it by phone call, email or text). Rule number one, as already commented upon, is never do it on home soil. There's nowhere to escape to if things get too heavy. You're trapped. During the incident in question, I'd adhered to this rule, opting to say my piece whilst dropping her off at her home in the car. The second law is trickier, knowing when to spill the beans. As with many things, timing is crucial. On that occasion, I'd spent far too long thinking about it: if I told her too early I'd have to spend the remainder of the car journey dissecting the whys and wherefores; if I told her too late, I'd have to complete the remainder of the analysis stationary in the car or worse still, be dragged in for an autopsy over coffee. Saying what you have to say and wording it efficiently is an art form, an art form I don't possess. Worrying about exactly when I should drop the bombshell forced it to come out involuntarily. We had the full dissection in the car, then feeling so guilty, I ended up going through the whole dissection-over-coffee palaver as well.

Once Rebecca had got the small talk out of the way, she'd probably ask if we could go out for a walk. She'd then ask if we could hold hands and suggest going for dinner. In the end we'd probably come back to mine and discuss for the next couple of hours why packing her stuff into the car was a bad idea. She'd decide it was pointless, on the basis we might get back together again. She'd cry with the emotion of it all and leave sometime around mid-afternoon. Me being the soft, guilt ridden sod that I am would let her do all these things and waste a day which could be much better spent watching sport on the telly. Nothing would have been moved and the house would still be in the same state as it was before she arrived. No, I didn't think this 'bit of a chat' idea sounded very promising at all. Yes, I felt guilty and yes I wished there was something I could do but other than saying everything was alright and kidding her we'd both be happy together forever, there wasn't. I decided to ignore what she'd just said and stay on the 'moving stuff out' track.

'Well look, it's not a problem, I'm sure between us we'll be able to get the stuff in our cars even if we have to make a couple of trips.'

'And you don't mind?' She sounded surprised. Mind, why would I mind? I wouldn't have to be constantly reminded of her by looking at her stuff. Hopefully her smell would evaporate from the house and I could really start to go to town with the beer can and empty takeaway-carton look. It was going to be a long drawn out debacle, I could feel it, but I had to remain patient and understanding and look forward to moulding my bachelor pad when it was all over. It was all about getting the balance right again. I needed to be compassionate to a degree but not so much that she might think we were back on again.

'Of course I don't mind, you know I'll help.'

'I could always get my Mum and Dad to come if it was a problem.'

'No,' I shouted involuntarily down the phone. I took a deep breath and regained my composure. 'No, really, it's fine. We can just take our time and do it at our own pace.'

'You don't still hold my Mum and Dad responsible for us splitting up do you?' I had to choose my words very carefully.

'Umm, not entirely, no.' It was my best attempt at diplomacy.

'What do you mean, not entirely?'

'Well their constant meddling and interference didn't help matters did it?' I could feel myself grimacing as I said it, but it just came out. She started to cry.

'Is that how you really feel?' she blubbered. I sensed it was a rhetorical question. 'If that's the case I don't want anything more to do with them.'

'Well let's not get hasty about …'

'I'm going to tell them,' she continued, 'I'm going to tell them it's all their fault.'

'I don't think we should …'

'I hate them,' she screamed before abruptly hanging up. I sighed, bashing the phone against my forehead.

I made my way back into the club, uneasy about the whole situation. Bob was still sat at the bar.

'That couple over there want to challenge us to a game of

pool,' he said excitedly. I squinted over to the far side of the hall.

'Are they any good?'

'He's pretty good.' Bob pointed to a guy in his mid-thirties. He was built like a brick shit house with long greasy hair and a moustache, pretty much how I would expect Vlad the Impaler to look, but in a leather jacket. A cross between Vlad and Lemmy you might say.

'What about her?' I looked towards his partner. In her early thirties, her hair was cut into a pumpkin coloured bob. Her face was thin but attractive and she had what I can only describe as feline eyes.

'Absolute dog shite mate, diabolically bad,' explained Bob. I nodded.

'Game on then?'

'I guess so.' Bob downed the last of his pint. 'So what's up with the phone?'

'Oh it was Rebecca.'

'I gathered that. What's the score?'

'Oh I dunno. Sometimes I just wish I could say everything was going to be OK and make her happy.'

'You can't do that mate.' His tone was grave.

'I know, I think about what we've both been through to get this far.'

'This isn't the time for reminiscing.'

'No I mean this far in the break-up. The tears and guilt and everything else, I can't go through it all again and although it might be a short-term solution, us getting back together isn't the answer.'

'Well at least you know that much.'

'Yeah, I know,' I said dejectedly.

'So when's she coming to get her stuff? That'll be a big hurdle out of the way.'

'That's what we've just been talking about,' I said. Bob grabbed my forearm.

'Don't let her talk you into taking her out! You know it'll drag on all day. Remember what happened with Helen?'

He was right; meeting up with the ex was, in the majority of cases, bad news. He had however got it wrong when referring to my previous girlfriend Helen. She'd actually avoided patching things up when our reconciliation meeting at the local fair took a nasty turn for the worse. In my opinion, she only had herself to blame. We'd gone on some of those flying teacup things. A barrier came across the top of our legs to stop us from falling out. It wasn't my fault she couldn't get the guardrail up quickly enough when we came to a stop (the catch had been on her side you see). Furthermore, I distinctly remember telling her I felt queasy before we embarked on the ride and when I was initially sick I did try and hold it in whilst she fiddled around with the catch. It was only when the sick had started to dribble from the corners of my mouth that I thought it best to swallow it again. Needless to say as soon as it hit the pit of my stomach it proceeded to come straight back up again, out of my mouth and over Helen's legs. Not content with that, I was sick inside her new car on the way home. Again, not really my fault. I had wound the window down and was happily chucking up down her car door onto the road until she panicked and lurched to the side. I swear it was her erratic driving which forced my body weight back into the car, banging my head and forcing me to throw up again. I offered to buy her a new mat for the foot well. She didn't want to see me again. Whether being sick on Rebecca would have the same effect I couldn't say but seeing as how I hadn't perfected nausea on demand it wasn't worth worrying about.

'So is this game for money or anything?' I asked.

'I doubt it. Like I said she's pretty bad. I think he just wanted a half decent frame and came over when you left. I didn't think you'd mind.'

'I don't. There just might be a couple of quid to be made here.'

'Maybe,' Bob said reluctantly. I don't think it was a lack of confidence in winning. He merely couldn't be bothered.

'You follow the bloke and play quite well. I'll follow the girl and just keep leaving him on. Give it a couple of frames and we'll introduce a wager.'

'Yeah, whatever, let's just get on with it, eh?' We made our way over to the table. The girl greeted us with a cold glare and the response from the bloke wasn't much better. He eventually forced a grin and introduced himself as Boris. He gestured towards his partner.

'This is Jovana.' Vlad's deep rasping voice was as foreboding as his appearance. She nodded curtly and walked towards the table - loosely swinging her cue between her thumb and forefinger - scanning Bob and me up and down with her dark Eastern European eyes.

'Do you vont me to break?' she purred. Quite who this question was directed at, I wasn't sure but she seemed confident that nobody was going to argue. Now I swear I wasn't looking on purpose but I couldn't help noticing how tight her jeans were when she bent over in front of me. Nor could I fail to notice the black lace thong she was wearing. That being a thong made from a black lacy material and not one endorsed by the 80's band of *Agadoo* fame. I looked up at Bob on the opposite side of the table. I assumed from his facial expression he'd inadvertently got an eyeful of Jovana from the front. This was confirmed as he anxiously looked over at Vlad to see if he'd noticed him ogling down her top.

Unlike the scenery, the break was awful. She miscued the white, which proceeded to trickle down the table, barely touching the pack. I grabbed a cue and gave them a smack. Luckily, I didn't pot anything. I was still up for hustling even if Bob wasn't. Vlad followed me and wasn't a bad player to be fair, although he didn't need to be. I think Jovana could have polished off some of the gifts I'd left him. No, actually I take that back. She was awful. She managed to hit the cue ball off the table three times in the first frame. Vlad winced every time she stepped forward. The longer we played, the more agitated he became. I was quite enjoying myself. Playing to miss and making it look credible is more difficult than it sounds. Other than Bob and I uttering the odd 'oooh, bad luck,' or, 'good shot,' now and again, nobody said a word. Vlad's steely glower convinced us it was best to keep our comments short and sweet. I don't quite know what his problem was. I mean why ask us if we wanted to play and then have a complete strop about it. We were even letting them win for Christ's sake. The fact Jovana was so crap infuriated him but there wasn't really a fat lot we could do about that. As she continued to bollocks up the majority of her shots, Vlad's visual disappointment turned into muttered comments, directed at her in a foreign language, Russian I guessed. She got more and more agitated and it wasn't long before they started to row. Vlad thumped his fist on the table, pointing at various pockets. I felt myself cowering as he raised his hand as if to strike her. We quickly thanked them for the game and suggested it was time for us to leave. Downing our drinks, we made for the exit. The last thing I saw as we left the club was two guys from behind the bar approaching the couple to try and calm the situation. Vlad had a tight grip on Jovana's arm.

It was good to get some air. I lit a cigarette whilst Bob sidestepped into a burger bar to get some chips. He emerged some time later with red sauce smeared around his chops.

'Have you enough money for a cab home?' he asked.

'Just about, yeah, why?'

'I dunno what's happened to my fucking wallet.'

'What do you mean you don't know what's happened to it?'

'I don't *know* where it is.'

'You've lost it in other words.'

'Um, yeah.'

'You tit.'

'Me tit, what happened to Mr Hustler?'

'Bob, if he was that upset about winning, just imagine what he'd have been like if we ended up taking money from him. Anyway what about your wallet. Do you want to pop back to the club and see if you left it there?'

'You're joking aren't you? Naah, it's no drama, I'd taken all the cards out. There was only a few quid in there.'

'You had enough for bloody chips though didn't you?'

'Yeah well I had some loose change in my pocket.' He looked down at the few remaining fries in the greasy paper and pulled a face. 'I don't think I want these.' He threw them away, I put out my fag and we hailed a cab.

'Where to mate?' asked the driver. We didn't have time to respond. The back door of the cab flew open and Jovana bundled her way in.

'Drive, juz drive,' she screamed.

Chapter 7

'Red Alert' – Basement Jaxx

'Putney please mate,' Bob said as Jovana settled herself in the back of the cab.

'Thank you, thank you, thank you.' She kissed me excitedly, her hands either side of my face in a vice-like grip.

'I haven't done anything … have I?' I stammered.

'The cab, you let me share your cab, my little luby,' she purred. I wasn't quite sure what a 'luby' was but in that accent it could have meant 'shit head' for all I cared.

Women who are particularly forward, as with Rachel Summers in the cream room, scare the shit out of me at the best of times but when her partner was what can only be described as a thug, it added an extra element of fear. Nevertheless I had to admit the accent was soothing, almost hypnotic.

'Where can we take you Jovana?' Bob asked. He seemed unnaturally calm considering the circumstances.

'I haz nowhere to go,' she said fluttering her eyelids, 'I cussin go back whiz him, not tonight anyway. Can I stay whiz you?' she whispered staring deeply into my eyes.

'Don't look at me. Ask him, it's his flat.' I knew he was going to say no but I didn't want to be the one to give her the bad news. Jovana leant forward over Bob's shoulder waiting for a response.

'Yeah, whatever,' he said waving his hand dismissively. I couldn't believe my ears. I could only assume the fresh air had gone to his head. Then again, it was no skin off my nose if he wanted to allow a complete stranger to kip over at his place. I mean if Ellie found out and gave him any agro at least I'd be able to tell her it was all perfectly innocent. Jovana kissed Bob on the top of the head. She then sat back down and started stroking her hand up the inside of my leg. She didn't look at me, just fixed her gaze out of the cab window as if to give the impression she didn't know she was doing it.

'Where,' I said in an unnaturally high voice. I coughed and regained my composure, 'where is she going to sleep though Bob?' I asked.

'Can't I cudzelle up whiz you luby?' she whispered, biting my earlobe. My body went rigid with panic.

'We can always pull the sofa bed out. It's really not a problem,' Bob was oblivious to the carryings on behind him. His blasé attitude wasn't helping matters. I looked out the back window of the cab to check if we were being followed. For all we knew Vlad could be in hot pursuit.

'What about your partner, Boris?' I asked.

'My huzband you mean?' She must have seen the fear in my eyes so elaborated, 'my ex-huzband that is.' Paranoia really kicked in. Was she just saying he was her ex-husband because she'd seen my reaction? Granted, she wasn't wearing a ring but that didn't mean anything. I didn't want to get on the wrong side of him whatever the circumstances. Our game of wrestling chess continued for the rest of the journey. She'd make a move, I'd try to counter it whilst Bob made semiconscious gurglings from in front. He jolted to attention as the cab pulled up outside his flat. I paid the cabbie and helped Bob up the steps to his front door, closely followed by Jovana. The hall was pitch black and as I struggled to prop Bob up and flick the light switch, my foot slipped on the rug and we both crashed to the ground. If he wasn't already due for a sore head in the morning, he was certainly going to get one now. I tried to move him before realising the best option was just to drag him across the timber floor. I ushered Jovana into the lounge whilst sliding Bob to his room. By the time I'd got back to the lounge, the lights were low and Jovana lay seductively across the sofa. It might have been the scene from a film except the sofa had seen better days and the bits of stuffing poking out of the arms didn't really enhance the atmosphere she was trying to create.

'Let's just get this pulled out then so you can get some rest shall we?' I tried my best to ignore her flirtatious behaviour.

'Why so zoon? I is not tiredz yet.'

'Yeah but I am, so at least if you're settled I can get to bed myself.' I had no idea what I was saying, I just knew the longer I waffled on, the less chance she had of saying anything.

'Oh you can stay for a while,' she said, stroking the cushion beside her. I could see she had no intention of moving which made it difficult to pull it out into a bed, so against my better judgement, I cautiously sat down next to her.

'Dew vant to play a game?' she purred, stroking the side of my face.

'Errm,' I started, staring up at the ceiling, 'not, not rea …' I stopped mid sentence whilst her hand slid down my chest and stomach. 'What sort of game?' I asked reluctantly. She didn't answer. The game seemed to consist of her gyrating about and me sitting frozen to the spot. I couldn't stop thinking about Vlad pummelling my head in. 'Look, I can't do this,' I said trying to squeeze myself along the sofa.

'Vhat iz your problem?' she asked sternly.

'To be perfectly honest, it's your husband.'

She sighed and threw her hands in the air. 'I told you, he's my ex-huzband.'

'Well, whatever, he's still likely to do me over if he thinks we got up to anything.'

'Do you vhat?'

'Do me over, you know, be angry, come looking for a fight.'

Jovana looked puzzled, 'but how would ezza find out?'

I didn't actually have an answer to this, 'Well, he just might.'

'Awwh, come on, are you a man or a moose?' I wasn't sure if it was her accent or she'd got the wrong animal.

'Most definitely a moose … mouse,' I said moving her arms and legs over so I could get off the sofa. 'Now if you'll excuse me, this mouse needs to go to bed. I'll get you a duvet and you can sleep here.'

I was woken in the morning by the doorbell. It rang a couple of times without anyone reacting so I thought I'd better take the initiative. I walked into the lounge to find Bob asleep on the sofa.

'What the bloody hell are you doing there?' Bob was a little dazed to say the least.

'Uhh,' was the only response he could muster.

'Why are you sleeping on the sofa?'

'Oh right, yeah. I had quite a scare in the night. I was lying in bed, just nodding off, when someone got in with me. I thought it was you mucking about but then they put their hand down my boxer shorts!'

'Jovana,' I said.

'Yeah, her hands were freezing.'

'Never mind the temperature of her hands. I can't believe you Bob.'

'Hang on a minute, nothing happened. She thought I was you. She asked me if it was my girlfriend I'd been speaking to on my mobile outside the club and was that why I'd rejected her advances. I legged it and kipped here.' The doorbell rang three times in quick succession.

'Is she still here?' I asked. Bob just shrugged his shoulders. 'Don't you think we should find out?'

'Don't you think you should get the door?' said Bob.

'Fine, I'll do that, you check your room.' I walked up the hall and opened the front door.

'So, we meet again.' To my horror, it was Boris. I stood in shock trying desperately not to look guilty. Not that I had done anything wrong, but I doubted he'd believe that. I swallowed and composed myself as best I could.

'Well… hello there, fancy …' taking another gulp of air, 'fancy seeing you here.'

'Yes, fancy,' replied Boris.

'So what brings you here on this fine … day?'

Boris turned his head slowly to look back towards the road. The rain was pelting down.

'I thought I'd do my good deed for the day,' he said sarcastically. It sounded like something Clint Eastwood would say seconds before blowing someone away.

'And what would that be?' I asked nervously. I had an inkling that I probably didn't want to know the answer, but I didn't think I had much choice.

'Jovana and myself went, how shall I put it, our separate ways last night,' said Vlad making a feeble attempt at an embarrassed laugh. He pinched his nose and sheepishly looked down at his feet. 'We had a little argument outside the snooker hall and she ran off down the street.' I found his calm tones increasingly unnerving. I wasn't quite sure where this conversation was going. 'I went back to the club and the guy behind the bar spotted me and handed me your friend's wallet.' I stared at him blankly. 'He dropped it?' he continued.

'Oh, right I see … yes, yes he did. You're damn right,' I said scratching my chin fretfully. 'So the chap behind the bar assumed we were together … what a stroke of luck,' I laughed nervously.

Vlad pulled Bob's wallet from the pocket of his trench coat and waved it gingerly, the reluctant hero. 'I looked in it to find your address and here I am.'

'Yes and here you are. Well, he will be pleased.' We stood in silence on the doorstep just looking at one another. I couldn't think of anything to say.

'Do you mind if I come in and give it to him personally?' asked Boris.

'Hmm, well I'm not too sure what he's up to at the moment,' I said looking gingerly back down the hallway. 'Bob?'

'Yep,' he replied.

'Are you busy?'

'Errm, yeah kind of,' he said after a short pause, 'I'll be with you in just a sec.'

I waited uneasily with an embarrassed smirk on my face, tapping my fingers on the doorframe. Glancing briefly down the hallway I caught sight of Bob grappling with Jovana in the lounge. I could only imagine that he was trying to get her back into the bedroom.

'She didn't come home last night,' said Vlad.

'Did she not?' I said, far too cheerily. I shook my head in dismay, realising that this was a flippant response to someone who hadn't seen his wife all night. I was still confused about this whole 'ex' business. They obviously still lived together. I tried to sound more concerned. 'Oh my God, really? Do you know where she is?'

'No. You didn't see where she headed? She left just after you.'

'Bob?' I shouted trying to buy time, half shutting the door on Vlad whilst he attempted to look down the hall over my shoulder.

'Yep.'

'What are you up to mate, this kind gent wants to give your wallet back.' I laughed nervously. There was no response.

'So have you any idea where she might be?' Vlad repeated. All I could manage was an exaggerated 'umm', pursing my lips and furrowing my brow as if deep in thought.

'I mean, did she say anything about where she may have gone?' It seemed a strange question to ask when to all intents and purposes we'd left the club before she had. Maybe he'd seen her get into our cab. Maybe we'd been rumbled. I tried to choose my words carefully.

'Errm, well …' I said, still looking like a mad eccentric contemplating the meaning of life.

'When did you last see her?' He wasn't going to let it lie. How I wished that I'd gone to check on Jovana and Bob had answered the door.

'Hmmm yes, when did we … when exactly did we last see her? She errm, well she shared a cab home with us.' If I'd taken the easy option and said the last time we'd seen Jovana was in the snooker club then I could have been digging a seriously deeper hole if Boris had followed us and watched her get into our cab. I continued, 'well y'know, we didn't want to leave her in the middle of town on her own, and . . . and she got out before we got home.'

'So where did she get out?'

'Well I can't be sure, I was a little bit worst for wear.'

'You didn't seem too bad last night.'

'I don't really know the area too well …'

Not a moment too soon, Bob came bustling to the door. 'And she didn't pay her part of the fare,' he interjected.

I looked at Bob, my eyes open wide as if to say 'shut the fuck up'.

'Oh, I'm so sorry,' said Boris apologetically, fumbling in his wallet. 'Please accept … I mean I'd hate to think she hadn't …'

'No really, it's not a problem,' I said.

'Well it was a bit pricey, I mean you know the cost of cabs these days,' said Bob, sticking out his hand for the money.

'I fully appreciate that,' said Vlad handing Bob a £10 note. Bob gleefully pocketed it.

'So you have no idea where she could be?' Vlad repeated for a third time.

'Naah, sorry mate, she could be anywhere,' Bob was playing it very cool but I was sensing he was trying to hurry the conversation along now he'd made some money out of the situation. I couldn't believe he'd taken a tenner off a bloke who'd come to return his wallet. It was completely unlike Bob to be so bold and impertinent. I could only assume the situation had forced him to take leave of his senses.

'I'm sure she'll turn up,' I said looking back down the corridor to see Jovana standing in the lounge in nothing more than a pair of white cotton pants. Bob had also spied her out of the corner of his eye and shut the door further still.

'Yeah, like he says, I'm sure she'll turn up. Thanks again for returning the wallet.' He snatched it from Vlad's grasp. 'Well lovely to see you again. Sorry we couldn't be of any more help.' He started to close the door. 'Oh we'll be sure to let you know if we hear anything.' He shut the door in Vlad's face. I gingerly peered through the bull's-eye window. Vlad stood on the step for a few moments, a bemused look on his face before turning and making his way back down the path. I sighed with relief and glanced round to find Bob transfixed on the lounge. Jovana was bent over the coffee table.

'Morning boyz,' she said cheerily, 'can I get you anyzing?'

Chapter 8

Despite Jovana's tempting invitation, the morning's run-in with Vlad had confirmed my initial judgement that steering clear of her was the wisest move. I left Bob to sort out the mess, only hoping he got rid of Jovana before either Ellie made an impromptu visit or Vlad reappeared. Bob tried to talk me into going to the match with Alan and Jimmy but an afternoon on the terraces didn't appeal. I had a weekend with Stacey to look forward to.

'We'll be leaving at ten-thirty if you change your mind,' he said as I made my way towards the car. I waved dismissively and started my journey back to Bournemouth, confident this 'thing' with Stacey would give my newfound freedom a real kick-start. That was until I got home to a message on the answer machine.

BEEEEP! 'Yeah Hi, it's Stace (*she coughed loudly; sounded like a put on*). Don't worry about picking me up from work, I feel as sick as a dog. Guess I must have had too much to drink last night, oh and I've got a bit of a cold coming. I'll see how I feel tomorrow. Give me a ring at my friend's place.'

That was it. She didn't sound apologetic for calling it off or even faintly enthusiastic about the cinema trip. Further more she didn't actually sound ill. As for a name or number of this friend that I was supposed to ring, heaven only knew. The weekend's plans were in ruins. I couldn't understand how the mood had changed so radically since our last meeting. She'd seemed genuinely excited about everything we'd discussed in the pub the other night and now she gave the distinct impression she didn't give a shit. I wandered dejectedly into the kitchen. Eating something would while away a few minutes but the state of the kitchen - the bread tinged with blue and grey mould and the fur floating on the dregs of coffee in the percolator - put me off the idea.

I switched on the computer: I thought I'd see what the chat rooms had to offer although I'd never actually met anyone with whom I could strike up a decent conversation. I'd always found it ironic: the guys tried to portray themselves as macho danger freaks for the benefit of the girls. Maybe I was being stereotypical but I imagined these computer geeks, hunched over their keyboards, trying to get one over on other blokes in the room or trying to justify why, if they were so interesting, they were sat at home bored and lonely. Intermingle this with being offensive or, at best, over-forward to supposed members of the opposite sex (who could just as easily be some forty-six year old pervert from Durham) and you end up with a reasonably fair impression of what a chat room was all about. The 'girls' could be broadly stereotyped as well. They were usually engrossed in chat with other 'girls' about such philosophical topics as *Britney Spears*, *Steps*, *The Backstreet Boys* or errm, *Steps*, or else they were seemingly frustrated wannabe prostitutes only interested in cyber sex or the size of your penis. Regardless, here I was logging on, looking for someone to chat to. What did that say about me? I changed my username; *Solo* seemed appropriate.

The names of the people in the room - *Bigfcuk*, *Randyshag* and *Deepthroat* were doing the majority of the chatting - didn't exactly fill me with confidence. I watched the usual dross scroll up the screen trying to latch onto anything remotely sensible. I'm always amazed at how much time you can waste flitting from room to room in the hope of finding someone with at least half a brain. I never learn, reluctant to log off in case I miss something. Finally I found something …

'Hi, is any1 from England?' typed *Kristy73*. I stirred myself into a reply. After all, I was from England and always found it best to be honest online. I mean I don't see the point in pretending to be someone I'm not. I suppose it's escapism for some people but then I have the disadvantage of not being a very good liar. If I do tell lies, either online or back on planet earth, I can never remember what I've said to whom. Little white lies, well that's different. We all have to tell them now and again don't we?

'Yeah, I'm from England' I replied. *Bigfcuk* also claimed to be from England but concluded his opening gambit to *Kristy73* with asking the size of her tits. It could have gone either way. Was she the archetypal frustrated pro? Apparently not, for she replied to me in a private mailbox and we actually struck up a conversation. Her nametag was based on her name being Kristy and being born in 1973. Not highly original, but at least it wasn't crude and it was on the face of it, honest. She lived in Ontario, Canada. We chatted for over an hour about all sorts of things: what sports we played; what we liked to do in our spare time; what it was like where we lived; what we did for a living (although she was at college studying teaching) and by the time we finished I guess I'd got to know Kristy pretty well. She was due to come to England with her friend in a few weeks and was interested to know where to stay and what to do, hence her opening question. We exchanged e-mail addresses before she logged off. After spending a few moments watching *Bigfcuk* ask a few more people how big their tits were, I decided to do the same. (Log off that is, not ask someone how big people's tits were).

The moment I disconnected the PC, the phone rang.

'Who the hell have you been on the phone to all this time?' asked the voice. It was Becci.

'I've been on the computer,' I replied. There was a few moments' silence. She didn't seem to have heard what I said.

'I've done it,' she said.

'Done what?'

'Told them,' she began to get tearful.

'Told who . . . what?'

'I've told my parents. I hate them.' I suddenly felt sick.

'You told your parents you hate them?'

'No,' she said choking back the tears, 'I told them that it was all their fault we split up and if they hadn't have gone poking their nose in all the time, it'd have never happened.' The more she spoke, the more I felt ill.

'Right,' was all I could muster.

'I hate them,' she repeated.

'Where are you now?'

'I'm at a friend's.'

'You over at Jude's?'

'I'm with Roger.' Roger? Who the hell was Roger?

'Who the hell is Roger?'

'He's a friend of the family, rents out rooms at his house and has got one spare.' In the years we'd been going out, I'd never heard of anyone called Roger. I suddenly wanted to find out though.

'How old is this Roger then?' I found myself saying, rather pettily.

'Look I just want to pick up my stuff but my parents aren't going to help me now.' My instinct was to tell her to get whoever the fuck this Roger was to help her but then the realisation her parents weren't coming round led me to be more reasonable.

'It's not a problem is it? We can use both our cars and take our time, sort this out amicably.' The sooner I got her stuff out of my house, with the least bother, the better.

'Are you sure? I doubt we'll get all my things in two carloads.'

'Well, whatever, we'll just have to make a few trips until it's done.'

'And you're sure you don't mind?'

Anything which bypassed her parents' involvement was fine by me and so the plan was formulated. She was to ring me in the morning to confirm her arrival time. I didn't manage to learn much more about Roger, except he was in his forties, receding and she thought he was gay. I'm sure there was something she wasn't telling me though. Why I should care either way? It bugged me somehow though.

The rest of the day dragged. I just wanted the next morning to come and to get Rebecca's kit out. Her things dotted around the house, the constant reminder of her having lived there, was starting to get to me. I decided to make inroads into sorting some of her things, to speed up the process. Her CD's (Ibiza Gold, Cream Anthems and other such titles) went in one pile whilst mine went in another. After attempting to rearrange the CD rack in meticulous detail three times (should U2 – Achtung Baby come before the Red Hot Chili Peppers – Blood, Sugar, Sex, Magik because of the order in which I bought them or should I just put them in alphabetical order?) I gave up and committed the remainder of the Saturday afternoon to watching *Grandstand.* I must have fallen asleep. There was a message on the answer machine from Alan when I woke to say they were on their way back to Bournemouth and would be in the pub at about 8.30pm if I wanted to join them. Needless to say I couldn't get hold of Alan to find out which pub, so I guessed. I had nothing better to do after all. Nothing better that is than sit in a pub drinking on my own for a couple of hours feverishly looking round every time I heard the door open. They never arrived. I must have guessed the wrong pub.

The shrill ringing of the phone broke the ghastly silence of the following morning. It wasn't particularly early. I'd been awake for a while. Answering the phone was the only impetus I had to get my lazy arse out of bed and stop wallowing in self-pity.

'Hi babe, it's only me.' It was Rebecca. Obviously Roger's hospitality had given her a new lease of life.

'You all set then?' It didn't mean to sound like we were going on some sort of adventure; it's just the way it came out.

'I guess, yeah. It all seems so sad though.' There was a downturn in her tone. It really was starting to feel like the end of an era. Hearing her voice made me nostalgic. Nevertheless the inevitable had to be sorted.

'Are you coming over shortly?'

'That's why I was ringing actually. Is there any chance we could make it this afternoon?'

'I don't see why not. Why, what's cropped up? Is everything alright with your parents?'

She hesitated for a moment and said 'It's just this afternoon would be better.' I suddenly remembered I was supposed to be seeing Stacey. Maybe that's why Rebecca couldn't make it: Maybe she was going out with bloody Roger. Whatever the reason, I had to do some backtracking even though I wasn't wholly confident mine and Stacey's date was still on.

'Actually,' I hesitated, 'this morning would suit me better.'

'Why, is there a problem with this afternoon?' she huffed, her voice taking an argumentative tenor as if talking through pursed lips.

'It's just … I said I'd do something else.'

'Oh you did, did you?'

'I thought you were coming round this morning you see.'

'You're going out aren't you?' she continued her belligerent stance.

'Well…'

'With another girl … you're seeing someone else aren't you?'

'Umm.'

'I knew it.'

'Look, hang on.'

'I knew it. Well you can kiss goodbye to your amicable move out … thing. Me, Mum and Dad will be round in an hour.' She slammed the phone down. Panic set in. How the hell was I going to cope with the three of them dismantling the place? Desperate times called for desperate measures. I rang Jimmy on his mobile.

Chapter 9

'Every you Every me' – Placebo.

I'd chained smoked my way through six cigarettes before Jimmy's arrival. I jumped at the sound of him knocking at the door, fearing the bailiffs had beaten him to it. He barged past me and threw himself on the sofa, frantically waving his hand in front of his nose.

'Phoawww,' he remarked, 'is the bloody house on fire?' I had to admit, it was a little smoky in the lounge. That was one of the problems with my one bedroom house. There was nowhere for the smoke to go. I'd made a pact with myself I'd pack it in when I'd finished decorating the place, I'd just never followed it through. Rebecca knew I smoked before she'd moved in but that didn't stop her making a song and dance about it every once in a while. One particular night I'd had two cigarettes whilst watching the TV and had gone to bed just before she returned from a clubbing escapade with her mates in town. Despite it being 1.30am in the morning and sub zero temperatures outside, she opened all the windows and spent the next half an hour going up and down the stairs huffing and puffing and spraying air freshener everywhere. I pretended I was asleep. Now though I didn't suppose it really mattered.

'We could pretend to be out,' I mumbled weakly.

'Nope, you're only going to prolong the agony you coward.' To my surprise Jimmy was being quite sensible about the situation. 'Just kick the bitch out and get it over with.' Then again, maybe he was less interested in being supportive and more intent on being part of the whole misogynistic demise. He'd have kicked her out without hesitation. Her stuff would probably already be on the pavement, in bin liners *if* she was lucky. What's more, he certainly wouldn't have needed a mate for moral support. That said, he had turned up, which to me at the time meant everything. I paced around the lounge, continuing to smoke whilst Jimmy helped himself to the TV remote and was soon engrossed in *Football Italia*.

Two cars eventually pulled up outside. The onslaught was about to begin. I opened the door. Rebecca's mother bundled her way past me in much the same way Jimmy had done. She was closely followed by her troops, namely Becci and her Dad. She stood in the middle of the lounge with her hands on her hips, surveying the task in hand.

'Right, I'll start in the kitchen,' she bawled. Acting on her high-pitched war cry, her troops rallied into action and the onslaught began. It was like standing in the middle of a whirlwind. The operation had been planned with military precision. She started loading everything in the kitchen into boxes, and I mean everything, even stuff that was mine. I felt powerless. As I went to say something I looked round to find her Dad disconnecting the video recorder. Becci was clattering through the drawers of my computer desk. Jimmy remained transfixed on the telly throughout.

'I don't think there's anything in there that belongs to you. I've already packed your things into that box over there.' I pointed to a pile in the corner. At that, her mother stomped in from the kitchen.

'Huh,' she said, 'I think we'll be the judge of that.' And then they were both at it, rooting through my drawers with vigorous gusto. 'Are these yours darling?' she said holding aloft a half empty plastic carton of drawing pins.

'Yes,' said Becci and into the box they went.

'What about this?' We had now moved on to lot 124, a ball of BlueTac. The answer was in the affirmative and it too was packed.

'I'll go get your things from upstairs,' I said gingerly. No-one appeared to hear me, so I sloped off to pack up the duvet cover Becci and her Mum had bought behind my back after I'd said I didn't like it, along with all her lotions and potions from the bathroom. It wasn't long before I heard someone coming. It was Becci. She stood in the doorway looking down on me.

'I'm sorry about this,' she said, 'I thought we might have a couple of moments to ourselves.' At that she undid her blouse and bra and knelt down beside me putting my hand to her breast. 'Touch them,' she said softly, 'they're all yours, and they always will be.' She lowered her head and kissed me passionately. It was like a surreal dream. Here I was with my ex-girlfriend playing doctors and nurses to the backdrop of her parents banging and clattering downstairs whilst they riffled through my gear and Jimmy continuing to rant at the television. For a few brief moments I went along with the charade, selfishly realising it might be the last chance I got. My head soon began to spin with confusion however and I pushed her away. I made myself presentable and went back downstairs. Both cars were by now packed to the gunnels. Her Dad continued to tinker with the video, much to the annoyance of Jimmy who'd repeatedly told him to stop bobbing up and down in front of the television.

'Do you want to take the video?' I questioned, noticing there didn't appear to be enough room for another paper clip in either of the cars let alone a video recorder.

'Want to take the video? Of course we want to take the video, it's our video,' her mother piped up. That wasn't strictly true. It was a beaten up old thing that had belonged to her brother until he'd given it to me as a birthday present. I wasn't going to argue. Eventually they managed to free the video and made their way to the door.

'Thank your lucky stars we're not taking more,' her mother remarked. I didn't respond, I wouldn't have dared, but it didn't stop the anger from welling up inside. Was I supposed to be grateful? 'She's been to a solicitors, haven't you darling,' she continued, glancing at Rebecca. She nodded reluctantly, almost ashamedly. I imagined her parents, or rather her mother, had put her up to it. In fact I would go as far as to say that her statement should have been, '*we* have been to a solicitor.' They were the only people I knew who had one, unless you include the bloke who always acted on behalf of the Mitchells in *EastEnders*. That aside, I'd never actually known any real people to have one.

'Oh,' was my gargantuan response.

'Yes,' she continued, 'luckily for you, the mortgage and all the bills are in your sole name (yes, lucky old me) so *we* have no stake in the house.' I couldn't believe she'd been to see a solicitor. Rebecca had lived here rent-free for nearly twelve months, her only contribution towards any of the costs being to buy the weekly shopping. Any major purchases such as furniture, carpets and the like had been paid for by me and anything she'd had any financial input towards, and more besides, had now been stuffed into their cars. Yet here she was telling me I was lucky not have to sign over half the house? It struck me she'd used the word *'we'* … *'we'* would have no claim to the house. Aha, so it had been a joint effort. Was I going to let this woman speak to me like this in my own home? I looked at Jimmy; he'd leapt to his feet as Juventus slotted another one home. He lifted his shirt over his head in celebration revealing his rotund midriff. I'm sure it was seeing Jimmy's wobbling gut that put me off forming any sort of cohesive argument in my defence. No, I couldn't blame him. I was chicken. All I could do was stand there and take it. My expression erred on the side of gratitude rather than anger. I put it down to relief, knowing that the uncomfortable experience was nearly at an end and the bailiffs would soon be on their way.

'But then,' she continued, 'I suppose you knew that when you set up this little deal.'

No actually, because I didn't venture into 'this little deal' as you put it with the belief it was eventually going to go tits up. More to the point, I was the only one with any fucking money and I seem to recall that instead of being happy for your daughter on the night she moved, your words to her were something along the lines of 'If you move in with Connor, you move back in here over our dead bodies'. But that doesn't matter, we brush all that under the carpet because the upset and tears caused by your outburst were forgotten two days later when you threw a big 'making up' party at your house complete with the obligatory banners and balloons. And you stand there, like Lady Muck, with the cheek to make out I'm the one who's being unreasonable?

'Come on, we're going,' she barked and with that her little followers frogmarched passed me. I shut the door in relief. Jimmy seemed oblivious to anything that had gone on. I wandered upstairs and rang Stacey's house on the off chance we were still going to the cinema that afternoon. Brenda seemed overly keen to give me the phone number of the friend's house where her daughter was staying. Reading far too much into things once again, I took this to mean that Stacey had filled her mother with good vibes following our initial meeting and that Brenda approved. I eagerly rang the number. There was no answer. I waited a few moments and rang the number again. This time a female voice answered.

'Hello?'

'Hello, yeah, my name's Connor. I was told I might be able to get hold of Stacey on this number?'

'Stacey?'

'Yes, you're friends with her aren't you?'

'Yeah, but I haven't seen her since Friday night when she left the club with…' she tailed off.

'With who?'

'With one of our other friends,' she said unconvincingly. 'I think we've met before Connor, a long time ago. I'll be sure to let her know you called.' Her voice sounded sympathetic.

'Right, OK then, thanks very much,' I rang off.

'Got anything to eat?' Jimmy shouted up the stairs. Unfortunately for him, but ultimately me, the kitchen appeared to have been the worst casualty of the bailiff's onslaught. I looked in all the cupboards and drawers to find what they'd left: one kitchen knife (the blunt one), a cheese grater and one of those things to separate the egg yolk from the white. I always found the last item in particular, to be tremendously useful in the kitchen.

'Errm well, even if I had anything there're no saucepans to cook anything in, or plates to serve it onto or knifes and forks to eat it with.'

'Good, let's go down the pub then and get some tucker.' Jimmy had actually come up with a good idea. He even treated me to lunch. It was then we began probably the most sensible conversation we'd had to date.

'Bet you're glad that's over,' he blurted, his mouth half full of chicken madras.

'You could say that,' I sighed, 'I don't want to have to go through that again in a hurry.'

'Nah, I bet you don't.' He was now chomping on some naan bread, 'I hope for your sake the silly bitch doesn't try a pull a stunt like she did last time.' He paused for a moment to take a swig of bitter. 'Leave the stupid cow to die this time. I would.' He was referring to the time I'd tried to break it off before. We weren't living together then, but the day after I said that enough was enough (my reasons had been the same) I got a phone call at work. I couldn't make out who it was at first, there was just a lot of wailing and moaning but I got the gist of what was being said. It was Rebecca.

'I can't live without you Connor. You know where I am and you know … what I'm going to do,' she kept repeating. Her voice was terrifying. The hysteria and panic was something I had never heard before. Nothing I said calmed her down.

'Bye,' she whispered, 'I'm going to do it.' She put the phone down.

I don't mind admitting I was frightened. I wasn't sure whether she was really going to do anything but I wasn't prepared to take the risk. I was a trainee at the time and my boss sat at the opposite desk. He knew something was very wrong by the time I came off the phone and he let me borrow his car (his Sierra being quicker than my Fiesta). Not that it really mattered though; the traffic was horrendous. There was a spot on the top of the cliffs where we used to hang out. I guessed, rightly or wrongly, she was there.

The car skidded to a halt in the gravel car park at the base of the cliffs. A number of old age pensioners sitting outside the little café enjoying cream teas and the like, tutted disapprovingly at the youth of today as they saw me speeding by. I spied the telephone box from where I assumed she'd made the call. A Telecom man had taken it to bits and wires were hanging out all over the place. I ran over to him.

'Excuse me, does this phone work?' I said panting.

'Huh?' said the man unhurriedly, not taking his eye from what he was doing.

'The telephone, does it work?'

'Are you taking the piss mate, does it look like it works?' He must have seen the distress on my face. He changed his tack. 'What's the problem son?'

'I had a phone call from someone about…' I looked at my watch hurriedly 'forty minutes ago and I wondered if they were still around.'

'Nope, I've been working on this for over an hour.'

'Are there any other phones round here?'

'Nope, the only other one is on the other side of the cliffs in the next bay.' Shit, I was in the wrong place. It must be at least a thirty-minute walk to get there; I'd have to take the car. 'I can phone if you like,' he said, seeing the desperation in my eyes, 'see if anyone's there.'

'I thought you said it was broken.' He didn't reply but slotted a card into the guts of the phone and dialled a code, presumably to connect him to the phone he'd been speaking of. We stood there for a while in silence.

'Well,' he said replacing the receiver, 'there's no-one there now.'

I thanked him for his efforts and ran back to the car. I didn't know where I was going but I just knew I had to get there fast, if that makes sense. I think it's known as panic. Whatever the reason, something made me look back up the road as I got into the car. Rebecca's car was parked half way up the street. She was there after all. I speedily made my way up the steep grassy track to the top of the cliff. The pensioners continued to monitor my progress. It must have been about half a mile to where the cliff flattened out at the top. I hadn't gone more than 200 yards when I had to stop and catch my breath. Taking in deep gulps of air with my hands on my knees, I looked up to see how much further I had to go. It was then I saw Rebecca making her way back down. I pushed myself on to get to her. She was no-where near the edge and didn't look suicidal in any way (apart from the fact she was sobbing her heart out) but I was filled with relief. I grabbed her tightly, both arms locked around her upper body. I couldn't let go, even when we were making our way back down the cliff path (I made sure that she walked on the inside of me and away from the edge, just in case). The pensioners were in for another treat as they witnessed a girl with a blotchy red face, crying her eyes out, seemingly being bear hugged by the boy racer idiot who'd shocked them all earlier with his *Dukes of Hazard* style entry to the car park. They probably thought I'd made her cry, but then in a way, I suppose I had.

'Do you want an ice-cream?' I asked as we neared the café at the bottom. It was if I was speaking to a little kid and that having an ice cream would make it all better again.

'No,' she sobbed, 'I just want you.' Never have I heard something so touching and yet so vomit-inducingly slushy at the same time.

Even more upsetting were the antics of the next day. I'd phoned her mother as I thought I had a duty to tell her what had happened. I was not going to shoulder this responsibility on my own. I arranged to see her the following lunchtime and spent quarter of an hour explaining exactly what had happened. I thought maybe she should be aware of her daughter's actions. After pouring my heart out and telling her how terrified and disturbing the whole episode had been, she looked me straight in the eye and said dismissively, 'Well, you didn't think she was actually going to do it did you?' She gave me a patronising smile. In hindsight I wouldn't be surprised if her mother's nonchalant response was down to the fact that she'd put her up to it in the first place. Whatever the case I should have formulated some kind of response.

'Fine, maybe not, but the next time your daughter calls me from a phone box on a cliff top crying her eyes out, intimating that she's going to throw herself from the top, I'll just get on with my work and hope she changes her mind; I'm not going to be made responsible if anything happens.'

In reality I left post haste with my tail between my legs. In view of her mother's dismissive stance and feeling I was left to carry the responsibility alone, I patched things up with Rebecca on the proviso she never tried to pull the same stunt again.

'Look,' Jimmy continued, 'why don't you come to footy tonight. We're one short at five-a-side. I could do with a laugh watching you lumbering around the pitch.'

I smiled thankfully and accepted his generous offer.

I must have been more out of practice than I thought. The game was no more than five minutes old when the ball came to me on the edge of the opposition's area. I swung my right foot with so much enthusiasm that my left foot came about six inches off the floor. Having missed the ball completely I landed awkwardly and my ankle buckled beneath me. It ballooned to the size of a baby elephant and I was carried off the pitch, yelping like a small child. I spent the next four hours in the local casualty department having torn the ligaments in my ankle. It was the final nail in the coffin of an unbelievably crappy weekend.

Chapter 10

Weeknights were spent mainly at my parents' house. Mum enjoyed having the family, albeit only the three of us, together at dinnertime and it meant I didn't have to cook. Mum's offerings were much more inviting than my usual burnt meals for one in any case, and it saved me from hobbling around the kitchen on my slow-to-recover foot. I even got my washing done on occasions.

We had a heart to heart one night. She tearfully told me she'd missed having me around. Despite only living down the road, I hadn't seen much of them whilst living with Rebecca. It was good spend time at home again.

On one particular evening, Stacey's was the only car parked next door. I took the opportunity to find out what the hell was going on and get the books back she'd borrowed. I knocked the door. No answer, but I could see a shadow bobbing in the hallway through the frosted glass. I knocked again, harder this time. A burly looking guy in his late 20's opened the door just enough to see who was there. He was enormous. I don't mean he was fat, just very broad and, despite being over six feet tall myself, the time it took to scan up from his torso to his face made me uneasy. He had a fairly dark complexion and his face was scarred and pitted. He'd either picked all his chicken pox as a kid or had been in a lot of fights. I assumed it was a bit of both with the emphasis on the latter.

'Yeah?' he said through the crack in the door.

'Is Stacey in please?' I asked nervously.

'She's in the shower,' he grunted, closing the door as he did so. I pushed my hand against the door to stop him.

'Wait!' It was as if I'd announced I'd been sleeping with his mother. A fiery hatred burned in his eyes. I was glad the door was virtually shut. I thought it best to just say my piece and shove off. I neglected to ask the questions I'd originally wanted the answers to.

'Can you just ask her to pop my books back next door?' His face was emotionless, continuing to stare at me with foreboding eyes. 'I live next door and she borrowed a few books from me.' I assumed this animal was the reason things hadn't gone according to plan with Stacey. Coward as I am, I hoped saying I was just the bloke next door would help deflect suspicion. There wasn't really anything to suspect, but I thought I'd err on the side of caution. 'I just want my books back,' I said pathetically as though I was a kid having kicked his ball over the fence. He shut the door in my face.

I spent most of the next week feeling sorry for myself. Keeping my foot elevated for ridiculous amounts of time and chatting on the internet didn't do much to inspire me. Chatting to Kristy was probably the only thing that kept me sane. We exchanged a few photos and rambled on about nothing in particular. She was actually really easy to talk to. I know that might sound weird seeing as how you're typing, but believe me, online chats can dry up as easily as real life conversations. She insisted I sort myself out with something exciting for the rapidly approaching weekend. I rang Ellie in the hope I could go up to stay with her; a house full of nurses for a couple of nights was surely better than any medicine. Unfortunately she couldn't put me up. She'd organised some antics with Bob and so my next best offer was treating myself to a thrilling afternoon at Dean Court watching AFC Bournemouth with Jimmy and Alan.

It was cold, it was wet and I wondered what the bloody hell I was doing there. I shuffled from side to side in an attempt to ease the discomfort of my ankle. Alan and Jimmy obviously knew all the terrace chants. I stood there feeling as though everyone in the stand was staring at me. I could sense them nudging each other and pointing.

'Ere, that bloke over there ain't singing George.'

I soon realised I needed glasses. I knew when Ian Cox and Mark Stein had the ball. One was tall and black, the other, a black midget. That isn't meant to sound racist, merely an example to show how bad my eyesight was. Thank Alan for small mercies. He kept me up to speed with events on the pitch with his constant commentary. He took being a football supporter to another level. He could tell you the match statistics from the last time these teams met; any midweek team news, including fitness and form; the highlights from the reserve team game, because he'd been to watch; the name of the person dressed up as the team mascot Cherry Bear on that particular day. I mean how would you know that? More to the point, why the hell would you want to know that? It's not exactly going to come up as the £32,000 question on *Who Wants To Be A Millionaire?* I can't imagine Chris Tarrant leaning forward in his chair, 'Take your time now Alan, you're free to walk away with £16,000. You've used your 50/50 and 'ask the audience'. You've phoned your Mum for the capital of Finland, but take a look at this for a guaranteed £32,000. Who was dressed up as AFC Bournemouth's club mascot, Cherry Bear in their home fixture against Notts County in the 98/99 season?' Imagine Mr Tarrant's surprise as Alan excitedly screams out the answer before the four options have even come up on the screen. Classic television.

I may have got wet, squinted for ninety minutes and had a crap burger but at least it had got me out of the house. I returned home to find another note on the doormat.

'To my dearest Connor; I can understand you being mad with me; at the time I thought I was being strong moving my bits out but now it's hit me and I feel a bitch leaving you with nothing. I really don't know what to do with my life, Connor. It feels so empty without you. Please, please don't hate me forever; you are still my life and soul. Can we see each other? It is my birthday after all. You're still the best in my eyes. Love Becci xx.' Her new address and phone number were on the bottom.

Now Jimmy would have done one of two things. Either screwed the note up and thought no more about it or rung Becci and told her in no uncertain terms to fuck right off and leave him alone. No, actually, he'd have probably have fucked her and then told her to fuck off. I, being the sucker that I am, did none of these things. I rang Rebecca and arranged to go to the cinema.

Chapter 11

'Funny feeling' – Reef.

The whole thing felt really quite strange, almost like a first date. Rebecca had obviously made an effort and dressed in a tight red top with poppers down the front and baggy black trousers. I, on the other hand, had slung on a pair of combats and a fleece. She was stood outside the cinema as I trotted up the steps. Strange, it was unusual for her to be early. I looked at my watch. No, it was usual for me to be late. She went to kiss me as I approached her; it was all a bit awkward. We gave up half way through and made our way to the ticket office.

'You go and get me some popcorn,' she said, 'you know how I like it. I'll get these.' So into the foyer I wandered not actually knowing what film we were going to see. I ordered two tubs of popcorn (she had always liked hers sweet, which I couldn't stand. I preferred mine salted with butter) and waited for her to come in.

'So what we seeing then?' I asked.

'*Scream*,' she replied. I stopped myself from cracking the obvious cheap gag and letting out a blood-curdling shriek. I assumed she was referring to the film title rather than giving an order.

I've never been keen on anything horror orientated. My philosophy has always been, why scare yourself more than you have to. That goes for ghost trains or haunted houses as well, even the crappy ones at the local fair. I won't get on them for love nor money. Although I'm now a lot more tolerant of scary things than I was – my Dad having pointed out the comic clumsiness of the villains in all three *Scream* films and ridiculing anyone scared by the dawdling unwieldy zombies barely able to walk in *House of the Living Dead* - on this particular occasion *Scream* really put the wind up me.

Although I tried not to show it, I left the cinema petrified. After saying my goodbyes to Becci (I can't remember how we parted, everything was a bit of a blur by then. I was more interested in getting home safely without being attacked by a man in a mask and black cloak), I swiftly walked back to my car, checked the back seat and boot for potential assailants and made my way home. I turned the radio off in order to hear any suspicious noises. I pulled up outside the house in silence. There wasn't a breath of air and the house seemed more dark and empty than usual. Despite the deserted streets, I wasn't sure whether I could make the transition from the car to the house. I contemplated sleeping where I was but thought it was probably more risky (and colder) than going inside. Even the slightest noise seemed to be amplified: locking the car; putting the key in the front door; wiping my feet on the mat. I ventured gingerly towards the light switch and felt slightly better with the instant relief from darkness. The next course of action was to move up to the bedroom. Other than my fleece, which I'd hung up in the wardrobe (whilst checking for boogiemen), I went to bed fully clothed and lay in silence. After a while I plucked up the courage to close my eyes. I couldn't have closed the wardrobe door properly however and it slammed shut on its hinges. I jumped out of bed and caught a glimpse of myself in the mirrored wardrobe doors. I grabbed my fleece, picked up Rebecca's note with her new address and headed for the car.

She'd obviously gone straight to bed as the house was in darkness. I looked at my watch, it had gone 1am and I couldn't exactly go banging on the door. Luckily I noticed a collection of

Rebecca's trinkets in the front bay window and decided to tap the glass gently. There was no response. I tried again a little harder this time. I thought I could hear some kind of movement from inside. There was a slight rustle of the curtains and then Rebecca's face appeared at the window. She let out a muted yelp and fell backwards. I waited anxiously for a moment till she reappeared at the window. She fanned herself with one hand, held her chest with the other and gestured me round to the front door.

'What the hell are you doing?' she whispered.

'I couldn't sleep, I didn't know where to go, my house was so empty.'

'You'd better come in,' she said shepherding me into her room. 'I'll go and make us a coffee.'

Her room was cramped but tidy. All the things she'd retrieved from our house had been crammed into the limited space. It was cosy. I sat down on the double bed with the hideous duvet cover and waited for her to reappear.

'So what you going to do?' she asked, slurping her coffee. She sat down next to me on the bed. In her night slip and dressing gown she looked reassuringly familiar. I hoped she would ask me to stay the night. It had to be better than going home. 'You could always stay over.' Her voice was soft and calm.

'Well OK, if you're sure,' I replied, feigning reluctance.

'Of course. It's no problem.' She must have seen me look cautiously at the bed. 'I think we've known each other long enough to sleep in the same bed for one more night.' I tried to hide the beaming smile that I was feeling inside and toned in down to a mild grin. 'It will be nice to have you to myself again,' she said pushing me backwards onto the bed. Whilst not complaining, I genuinely hadn't come intending anything to happen. I was just being a big girl's blouse after a mildly scary movie and needed a friendly face. The fact that she wasn't distressed in the slightest by the film made me feel more pathetic and I realised my innocent visit just looked like a cheap excuse to get into bed with her. My naivety sometimes knows no bounds. The rest is history.

When I woke, Rebecca was already up. I dressed and made my way into the kitchen where she was stood, scantily clad, talking to a man in his early 30's. They laughed and joked with one another until Rebecca caught sight of me.

'Oh, Connor, this is Roger.' So this was Roger. Despite being a bad judge of age, I realised Roger wasn't in his forties. He had a full head of hair and he didn't look in the least bit gay. He was more of a 'flash Harry' type. His wide-mouthed smile was full of perfect pearly teeth. He exuded an air of slimy confidence.

'So you're Connor. I've heard so much about you,' he grinned smarmily. I tried to match his slimy demeanour.

'Very pleased to meet you,' I said patronisingly through gritted teeth.

'You'll be pleased to know Rebecca has settled in very well here,' he looked across the kitchen, his creepy smirk still wide as ever. 'Haven't you Becci?' She smiled and let out a little laugh. Maybe I was being paranoid but I got the impression there was more going on than these two were letting on.

'Good, good,' I said awkwardly.

'So what are you guys doing today?' asked Roger intently flicking his gaze between us.

'I thought …' I started, wishing to make my excuses. I felt increasingly uncomfortable.

'We thought we'd go for a drive in the New Forest,' Rebecca interrupted, smiling.

'Oh,' Roger remarked, sensing my surprise.

'Yeah, I'll just, umm, get my things together,' I said, making my way from the kitchen. The sooner I excused myself from Roger's presence the better. Rebecca rustled up some toast and cereal and then we made tracks.

I would have been happy to go home but didn't feel walking out was an option considering the events of the previous night. I was more concerned about the direction the conversation might take. I needn't have worried. Despite our bedroom antics, Rebecca spoke as if she'd come to terms with the fact that we had finished. She asked what I was going to do now. Did I hope to meet someone else? The expected dialogue about 'us' didn't materialise. Maybe my conjecture on the Rebecca / Roger scenario was less speculative than I'd originally imagined. We made our way through one of the quaint villages in the forest in virtual silence until Rebecca noticed something out of the window.

'Stop,' she shouted.

'What?' I exclaimed.

'Stop the car.'

'Why?'

'It's … what's his name.'

'Who?'

'That man from *Only Fools and Horses* … Uncle Albert.'

'That wasn't him,' I said dismissively, 'it's just some old bloke with a white beard.'

'It was him,' she said snapped defensively, 'turn the car round.'

Reluctantly I parked up and we made our way back down the high street. It was only when we got close and saw the Buster Merryfield posters that I realised it was indeed *the* Uncle Albert. He was promoting his new book. We eventually got to talk to him after we bought a copy, which he signed for us.

'You make a lovely couple,' his well-spoken voice replaced the cockney accent I'd been expecting.

'Thanks, thank you very much,' I glanced uneasily at Rebecca.

'Make sure you look after this chap …' he said to Rebecca, putting his hand on my shoulder, 'and keep hold of him.' It all felt a bit surreal, especially when Rebecca told him she would.

We returned to the car and drove back through the forest to Bournemouth. We weren't far from Rebecca's new residence when she seemingly had a panic attack, riffling feverishly through her handbag.

'Oh my God,' she cried.

'What's up now?'

'My pill,' she said, 'I never took my pill.'

'Can't you just take another one now?'

'Of course not,' she growled.

'Alright, alright,' I said, 'I'm only trying to help. Can't you take one of those morning after pill thingies?'

'It's bloody Sunday, Connor,' she said desperately. I momentarily thought about cracking an insensitive joke about the massacre in Ireland but thought better of it.

'Well don't they have those all day chemists or clinics where you can get them from?'

'I don't know Connor, I don't know,' she sobbed.

'Don't cry,' I said reassuringly, trying to ignore my own panic, 'we'll sort something out.'

We pulled up outside her house and she quickly got out. 'I'll come in with you,' I said.

'No, no, it's all right, I'll sort it.' She didn't seem in any state to sort anything.

'Let me know how you get on,' I shouted helplessly but she was already half way up the drive.

I felt I should have been allowed more input into sorting this mess. I scoured the yellow pages the moment I got home for chemists and clinics. No luck; either no reply or answer machine. My attention turned to the local newspaper. Surely they must list emergency dispensers. The good news, they did. The bad news, there was still no reply. I couldn't believe that there could be a proportion of the population who were Saturday night babies conceived on a weekend purely because their parents couldn't find a twenty-four hour clinic. I felt useless, pacing around the lounge, smoking endless cigarettes and watching TV. I didn't go on the Internet in case Rebecca tried to phone. The longer it went on the more I began to panic. It got to 7pm and Rebecca still hadn't phoned. I thought I'd take the initiative and ring her. Roger answered.

'Hello,'

'Hello, is Rebecca there please?' I didn't feel like making conversation with the smarmy git.

'No, I'm afraid she's out with Clare.'

Clare? Who's Clare?

'Who's Clare?'

'Oh, she's one of the other girls in the house.' He said 'girls' as if they were members of his harem.

‘Do you know what time she’ll be back?’ I asked, ‘it’s quite important.’

‘Is it about this morning?’ he asked, putting me on the back foot.

‘What about this morning?’ I blurted.

‘The pill,’ he said matter of factly. I felt exposed, as if someone had read my teenage diary.

‘Errm, well yes.’ I couldn’t believe she’d discussed it with bloody Roger.

‘Oh you don’t need to worry about that,’ he said ‘it’s all been sorted.’

‘How do you mean, it’s been sorted?’

‘Well I don’t know the gory details,’ he laughed smugly, ‘but I know Clare and Becci have sussed it.’

And no one thought to ring me?

‘I’m surprised she didn’t ring to tell you,’ he continued. I’m sure he was trying to wind me up.

‘How?’ I asked.

‘What?’

‘How exactly has it … been resolved?’

‘Well, like I said,’ he said still chuckling, ‘I’m not party to the gory details … I hope you don’t mind me knowing, she was just very upset when she came in and I guessed she needed someone to talk to.’

Me, me … why couldn’t she have talked to me?

‘Well I’m glad it’s all OK,’ I said unconvincingly.

‘Yeah, if there’s any problems, I’ll get her to give you a ring.’

‘Thanks.’

‘No probs, hope to see you again soon, baah.’ Not only was I humiliated … I was infuriated. The situation had seemingly been sorted without any need for me. And Roger had annoyed me. He was one of these people who said ‘bye’ as if he was a sheep. ‘Baah?’ What the bloody hell was ‘baah’ supposed to mean?

Completely pissed off I went to bed to ponder my next course of action.

Chapter 12

The thought of going on holiday and getting away from it all only occurred to me when Alan unexpectedly asked me to go with him and a couple of his mates to Spain. Holidaying with Alan wouldn't be high on my priority list at the best of times. Despite now not being the 'best of times', the prospect of a week in Spain with Alan and what I could only imagine to be Alan clones was still not high on my wish list. I thought maybe I'd make my own enquiries at the travel agent and see what I could dig up.

'I'd like to do something … different. Go somewhere … different,' I said. 'Oh, and I don't want to go to Spain.' Knowing my luck I'd end up bumping into a tribe called Alan. The assistant, whose name badge informed me she was called Kelly, thought I was a little odd for not wanting stay in a bed sit over a night club in Tenerife or go on an 18-30 'holiday' to Corfu. Her pained expression became even more tortured when we established I would be holidaying alone. Thinking about it, I can't say I really blame her. The agent on the next desk interrupted Kelly's face pulling competition by sliding a brochure onto her desk. She looked at me reassuringly and smiled.

'There might be something in here that takes your fancy sir,' she said. I could see out of the corner of my eye that Kelly was now scowling across the desk at me with her arms folded. I attempted to smile back at the assistant who'd shown some interest in my vacation dilemma but Kelly had so disconcerted me it must have looked like I had trapped wind.

'Huhh, you do realise I'm supposed to be going to lunch in a minute,' said Kelly as she begrudgingly pushed the brochure across the desk with one finger. I must admit I was a little disappointed at her lack of enthusiasm and may I say damn right rudeness, but being me I didn't want to cause a scene. I said I would take the brochure home and have a scan through at my leisure to alleviate any risk of famine that might result from Kelly not being able to take her lunch on time. My attempt to diffuse the situation didn't work. 'That's an office copy,' scowled Kelly. I raised my eyebrows.

'I'm sorry?' I replied.

'That's an office copy. It can't leave … the office.' Her head was now cocked to one side and her mouth slightly open. She might as well have been saying, 'if you've got a problem with it being an office copy or make any attempt to leave the premises with the aforementioned publication I will have no other course of action left open to me than to press this red buzzer, alerting the brochure police and sit back whilst they burst out from the back room and proceed to give you a right good kicking.' She sat back and tapped her pen between her teeth glaring at me across the desk. For a moment I wondered if she was trying to alert the brochure police via telepathy. Before I decided to make a run for it, the girl on the next desk butted into our confrontation once more.

'Why don't you go to lunch,' she said looking down at Kelly's name badge. 'Kelly. I'll take over here.' She certainly didn't need telling twice. Her bag was over her shoulder in a matter of seconds and she proceeded to slope off towards the door.

'Now sir, if you'd like to move over to this desk we'll see what we can do shall we?' I didn't mind that her smile was false and her manner slightly condescending. She was being helpful and she was a damn sight more amenable than Kelly.

'Is she new?' I asked.

'Yes, she started last week. We're training her.'

'I think you're going to have your work cut out there if you don't mind me saying.' I replied. She smiled at me once more and asked if I'd care to take a look through the brochure. This suddenly seemed a bad idea. Yes, I wanted something different but that didn't constitute an 'Art of Oil Painting' holiday in Tuscany or a 'Yoga Experience' on the shores of the Gozo which was seemingly all this brochure had to offer. Admittedly, 18 to 30 holidays were not my thing but I hadn't bargained on going on a Saga holiday either. 'I was thinking more along the lines of, oh I don't know, something exciting.' I said. She took the brochure from me and thumbed to a page depicting the Greek Islands.

'How about scuba diving in Kephalonia,' she enquired, 'would that be exciting enough for you?' She must have read the panic in my face. 'Or would that be a little bit too exciting?' Not wanting to look like a lily livered jessabelle after all my fuss, I took the brochure from her and scanned the page in question.

'The, the apartments look very nice,' I stammered. At that my mobile rang. It was Alan to say he was just about to book the holiday and it was my last chance should I have changed my mind. Hmmm, holidaying with Alan and chums or going on my own and scaring the living shit out of myself everyday for seven days whilst scuba diving in the Mediterranean? I booked for Kephalonia.

Chapter 13

'Feel the Sunshine' – Alex Reece.

So this was to be my first holiday alone. It had its advantages. I only had myself to look out for after all. There was no quarrelling over tickets or passports. I could browse at my leisure through the duty free and when I eventually made my way onto the flight I was able to sit anywhere I liked. There were only seven of us on the plane. We almost had a stewardess each.

I felt like an ambassador for singledom - albeit nonchalantly straggling at the back - as we alighted the plane on to Greek tarmac and made our way into the arrivals lounge. Travelling alone seemed to heighten my senses or maybe I became increasingly nosey. Either way, I indulged in more people watching and eavesdropping than ever before.

'It's too hot George,' scowled one young lady in front of me. 'I told you I should have worn a T-shirt but you always know better don't you.'

'It's difficult to know what the weather's going to do this time of year, that's all babe,' George replied defensively. 'I didn't want you getting cold.' George's partner was having none of it.

Folding her arms, she stomped her feet like a spoilt child. I admit it was warm but there was nothing stopping her from removing her fleece. I felt the corners of my mouth turning skywards into a smug smile. Singletons like me didn't have to tolerate such crap.

My smugness didn't last long, the hollow clunk of the key turning in the apartment door made me feel horribly alone. It was the plushest accommodation I'd ever stayed in. A welcome pack filled with exotic fruit, wine, biscuits and fresh bread greeted me on the oak table in the dining area. I opened the fridge and stepped back in awe: cheeses, fresh milk, yoghurts, chilled wine and chocolate made a startling contrast to the mouldy contents of my fridge back home. I instinctively turned around to share the news of the treasures ... and immediately felt ridiculous. I sat down on one of the sofas, stroking the fabric as if I was in *Courts* showroom. The arms weren't worn through and the springs were still firm. No need for a throw on this baby. I made my way out onto the balcony via the patio doors , rubbing my eyes as they adjusted to the light. The view was fantastic. I stood mesmerised, watching the comings and goings in the bay below. I closed my eyes and imagined someone was going to slip their hands around my waist and rest their head on my shoulder any minute soon. I began to wonder what it must be like to meet the person of your dreams, thinking back to how I felt when I'd first met Becci. I opened my eyes. What would have been the next steps? Get hitched, spend X number of years in marital 'bliss' and then inevitably split up and spend thousands of pounds in the courts fighting over possessions, kids and rights of access? Maybe not so much fun after all and possibly a pessimistic view of marriage and relationships, but isn't that what happens to more and more so-called 'happy' couples?

What were my chances of moving on? Yes, I guess I could shack up with anyone who showed me the faintest interest but that wasn't really the answer, but then I wasn't sure the isolation of being single was any more uplifting. For all my externally perceived confidence, being back on the market only made me feel less self-assured than normal. The problem as far as I could see was my image. I was the proverbial boy next door. Clean cut, dependable, honest, and caring (not to mention modest ha ha), there is not an ounce of mystery about me. I wasn't a cad, nor mean and dangerous but unfortunately for me, this is what the female population were seemingly interested in. Ask any woman the characteristics she would look for in her ideal man and the majority would suggest the attributes I have just listed to describe myself. Quid's in me, you might think. Wrong! This is a complete blatant lie. What women fail to include in their statement is that to get to this idealistic man, they must first go out with a string of complete bastards who treat them like dirt whilst they attempt to change these pathetic specimens into the man of their dreams. If you're arrogant, over confident and/or generally laddish then you are a perfect candidate for the female correction process. Even on the odd occasion where I had been able to forge a relationship, despite my apparent lack of character, this had seemed to give my opposite number the green light to walk all over me. Not that I'm bitter and twisted about my philosophy you understand. No, I was much better off wallowing in the depths of self-pity. I decided to go to the welcome meeting.

'Hello and welcome to Greece,' shouted the cheery rep. I looked round at the couples, linking arms and attentively hanging on every word. I sneered and sipped my sangria. I imagined this was how Jack Dee would take a holiday alone. 'Now there's lots to do on the island of Kephalonia and even though you're all here for two weeks you will have no problems in filling your time.' Her voice inflected at the end of her sentence. It was as if she was expecting us to cheer or something. There were more punters in the bar than had arrived on our flight. I glanced around the room in an attempt to spot my fellow divers would be. They, like me, would only be here for a week for the PADI course. Nobody moved a muscle.

'So, we start off … yes?' said the rep, acknowledging my limp arm raised in the air.

'I'm only here for the week,' I said.

'Speak up at the back, I can't hear you.'

'I said,' speaking with more purpose, 'I'm just here for the week.'

'No,' she replied feverishly riffling through the papers on her clipboard. 'Ah yes, you must be Connor. Yes, you're the only one who's here for a week.'

'So where do I enrol for the diving?' I asked

'You'll have to see Konstantinos and see if he has any spaces. If you go out of the bar, turn right, and go up the stone steps on …'

'I booked … and paid for the diving before I left,' I explained.

'Well, if you just go and see Konstantinos. I'm sure he'll sort you out,' she shooed me out of the bar. 'Now, as I was saying …' she returned to her more appreciative audience. I necked my free drink and headed for the office.

I gingerly knocked on the already open door at the top of the stone steps. I assumed that the grunted acknowledgement from inside meant I could go in. The office was small and through the haze of dense smoke I could see a rather rotund unshaven character leaning back in his chair, his feet on the desk. He leisurely inhaled the cigarette hunging from his bottom lip, ushering me in.

'What d'ya want?' he said gruffly.

'Is this where I enrol for the diving?' I asked nervously. He looked around at his surroundings, shrugging his shoulders as he did so. The floor was covered in wet suits and masks. Air tanks were neatly stored in the corner whilst the walls were filled with pictures of expeditions.

'We are a diving school,' he raised his eyebrows in a rather dismissive way.

'Well,' I started, 'I'd like to enrol please.' This was a blatant lie. I wasn't sure I wanted to do it any more; nobody else had booked any diving that week. While most people would have jumped at the chance of one-to-one tuition, I thought it might have been easier to learn if there were more novices against whom to judge your own abilities. Part of the reason I'd decided on the diving was that I imagined it would be a good way to meet new people. There would be camaraderie among the respective idiots in the bar after a hard day's tuition. It wasn't to be. I was very much alone.

Konstantinos didn't exactly have the softly softly approach when it came to his teaching methods. We spent the first couple of days in a villa up in the hills overlooking Fiskcardo. Imagine feeling nervous about diving and then add to that being squashed onto the back of a tiny moped with a fat Greek going up a one in fifteen incline. Ok, now imagine carrying all your diving equipment for the day including weight belts, air tanks and wetsuits and you'll have some idea of the state I was in by the time we reached the villa. Coming down was worse, but at least I had the day's tuition out of the way, albeit in the villa's swimming pool.

On the second day Konstantinos wrongly assumed I'd retained all my knowledge from the first and was ready to go.

'Ready?' he said as I struggled with my buoyancy device and mask. Before I had the chance to respond in the negative, I was given a hefty shove from the side, straight into the pool. Konstantinos had been the Greek equivalent of a U.S. Navy Seal. This was how they were taught apparently and his philosophy was that if it had worked for him, it would work for anyone else. You were, quite literally, in at the deep end.

'You'll have to learn how to remove and replace all your equipment whilst you're in the water in any case,' he said. At least I think that's what he said. It was quite difficult to hear over the noise I was making thrashing around gasping for air.

Unbelievably, Konstantinos and I began to get on very well. The one to one tuition was a benefit and after the brutal initiation of the first couple of days I began to realise he was actually an alright guy. The more I showed interest and willingness to overcome (or attempt to overcome) my fears, the more he cut me some slack. The final dives off the Greek coast made it all worthwhile. They were breathtaking.

In a way I had my own holiday romance. Whilst staying in Greece my relationship with the island grew day by day. I'd gone to most of the local Greek bars, scuba dived, gone out for meals, and become friends with some of the locals. Call me old fashioned but I think friendship is the ideal basis for any relationship. As my holiday 'romance' blossomed I learnt more and more about a project which was being developed for the following summer. Various ecological schemes would be undertaken requiring a minimum of 350 students/volunteers. They would be recording the flora and fauna; re-establishing overgrown costal paths; building a boat from scratch and tracking the path of Odysseus. The main project was recovering a wreck, which seemingly only a handful of people knew about. From what I could tell it was a galleon of some description and due to its depth, as a diver, you weren't able to have very much bottom time. Hence the need for many divers working in relays to uncover the secrets of the sunken vessel. A camp was going to be set up, along with a purpose-built museum. I got involved in setting up the web site and wanted to learn more and more about how I could help. Konstantinos was keen for me to return to Fiskcardo the following summer to take up a supervisory position. This filled my head with a multitude of images: jacking in my job to live in Greece and sticking two fingers up at everything that had made my life a misery over the last few months. Maybe this was to be my escape, a chance to experience new and exciting things and to broaden my horizons.

There was one problem. If this was to come off it would mean a great deal of change and upheaval – and that's not something I'm good at. One of my many problems is my inability to adapt to change. If I'm honest I haven't come across too many people who are. I guess you could say people such as scientists and inventors enjoy change or else they wouldn't do what they do but I must confess I don't know too many of them. To be honest, I don't actually know any scientists or inventors although I should imagine that people like Carol Vorderman (well, she's not really a scientist, but she's pretty damn clever none the less) and that bloke who devised the clockwork radio (is his name Trevor somebody?) strike me as people who could probably deal with change quite well. Maybe they are safe in the knowledge that change is a good thing and that progression has essentially made the human race what it is today. Quite how the advancement of nuclear weapons and Dolly the sheep fit into this equation is still a little sketchy in my mind.

No, my gripe with the whole 'change' scenario is that even people who aren't convinced it might actually be a good thing are still a lot more capable of dealing with it than me. The stress induced by the prospect of change manifests itself in me as a fuzzy headed feeling which is very difficult to explain, and even when I try, the words used seem to be create a completely different phenomena completely alien to me. However, for the purposes of convincing you I am a complete freak I will endeavour to make sense of it all. It's kind of like walking around every day life without being too sure whether it's actually every day life or not. It hard to tell whether it's a film set or maybe a dream where you see the day's events through a camera lens positioned a few feet behind you. It's as if you interact with people in a sort of semiconscious manner. A bit like when you are really pissed I suppose, but without the staggering about with a bottle or can of something shouting, 'I really luv eewwwwee,' and throwing up. OK, so it's nothing like being pissed, I was just trying to make a connection with the fuzzy head, misty eyes and the general feeling that you're really not too sure what the bloody hell is going on. At least when you're pissed you don't care. Any the wiser? I'm sure I'm not.

I remember I tried to write a series of poems about it once. My Mum found them when she was tidying my room. She got quite upset and tried to talk about the way I felt. Seeing as how neither the poems nor my own vocabulary were capable of expressing my thoughts and feelings in coherent sentences, I decided it best to explain the poems away as a school project. The problem with change is that it can take on so many different guises. Change of feelings, change of surroundings, change in circumstances or even just the anticipation of change. By this stage in my life I had managed to control my reactions to change in most cases to a level of mild apprehension or worry. The last time I had felt the full effect of the mysterious beast was in July 1997 when I changed jobs. This had lasted for about two weeks, one week of apprehension and one week of settling in. Of course then I had the advantage of an understanding girlfriend. Understanding is probably not the correct word to use. I doubt she did. Nonetheless she was sympathetic, which in the circumstances was just as important.

Now though, I didn't have anyone. If it was going to happen and I was to face up to the prospect of change, I was going to need support. The 'feeling' had already sporadically returned since the break up and any further life tangents were sure to take their toll if faced alone. The parental route for help didn't appeal. I still wanted them to think I was relatively normal even if nobody else did. Anyway, I was 24 for Christ's sakes, I should be old enough to sort this out for myself. I had my friends to rely on though, Alan and Jimmy. Then again maybe I was right the first time. It was just me, myself and I.

It was obvious I really did need to grow up and learn to stand on my own two feet. Strange you might think for a guy of 24, but there had always been someone there to lean on, to share things with. Now I was in the big wide world with no back up, heart breaking eh? I needed to start making my own decisions without looking around to get an agreeing nod from someone. I needed to take responsibility for my own actions. Making decisions had never been one of my strong points. It was about time I learnt. The thing is it's not like learning to scuba dive or playing the guitar where you could get someone to teach you. I don't even take too much notice of these books you can buy. I'm sure that books with titles like 'How to be more assertive' and the like are only written to prey on bewildered people like me. I would just like to say that I have never bought such a book for this very reason. No, making decisions and adapting to change is just something you have to figure out for yourself.

I had always hoped that my ability to adapt to change would get easier as I got older. To a certain degree, based on my own experience, this seems to have been generally the case. In the last 18 months, I had studied for and completed my part time degree with a change of university from Bristol to London. I'd bought my own house, moved in with my long-term girlfriend, changed jobs, split up with my long-term girlfriend and made the transition from depressive solitude into the single world of pratting about and getting pissed. Now I was on holiday by myself with a further 12 months of uncertainty ahead. Would the 'feeling' intensify? Why after reminding myself of all the positives did I still feel so negative? Things could have been a lot worse. I could have decided to go on the lad's holiday with Alan and brought back nothing more than a sombrero and a wicker donkey.

Chapter 14

'It's not bloody fair,' said Alan as he stared into his half empty beer glass. Trust me on this one; in Alan's case his glass was definitely half empty and not half full. On our respective returns to the UK Alan and I had gone for a drink to talk holidays. It didn't take me long to appreciate he wasn't happy.

The problem with going on holiday is that more often than not you have to return home to the mundane load of crap you left behind. I believe it's commonly referred to as 'post holiday blues'. This however wasn't the reason for Alan having a face like a wet weekend.

'I mean, a whole two weeks.' Alan looked up from his glass, 'I'm definitely going to write them a letter.' It was safe to say his holiday to Spain had not gone according to plan. Apparently, 'Club Alan', along with a couple of other passengers, arrived at Malaga airport with only their hand luggage. After much delay they were told that for some reason their luggage was still at Gatwick but would be put on the next flight out and couriered to their apartments. Having now missed the original transfer in the nice air-conditioned bus, they waited an hour for a replacement which never materialised, and were eventually bundled onto packed local transport, standing room only, in the heat of the Spanish sunshine. After spending the afternoon around the pool in the sweaty pants he'd had on all day he (or any of the others for that matter) didn't much fancy going out in the evening in the body odour infested clothes they'd arrived in. The next couple of days were spent trailing to meetings with the rep to check where their luggage was. By the third day it still hadn't turned up and so the rep gave them £60 compensation among the three of them to buy some clothes until the luggage eventually made an appearance. Being a small tourist resort there wasn't much of a selection to choose from other than day-glow orange vest tops with 'I love Spain' embossed on the front.

'We burnt all the bastard clothes we bought on our last night,' Alan informed me.

'Shit Alan, your luggage didn't turn up 'till the last day?' I tried not to laugh.

'No, it didn't turn up at all. It's just that the clothes were so crap we couldn't be arsed to bring them home with us. My problem was trying to find anything big enough to fit. I spent the whole week in flip flops 'cus I couldn't find shoes big enough. The biggest shorts I could find were those swimming ones with the netting in. Not only were they a hideous colour but the netting kept chafing on me cobblers.' I had to look away for fear of hurting Alan's feelings.

'Oh dear, so have you got your luggage back now?'

'Oh yeah, we've got it back now. As soon as we got back to Gatwick they announced our names on the speaker system and told us to go to the enquiry desk where they duly presented us with our suitcases.'

'Any explanation?' I asked.

'No, other than the cases had their break in the Canary Islands.' I could feel the corners of my mouth turning upwards and had to take a swig of beer to hide my grin.

'So what did you actually have with you, in your hand luggage I mean?'

'Nothing much, just had a few sweets that had melted, our washing kit and my personal CD player.'

'At least you had some tunes to listen to then eh?' I was trying to be as sympathetic as I could.

'Not really, I'd put the CD's in my case.' Alan could see I was squirming in my seat. I couldn't hold out for much longer. 'Oh I had my camera as well.'

'So,' I tried to compose myself, 'did you get some good snaps of where you stayed?'

'Yeah,' Alan said reluctantly. He had a *but*-face, there was definitely a 'but' coming, 'but someone had been arsing around with my camera in the apartment.'

'How do you mean?'

'Well, I thought when I got them developed that I hadn't

taken as many photos, and then when I got them back …' he broke off for a moment and looked me straight in the eye, 'do you promise not to laugh?' I nodded, so that I couldn't be held to a 'not laughing' verbal contract. I thought maybe sucking my cheeks in might help me keep my side of the bargain. Alan leaned over the table and lowered his voice. 'There were all these pictures of the chambermaids with …' he broke off again and dropped his head, 'with my toothbrush poked up their arse.' That was it. I was a goner.

'I'm sorry Alan, you've gotta be winding me up,' I screamed. Alan looked around feverishly to see if anyone was looking.

'No, no straight up, they were like waggling their bums at the camera with the handle poking out. You said you wouldn't laugh.'

'I'm sorry mate,' I said, wiping the tears from my eyes. 'So you didn't have the best of vacations then all in all?'

'That's the understatement of the year. Getting those photos was just the icing on the cake. One of them was a bloke. I mean I thought it tasted funny but just put it down to the water …'

'Alan, Alan, stop for Christ's sake, my ribs are aching.'

'So did you have a good holiday anyway?' Alan asked. I thought about it for a couple of seconds and stared up at the ceiling. It would have been harsh to bleat on about what a great time I had had when he'd endured the holiday from hell. Telling him about all the thoughts, hopes and dreams the holiday had provoked wouldn't have been too tactful and besides, this is Alan we're talking about.

'Hmm, yeah,' I said, 'it was OK.'

Chapter 15

'Whatever' – Oasis.

Things went very quiet after returning from Greece. I hadn't heard from Rebecca since her birthday. There were no messages on the phone, no notes posted through the door, no crappy tapes for me to crush underfoot. It was the end of the end as far as I could tell. For some strange and purely selfish reason I found it difficult to take. I knew I'd made the right decision in ending it. The relationship wasn't going anywhere but knowing Rebecca now couldn't give a toss, or at least was capable of living her life without me, hurt. I used to work with a woman whose husband died tragically. She was in her 50's, he had been life assured up to the hilt and they had been married for thirty odd years. He'd put a lot of money away in various policies to make sure that she was sorted if anything should happen to him. Within six months of him dying, the love of his life had sold the house, met another gentleman friend, jacked in her job and spent the cash going on world cruises. It didn't seem right somehow. I guess everybody has the ability to move on. It's just a question of how quickly. You probably won't find it particularly hard to believe I'm usually in the slow lane. As I've already mentioned, change - whether it be for good or for bad - has a tendency to knock me for six. Rebecca had seemingly banished me from her system and it was about time I did the same. Although tempted, I refrained from phoning her. As I slowly became accepted back into my old friendship fold, we developed a loose routine. My life mainly consisted of the following:

1) Hanging out with Jimmy and Alan.

1a) Attending numerous football matches to watch Bournemouth play both home and away. I would even go as far as to say that I quite enjoyed it. I'd got to know the players' names and the terrace chants and in a sad kind of way was able to feel a part of something. When you start going to the games week in and week out it almost becomes a soap opera. From watching episode one and not really knowing what the hell is going on you slowly begin to pick up the storyline, get to know the characters and interact with the highs and lows. That said, I declined Alan's numerous invitations to watch the reserve matches; I wasn't overly keen on watching the behind the scenes making of the soap opera as well. My enthusiasm for the main fixtures did however lead me to the opticians so I could see what the bloody hell was going on. The eye examination at the goggle shop also provided me with an all too rare encounter with a member of the opposite sex. Stuck in a dark cramped room with a tall gorgeous optician was the nearest I got to any shenanigans. I mean, I didn't snog her or even get her phone number but she did seem inclined to push herself against me whenever possible. Her warm minty breath on my face and the chance to gawp at her cleavage was the best it got. Sad eh?

1b) Tuesday night pub quiz. More about the beer than the questions, so pissed by the end we never cared we'd come last … again.

1c) Thursday nights playing darts or pool to a very low standard and talking bollocks.

1d) Clubbing, usually when Alan had heard on the grapevine which establishment the Bournemouth team were likely to be in on a Saturday night after a home game. This wasn't always healthy. Alan had a tendency to turn worryingly homosexual. He was almost orgasmic having his picture taken with 'Super' Steve Fletcher in the *Empire*. But then, who am I to talk? I was equally weak-kneed at the sight of some of my old footballing heroes playing for teams in lower divisions. In our travels around the country I had the pleasure of witnessing the ageing skills of Peter Beardsley and stood only yards away from Nigel Spink. The fact I was more than mildly excited about seeing these players in the twilight of their career troubled me. It seemed only a matter of time until I turned into Alan.

2) Talking to equally sad individuals on the Internet. It instantly relieved boredom with the minimum of effort. Sorting the wheat from the chaff became increasingly easy with experience. I soon learnt that naively talking to anyone could be costly. Most of the people in the chat rooms were Yanks so when you 'met' someone who was actually from England it was a bit of a novelty. More surprising still if the person claimed to come from the same town as you. After initially dismissing *PornstarPeggy* as a time waster my curiosity got the better of me.

Without any prompting from me she started to list street names to prove she was local. I knew people she'd been to school with and it turned out she lived not far from me. Maybe we knew each other? We exchanged photos by e-mail. By the time they'd downloaded we'd swapped phone numbers and agreed to meet up for a drink. I wasn't disappointed when I eventually received her pictures. She looked quite attractive, sat cross-legged on the floor in a red night slip. We got chatting again and she asked if I liked what I saw.

'Yes, it's very nice,' I typed.

'You're not put off by them?' she replied. I was a bit confused as I'd only received one photo.

When I asked 'Is there more than one? she told me there were about ten photos on the same attachment. That explained why they'd taken so long to download. I'd failed to notice the grey scroll bar on the right hand side. As her name suggested, the remainder of the page was filled with gradually more explicit pornographic pictures. I stared at the monitor open mouthed. These weren't scanned in from a magazine. They were clearly amateur shots taken at home. She'd seemed such a pleasant girl too. Although shocked, my twisted curiosity wouldn't allow me to cancel our arranged meeting. I wished I had. It was around 11.30pm when her brother dropped her off in a desolate Tesco's car park in his beaten up Ford Cortina. With all the pubs shut and no-where really to go, we drove down by the seashore to the car park where I'd eaten my chips on New Year's Day. I should have known it was a bad idea. I'll summarise events by saying she was very forward. She was very insistent she should take the majority of her clothes off and it was as much as I could do to stop her cavorting around the car park naked. I drove her home as quickly as possible but of course she had my mobile phone number. She used to ring me up and ask, 'Are you ready for that shag yet?' I always declined as politely as I could. It didn't seem right somehow. Like Rachel Summers from the deli, she scared the shit out of me. Needless to say it wasn't long before I became a lot more cautious in chat rooms. On a more positive note, I got to know Kristy a whole lot better. We used to chat on quite a regular basis and even phoned each other now and again. She was a breath of fresh air. Venting our daily frustrations to a person on the other side of the world was therapeutic for both of us.

Going to London to stay with Ellie was a particularly favourite pastime of mine. Initially, I think she felt sorry for me. Although Bob always offered me a bed at his place, for some reason I always felt drawn to the house full of nurses. There were obvious advantages to staying with Ellie even if it did mean sleeping on a couch, in a hallway or half under the stairs. Being woken up from my makeshift bed, wherever it happened to be, to the vision of underdressed females could never really be described as a chore. There were house rules however. Ellie insisted that under no circumstances should I snog (or have any other sexual liaison with) any of the girls in the house. Again, this wasn't a problem. I was thoroughly looked after in every other respect and there was a certain confidence to be gained from going pubbing and clubbing as the only bloke with a multitude of young, attractive females. There soon came a time when I'd got to know three of the other girls in the house so well that Ellie would arrange to go out with Bob and pretty much leave me to it. Belle was the grunge girl of the house. Her jet-black hair and long fringe made her look paler than she really was, a highlighted red streak her only splash of colour. She could usually be found wearing combats and a T-shirt sporting whichever particular band was in favour that month. She made up for her quiet nature by belting out her music as loudly as she could. Contrastingly, Kat was the Irish, bubbly pop fanatic. She was always dressed ready for clubbing (even if she happened to be popping to the corner shop for some fags) and was always up for a laugh. Her round face generally beamed a radiant smile even if I happened to be ribbing her about her unhealthy appetite for 70's disco or Abba. Mel was completely different again. Classy and sassy, she spent her time stringing unsuspecting men along looking for the perfect, rich male who would be able to keep her in the manner to which she had become accustomed (her parents were very well off). With her looks, she could have had anybody but never seemed happy with whatever she had. Underneath her sophisticated, confident appearance was an insecure vulnerable girl with a heart of gold. I had a soft spot for Mel but despite her constant flirting I knew that I would never be able to live up to her expectations. Whatever the differences in our characteristics, we always had a ball on a Saturday night. Although we were all roughly the same age I felt like the big brother taking his sisters for a night out. We would arrive home in various states of consciousness but I always took great pleasure in looking out for them. Whether it was offering my coat to the coldest member of the team, giving piggybacks or simply hailing a cab because the others were all too pissed, we had fun.

I was actually starting to enjoy myself; I never knew where I would be going, who I was going to meet or even where I was going to sleep. On the occasions when I found myself alone, I was perfectly comfortable with my own company. I felt free and it felt great.

Chapter 16

Whilst I was getting to grips with single life, Bob and Ellie were going from strength to strength. When they announced their engagement I was very happy for them but not surprised. They were the perfect couple. There was a glint in their eyes when they were together and a flash of a smile when the name of their other half was mentioned. They were meant to be.

Bob and I went shopping in Camden on the weekend before the engagement party. He wanted to buy something snazzy for the big night but came away with nothing. Instead, he talked me into spending an extortionate amount of money on a gaudy Rothmans biker's jacket. It wasn't like me to buy something impulsively. I didn't even have a motorbike but I bought it all the same. After being enthusiastic in his support for my purchase, Bob spent the rest of the afternoon taking the piss.

'Where on earth are you going to wear that?' he scoffed. I knew he was right. It was probably over the top even for a Superbike Grand Prix. Bob's mocking didn't stop him from asking if he could try it on however.

'Funny how things work out,' said Bob as we made our way

back to the tube station.

'How do you mean?' I asked.

'I mean how things change. It wasn't so long ago you were happily living with Rebecca …' I looked at the floor. 'I'm not having a go. I'm just saying that you're coping with single life. You seem comfortable with it.' He continued. I gave a half-hearted smile. 'As for me, I'm happy with my lot. Marrying Ellie is a dream come true.'

'You're meant for each other mate.'

'Thanks,' he said laughing, 'I think I know that.' We walked through the ticket machines and made our way down the escalator. 'Even Alan seems to have stepped out of the shadow of Jimmy.' I raised my eyebrows in confusion. 'Well he's supposedly met this Terry chap who he hangs about with.' My blank expression told Bob I had no idea what he was talking about. 'Jimmy reckons this Terry is an Alan clone, another football anorak.'

'I don't know, I've not heard of this …'

'Terry,'

'Yes, Terry, but if it means Alan gets a break from having the piss ripped out of him by Jimmy all the time, good luck to him.'

'Exactly, that's what I'm trying to say … how things have changed.' We didn't speak on the tube. Nobody else seemed to be talking and although our conversation wasn't top secret I always felt uneasy about other people listening in. I didn't like making eye contact either. I admit that I people watched, but only out of the corner of my eye. It amazed me the number of individuals, ostensibly asleep, who jumped into life and exited the tube at their stop. Bob had told me that you got used to it after a while; you just got to know. There had to be, I therefore assumed, a transition period between the stage of looking feverishly through the window at every station, counting every stop and the stage of knowing instinctively where to get off whilst in a dreamlike state. My thoughts were confirmed when a guy leapt to his feet, scurried from the tube only to turn round halfway down the platform, presumably realising it was the wrong stop, and try to get back on again. The doors were already closing. He must have still been in 'semi-sleep' training.

'Jimmy,' I said as we climbed the steps back to the surface.

'What about him?'

'He's still the same old, well … Jimmy. Nothing's changed for him.'

'I don't think it ever will,' said Bob, 'he's quite happy larking about and doing what he does.'

For once Bob was wrong. When I got home from London I had a distressed message from Jimmy wanting me to meet him at the pub. It sounded pretty serious.

I walked through those oh too familiar doors to find him slumped over the bar looking longingly at the bottom of his pint glass.

'Can I get you another?' It was a rhetorical question; he was clearly in the mood to sink a considerable amount of alcohol.

'Mmmm, yeah, cheers.'

'What'll it be?'

'Stella.' Things must be bad. He only drank Stella when he was feeling really shit. It had a strange effect on him where by he would become very aggressive and melancholy at the same time. His mother had actually banned him from drinking it at home. During one particular 'Stella' moment some years back he'd had a slight disagreement with his brother. His brother ended up in hospital after Jimmy had repeatedly smashed his head on the pavement outside the pub. As far as I was aware, he hadn't ever drunk it since, until now.

'When's Alan getting here?' I enquired.

'He's not, he's going out.' Jimmy made a 'tosser' gesture with his hand.

'Going where?'

'Dunno.'

'But Alan never goes out anywhere unless it's with me or you.'

'Look, I asked him if he was coming out for a beer, he said no. I gave him some grief about being a big wuss, and he said he was going out with Terry.' Ah, the infamous Terry.

'And that's it?'

'No, I gave him some more grief and he told me to go stick it up my arse and put the phone down on me.'

‘Oh.’ It was shocking yet refreshing that Alan had stood up to Jimmy, but I got the impression that this wasn’t the root cause of the problem.

‘The bloke’s a prick,’ Jimmy continued.

‘Errm, are we talking about Terry or Alan?’ I pondered.

‘Terry … well both, but I meant Terry. Did you know he drives a yellow car?’

‘Does he?’ I must admit I’ve always viewed bright yellow car drivers with an air of suspicion but the descriptions of ‘football anorak’ and ‘yellow car driver’ seemed somewhat contradictory.

‘Yeah, why don’t they have ’I’m an egotistical self righteous twat’ daubed on the car instead?’ Jimmy clearly had it in for poor Terry.

‘I don’t know but there’s probably a law against driving round in a car covered in obscenities. It’s probably easier just to buy a yellow car and save yourself the bother.’

Jimmy nodded knowingly. ‘Anyway it’s you I wanted to speak to, not Alan or fucking Terry.’

‘Why, what’s up?’ I asked.

‘I just need to talk a few things through.’ Jimmy let go of his vice like grip on the empty pint glass and scratched his head, sighing as he did so.

At that, a girl walked into the bar. In her early 20’s, she was wearing white hot pants and a tight ribbed top. Very little was left to the imagination. In an attempt to divert Jimmy’s attention from whatever was bothering him, I felt I should make him aware of this vision of loveliness.

‘Bloody hell, take a look at that.’ Jimmy never moved. He didn’t look up or turn around, just continued gazing at his empty glass. I waited for a few seconds to see if there was going to be a delayed reaction. There wasn’t.

‘Get the fucking beers in.’ This was serious. Jimmy not looking at ‘totty’ and making suggestive comments was like, errm, well it was like Southampton winning the Premiership. It just didn’t happen. I went in search of refreshments.

‘So, what’s this all about?’

‘I need to get a few things off my chest and, well, you’ve always been the more sensitive one amongst us.’

I didn't know quite how to feel about this. In a way I was flattered but I'd taken so much crap over the years about my supposed oversensitivity, I felt resentful that, when it suited him, Jimmy figured he could pick my brains. Quite where he, or any of the others for that matter, had been when I needed a shoulder to cry on, I wasn't sure. Well, that's a lie actually, they had been no-where in sight. Why exactly I should help him now was beyond me, but I tried to. Maybe he would remember this in the future if the roles were reversed.

'So, come on then, spit it out.'

'Well, the thing is, I'm not quite sure what is going on with Maria.'

'Maria?' I'd not heard him mention her name before.

'This girl I met a couple of weeks ago.'

'You never told me.'

'Well I didn't want you lot taking the piss.' In other words, he didn't want a piece of his own medicine.

'So you're seeing this girl called Maria?'

'Yep,' said Jimmy gulping down another large mouthful of Stella, 'saw her last night actually.'

'And?'

Jimmy burped.

'So how did it go?'

'Yeah, very well. Well I think it went very well.'

'But you're not sure?'

'Errr, no.'

'Why not?'

'Errm, I dunno.'

'Ah, come on Jimmy, you're not exactly giving me a lot to work with here. So just tell me what happened. You picked her up, took her out, back to yours and pardon me for using one of your expressions, you banged one into her.'

'No I fucking didn't.'

'So, come on then, what *did* happen?'

'I picked her up, we went to the pub, had a quick drink and then I invited her back to mine.'

'So you did bang one into her?'

'Will you just shut up! Do you want to know or not?'

'Mmm,' I murmured, half smirking. To be honest I was enjoying this. It made a change for the boot to be on the other foot. 'So which pub did you go to?'

'I took her down the *Flying Dog* which was ideal really, quite intimate as there was this nice little table right by the window.' This was surreal, groundbreaking stuff. I'm quite positive that words such as 'intimate' and 'nice' hadn't previously resided in Jimmy Brown's vocabulary. The other shocking revelation was his attention to detail; going to country pubs was one thing, taking notice of 'intimate' tables by windows was something else.

'Sounds, errm, lovely,' I tried not to curl the corners of my mouth up.

'Yeah, it was,' said Jimmy, oblivious to my subtle mocking. He was in his own little world.

'So, did you get on? What did you talk about?' I asked.

'I dunno.'

'What, you don't know whether you got on or what you talked about?'

'We definitely got on. I'm just not sure what we talked about. She did most of the talking.'

'Well, that's OK isn't it?' I said trying to sound sympathetic.

'Yeah, I guess.'

'Maybe she was nervous and just prattled on a bit.'

'She, she did not prattle on,' Jimmy raised his voice and stared into my eyes with a look of disgust, 'I, I just had no idea what she was talking about half the time. It was like being in a whirlwind.'

'What do you mean you don't know what she was talking about? Is she foreign?'

'For Christ's sake Connor, no she's not foreign. She just talked about things that I knew nothing about.'

'That's not fucking difficult,' I mumbled.

'I heard that.'

'Sorry.'

'She just talked about bands, music, films, art, actors, actresses, food, things and people I'd never fucking heard of.'

'And that's bad is it?'

'Yeah, I felt like a complete divot.'

'You are a complete divot,' I said jovially. Jimmy didn't respond. He looked … well, he looked absolutely fucking knackered if the truth be known. It seemed to be more than his energy was worth to rise to any comment I had to make.

'So this bewildering conversation carried on at your place did it?'

'Yep, until 5am this morning.'

'I see, so you had plenty of time to inject your pearls of wisdom into the conversation as well then?'

'Not really.'

'So all that time and you didn't utter a word?'

'Yeah …of course I did, but after you've listened to her talking about that sort of stuff, her worldly travels, living and working in Australia and New York, setting up her own business, her ex-boyfriends, of which it would seem there are quite a few …'

'You're a fine one to talk.'

'Yeah, it just seemed pathetic to talk about the stuff I knew. She's just on another level. I'm sure she couldn't give a fuck about my footballing trivia. She certainly couldn't care less who the old bloke who is on that Anne Robinson programme …'

'*Points of view*?'

'Naah, the other one.'

'*Watchdog*, the programme you cannot afford to miss?'

'Yeah, whatever, well the old bloke off that is Harry Enfield's Dad.'

'I know.'

'I know you know, but she didn't.'

'But why would she want to know?'

'She wouldn't, she doesn't even like Harry Enfield.' I must admit I wasn't his greatest fan any more either but in the interests of keeping the conversation going…

'Philistine.'

'She's never even seen *The Fast Show*.'

'Shame on her.'

'I said 'oooooh suits you' to something she said and she had no idea what I was talking about.' Jimmy was becoming hysterical. 'She didn't even know who Damon Albarn was.'

'Well there you are then; she didn't know what you were talking about either.'

'But that's not the point.' He was definitely getting worked up now. I could tell. His face was going red.

'So what is the point?' I knew very well what the point was. Jimmy, for the first time in his life, actually respected a prospective girlfriend. He was fascinated, intrigued, interested in what she had to say. The disturbing thing for Jimmy was the realisation that he actually didn't know everything there was to know about everything. She had travelled, seen the world, had had lots of boyfriends and various one-night stands. She was independent, came from a reasonably wealthy background but had both feet firmly planted on the ground. She certainly wasn't going to take any shit, or need looking after and Jimmy wasn't entirely sure where he fitted into the whole equation. She opened up a whole new world for him with her views, knowledge and experiences and Jimmy had no come back. His day-to-day life was based around football, beer, women and trivia. He hadn't had to confront his feelings before as he'd never given a shit. He'd always been top dog, king pin, wooing the world with his irrelevant facts and figures. Now he'd realised that there was more to life than his previous shallow existence. You may think that last statement was harsh on Jimmy. I don't. Harsh, yet fair, but not exclusively reserved for Jimmy. I think it had a lot to say about all of us.

Chapter 17

'Something wicked this way comes' – Barry Adamson.

The following weekend was Bob and Ellie's engagement party. I was bemused for two reasons: it was being held on a Friday night and at a vegetarian restaurant. Being Friday meant I had to rush up to London after work, dump my car at Bob's (Ellie wasn't sure how many were staying over at hers so I'd been forced to seek alternative accommodation) and follow his confusing directions to the restaurant. By the time I got to his flat he'd already left for pre-engagement party drinks. I didn't have the chance to ask him why, when neither he nor Ellie were vegetarian, dinner was booked at a veggie restaurant. Maybe Laura had the aversion to meat. She was one of Ellie's friends whom she'd been trying to set me up with for a while. Laura seemed to have an insatiably busy lifestyle so something had always cropped up to thwart our, or rather Ellie's, plans. I couldn't believe that someone could actually be that busy. Neither was I sure I wanted to attempt to get it together with someone who could only fit me in at pre-arranged functions. Nonetheless I was curious to meet her. It wasn't until I got to the entrance of the restaurant that I thought it was maybe a bit contemptuous of me to wear my leather Rothmans jacket. There were about fifteen people already sat at the table by the time I arrived. I scanned their faces to see which one might be Laura. Maybe she'd had a previous engagement, if you'll pardon the pun, and not been able to make it. Bob and Ellie were obviously there and beckoned me over. I could see Mel, Kat and Belle so I thought it best to sit amongst people I knew.

'No Jimmy and Alan?' I asked.

'No, Alan's on his way to an away game …' said Bob.

'With Terry?'

'Yes, Terry. Jimmy's seeing Maria.'

'Could he not have brought her with him?' Bob just shrugged his shoulders and an uncomfortable silence followed. I was too busy scrutinising the female faces around the table in search of a possible Laura to realise someone else had taken up the conversational reigns.

'Did you come on a motorbike?' I looked in the direction the question had come from and then looked round the table to see who she was talking to.

'No he didn't,' said Mel looking straight at me.

'Who me? Sorry, no I didn't what?'

'Come on a motorbike,' smiled Mel, sipping on her glass of meat free wine.

'No,' I said derisively, 'why, who said I came on a motorbike?'

'I was just asking,' said the original girl awkwardly, 'because of the jacket.' I think I must have blushed.

'He hasn't got a helmet,' said Mel. I definitely blushed.

'So what's with the jacket?' asked Kat. It seemed as though my jacket had hijacked the proceedings. I briefly saw Bob smirking at me before I buried my head in the menu.

It's the kind of thing that annoys me. If you went to a 'normal' restaurant, vegetarians would be the first to complain if there was nothing veggie on the menu. Here I was, perusing the dishes on offer and not a meat feast in sight. I looked up, considered a revolt, saw that there were still members of the group discussing my jacket and decided against it. Pasta was the only thing I could see that didn't have any vegetables in it (if you ignore the tomato sauce) and so I ordered it out of principle.

By the time I took my head out of the menu it appeared that everyone had formed their own little groups and were chattering to their hearts' content. All apart from Belle that was, her shyness and admirably unconventional tastes had seemingly excluded her from any of the yakking. I opened my mouth to speak to her but at that moment she got up to go to the toilet. Feeling slightly awkward, I overheard Ellie talking about holidays and thought I'd seize the opportunity to join in.

'I've been on holiday,' I enthused. Ellie frowned at me.

'Yes Connor, we know you've been on holiday but we were talking about our New Year break.'

'What New Year's break is that then?' I asked.

'We don't know yet,' said Bob, 'that's why we're talking about it now. We thought we'd go to Barcelona.'

'Or Ireland,' said Ellie.

'Oh yes, or Ireland,' agreed Bob submissively.

'Well wherever it is count me in,' I said confidently. Ellie raised her eyebrows. 'If I'm invited that is,' I added.

'So where did you go on holiday?' Alarm bells rang in my head. That was definitely an Australasian accent. I'm sure Ellie had mentioned Laura was from New Zealand. It had to be her, at least I hoped it was. She was a good-looking girl with a composed air about her. Here was my chance to make a striking first impression.

'Oh, I just went to Kephalonia to complete my PADI scuba

diving training,' I said nonchalantly. I was expecting a flood of enthusiasm from the girls but a couple of them turned away and started their own conversation. After a short silence I thought I'd have to up the tempo. 'You don't quite appreciate how dangerous it is until you actually do it,' I added coolly. Still receiving a tepid response, I felt in necessary to continue. 'Diving down to the Beaufort Bomber that was shot down by the Germans,' I looked across the table to gauge reactions in case there were any Germans in the group, 'had to be the highlight for me.'

'Sounds … interesting,' said the Australasian, but I realised the people around the table were less than impressed with my exploits. 'Isn't your boyfriend a diver?' she said to Mel.

It turned out that Mel, unbeknown to me, had starting dating a guy called Ritchie. He was a fully qualified deep-sea diver, obviously putting my experiences to shame. It got worse.

'Is Ritchie not coming tonight?' asked Kat.

'Yeah,' replied Mel. I tried to disguise rolling my eyes by making out I had an eyelash caught. 'He'll be here a bit later on. He's just working a little late tonight.'

'Where's he working at the moment?' I asked. If he was a deep-sea diver I couldn't quite see how he was going to get back from whichever deep sea he was diving in to make it to a vegetarian restaurant in the middle of London.

'Pinewood,' replied Mel. She must have seen the puzzled look on my face. 'Pinewood Studios. Ritchie's working on the latest James Bond movie. He's a stunt double for Pierce Brosnan.' I wished I'd never brought up the subject of diving at all. The girls all huddled closer to Mel to hear the latest gossip from the set. I wasn't interested any more. Neither was Bob, his masculinity also taking a denting. He wrestled his way from the mêlée of women and came round to my side of the table. He crouched down by the side of the chair.

'So what do you think of Laura then?' he whispered.

'I never knew Mel had a boyfriend,' I sulked.

'Forget it mate, move on. It was never going to happen,' he said bluntly. 'Laura?'

'I dunno,' I said, hanging my head, 'no bastard's introduced us yet.'

'That's her,' he said, flicking his head in the direction of the Australasian. So I was right. I slowly turned my head to get a better look at her. She had shoulder length blonde hair and the cutest dimples. She seemed self-assured and the kind of woman who knew what she wanted. Unfortunately this didn't seem to include me. The evening went from bad to worse. I didn't speak to Laura during any stage of the proceedings (although Lord knows I tried) and Ritchie turned up just after the main course to enthral the women with his adventures with Mr Brosnan. He was everything I expected him to be; tall, tanned with dark hair and big muscles and as cool as you like. He didn't look like Pierce but to rub salt in the wounds he seemed like a bloody nice bloke. As a final straw, the pudding didn't have any meat in it either (give me a break, I was living in hope). Bob and I decided to get pissed.

Chapter 18

We got to the club after the meal and still the air was filled with tales from the deep. Belle, Kat and a few others had made tracks by now so I was even more limited for folk I could talk to. Bob was completely inebriated and Ellie had wedged him in a chair in the corner next to her to keep him out of the way. Laura was in her own little faction with a bunch of other people I didn't know. The rest of the group were with Ritchie Brosnan and Mel. I sat in the corner next to Bob trying to make out that I wasn't sulking. I started to flip beer mats and throw peanuts in the air and catch them in my mouth but I thought it might look like I was seeking attention rather than trying to keep myself amused so I looked out of the window instead. I began to wonder whether Ellie had thrown me a bum steer. She'd told me that Laura had been really excited about meeting me but she didn't seem to give a toss. Maybe she didn't know who I was. Maybe I should throw caution to the wind, bowl on over to Laura's group and introduce myself. No, hang on, she did know what I looked liked. She'd seen a photograph of me. Maybe she'd said she was excited about meeting me before she'd seen the picture. Perhaps she's seen me in real life and decided not to bother.

Before any other possibilities entered my head, the lights went down and everyone started cheering and whooping. I looked over to an alcove of the club where a spotlight was shining brightly on the scruffiest individual I'd ever set eyes on. He sat on a stool, cradling a guitar. I couldn't see the guy's face. His long, greasy, matted hair covered his features. As the appreciative din subsided the man mumbled something into the microphone in front of him. I couldn't understand a word but I must have been the only one. The whole place erupted again. He motioned for his adoring fans to calm down and brushed his hair from his face to reveal a fine set of Hampsteads and bloodshot eyes. The contrast between his shiny teeth and lifeless eyes was really quite creepy. I could only presume that he'd smoked a few biftas before he'd come out. Either that or he was wearing black eye make-up. He muttered something else incomprehensible, distorted further by the fact that he was too close to the microphone. The whooping started once more and he began to strum the guitar. I could only imagine he was a regular. I looked at Bob. He was probably the only other person in the joint besides me who didn't know what the fuck was going on. His head was swaying wildly backwards and forwards. My glance turned to Ellie. Her tearful eyes were fixed on Stig of the Dump and his guitar. I looked around our grinning group, all of them on their feet, gazing happily between Ellie and the guitarist. I realised the guy must have been something to do with the engagement party. Yep, that was definitely an 'Ellie' in the lyrics. OK, so it would appear that Bob had been mentioned too. Other than that, I really couldn't tell you what he was singing about except it seemed like a celebratory song in honour of the happy couple. Was I the only person to think he was dreadful? I looked around once more. It appeared so. I guess I should have embraced this joyful contribution to the evening's proceedings in the spirit in which it was intended. But sickly sweet love songs had never really done it for me and despite the occasion, Stig's off key murmurings were no exception. He did about three numbers in all but was forced to pause during his second effort as his hair had become tangled in the strings of his guitar. He didn't give a shit though and neither it seemed did anybody else. He eventually left the alcove to a standing ovation with his guitar held over his head like a trophy. Almost immediately a live band started right at the back of the club. I couldn't see who they were from where I was sitting but I decided not to be a party pooper any more and made my way to the bar. There was a tap on my shoulder soon after.

'You must be Connor then.' I turned round to see Laura. I realised for the first time she was quite short and possibly a bit older than me. She held out her hand for me to shake. I did the honours and acknowledged my status as Connor.

'We seem to keep missing each other,' she smiled. I'm not sure whether it was because I'd had a bit to drink but her accent seemed more endearing than I'd originally appreciated. She wore a shapely purple skirt that just covered her knees and a matching shoulder-less top that stopped short of her waist. Two purple clips in her shiny blonde hair completed the look. She was stunning and despite her size, I found her looks and confidence intimidating. I would normally have clammed up or said something stupid but although I knew she was completely out of my league, I was surprisingly, well … me. I put it down to the four pints of Kronenbourg lending a helping hand.

'Yes, we meet at last,'

'You don't look anything like your photo,' said Laura, her hypnotic smile completed at either end by those dimples.

'Err,' I mumbled, laughing. 'Is that good or bad?'

'Oh good,' she said, 'you were throwing up over Vauxhall Bridge in the one I saw.'

'Well I would hope that I looked slightly better now,' I said, cursing Ellie.

'Ellie's been trying to get us together for ages.'

'So it seems. You appear to lead a busy life.'

'I just think it's all crazy. I mean just because they're happy they seem to think they can get two complete strangers together and it's all going to be good.'

'Yeah,' I laughed, 'unbelievable.' Although, like I said, I knew I didn't stand a chance, I felt slightly wounded that she found the whole thing so black and white.

'I mean don't get me wrong, you seem a really nice bloke and all, but what are the odds …' she broke off, laughing.

'Like I said, unbelievable.' I suddenly thought that maybe I shouldn't be giving in so easily. I had nothing to lose after all. 'Although, it's not like we're complete strangers. I guess Ellie and Bob must have thought we'd get on with one another to suggest it.'

'Oh you,' she said pinching my cheek. 'Ellie always said you were an old romantic. Hey, I'd better get back to the group. Nice talking to you Connor, I'll catch up with you later.' She waved with just her fingers and made her way back to her party. I wasn't really that bothered. I felt relieved that I knew where I stood and I suppose in a way I knew she was right. It was nice to dream though.

I ordered another drink and made my way through the dense, sweaty gathering congregating to watch the live band. They were a four-piece indie band consisting of a drummer, two guitarists and a singer and I had to admit they were very good. At least I could understand what they were singing about which is more than could be said for Stig, the inaudible support act.

I'd been stood there for about half an hour when someone behind me placed their hands either side of my waist. Initially I thought it might have been Bob but soon realised he was far too smashed to have made it out of his chair. As much as I'd like to have thought it was Mel … that was never going to happen. The hands slid softly around my midriff and joined together in front of me.

'Hi,' whispered a voice tenderly in my ear. It was Laura. I felt the hairs go up on the back of my neck. 'Enjoying the music?' she asked.

'Yeah, this is my kind of stuff.'

'Me too,' she said and not another word was spoken. We stood in our makeshift reversed embrace and swayed gently to the music. This continued, ooh, for at least a song until Ellie bundled into our intimate moment.

'Bob's been sick, we're going to make a move.'

'Oh, OK,' I said. Ellie stood there for a while with her hands on her hips.

'Are you coming then?'

'Oh, yeah sorry,' I said, waking from my trance. I turned to make my excuses to Laura but she butted in.

'He's enjoying the band. He can stay at mine if he wants,' said Laura.

'Well if that's alright?' I added hastily. Ellie shrugged her shoulders.

'Sorted,' said Ellie. She was clearly more concerned about Bob. 'You behave yourself,' she smiled sardonically before kissing me on the cheek.

Chapter 19

'Beautiful night' – Prince.

Laura shared a first floor flat in Swiss Cottage with four Moroccans. They were away so she had the place to herself. The place had a cosy Mediterranean feel with dark wooden floors, a gorgeous open fireplace and ethnic décor. A large bay window looked out over the busy London streets below. Laura led me along the narrow hallway, past the bathroom to her bedroom. It was small and cluttered, barely big enough for the ornate double bed, which was wedged up against the far wall under some homemade curtains. She must have read the anxiety on my face.

'Oh don't worry,' she said laughing, 'you're sleeping on the couch in the lounge.'

'Right, that's … that's fine,' I was relieved. Although the thought of sharing Laura's bed was appealing there was still the intimidation factor. Mix that with my own inhibitions, and I felt kipping on the sofa was the best option. Friends or no friends I'd only met her that night and I wasn't in the habit of sharing beds at this early stage.

'Have you got a duvet or something?' I asked. She just laughed.

'Don't be silly, I'm sure we're grown up enough to share the same bed,' she giggled. She was right, we were old enough but that didn't stop the butterflies trembling in my stomach.

Unsightly visions flashed through my mind; stripping to my boxers and revealing my slightly flabby stomach in front of her; subconsciously farting in my sleep. Worse still it could be a really smelly one. No, worse than that, I could wet the bed. (It hadn't happened for years but that didn't mean it wasn't going to happen tonight). That would … possibly be worse than poking her in the back with my almost guaranteed morning glory.

'Look, it's OK really. I don't mind sleeping on the sofa.'

'I wouldn't hear of it,' she said, 'I don't want Ellie to think I'm not looking after you.'

'If you're sure,' I said reluctantly. I say reluctantly but I think there would be something wrong with me if I hadn't been feeling a slight thrill about the situation. I comforted myself with the thought that if there was any bed wetting to be done, it was marginally better if I did it in her bed as opposed to drenching the sofa. I dithered for a moment. Was it better if I went to the bathroom first and risk walking in on her whilst she was getting undressed or to get changed in front of her and climb in myself? Deciding that the wee I'd had back in the club was probably sufficient to see me through the night, I hastily stripped to my boxers and got into bed. I briefly saw Laura smirking to herself, presumably at my indecisive behaviour and general unease, before I turned over so that I couldn't be accused of ogling her. Hearing her clothes come off was probably worse than seeing anything. I lay there as stiff as a board if you'll pardon the expression. She eventually turned off the bedside light, wriggling further down under the sheets as she did so. I continued to lie motionless in the dark. Other than Laura's occasional fidgeting, you could have heard a pin drop. I began to relax and casually turned over to convey my newly found confidence. It was only when I felt her warm breath directly in my face that I realised she was lying right next to me. I froze again. She didn't fidget and I didn't move until … she cautiously edged the last few millimetres and kissed me tenderly on the lips. The kisses became increasingly intense until she climbed on top of me, pinning me to the bed. She started nibbling … no, biting my upper body. My initial inhibitions had gone away, somewhere, I didn't care where, and the whole thing got a little bit heated, until …

'I'm not shagging you,' she said harshly. My head started to spin. The thought of '*sleeping*' with Laura, however completely awe-inspiringly sublime I was sure it would be, scared me shitless. I should point out at this stage that I didn't actually shit the bed. I just wasn't ready for this. I hadn't, I couldn't do this sort of thing and there was some sort of twisted relief in her last statement. What I couldn't quite come to terms with was that I hadn't done any of the groundwork here. This was all her doing and although relieved, I was confused at the harshness in her voice.

'I'm not shagging you, Connor,' she repeated less abrasively. She rolled off me and turned over. I released a huge sigh as quietly as I could and settled in for my nightlong vigil of rigidity. It didn't last long.

'Oh fuck it,' she shouted and within a blink of an eye she'd whipped off both her camisole top and my boxers and set to work so to speak. It all happened so quickly I had no time to be anxious. There was no discussion, no awkward preamble, no time to worry about coming too quickly, it just happened. Without wanting to sound melodramatic, it was like nothing I'd experienced before. She was so full on it was just completely and utterly gob smacking.

I was woken the next morning by the sound of the running shower. I assumed it was Laura as there was no one in the bed next to me. I got to my feet in a daze, wiping the sleep from my eyes. The wooden floor felt cold as I tiptoed up the hall past the bathroom.

'Make yourself at home,' she shouted through the crack in the door. Her tone pleased me. There didn't appear to be any morning after repercussions.

'Is it OK if I have a smoke?' I asked.

'Hmm, if you must. Go in the lounge, the others won't be back for a while. There's an ashtray on the coffee table.'

Feeling like a million dollars I strutted down the hall in my boxer shorts, made myself comfortable and balanced the ashtray on the arm of the sofa. I savoured that cigarette as if it was the last one on earth. It felt good. I wandered over to the window and stood proudly, wanting to tell the whole world what had happened the night before. I made my way back to the sofa, examining various works of art as I did so. The shower was still in full flow. I lit another cigarette. The door in the lobby downstairs banged and I heard muted foreign voices and more than one set of footsteps. I looked agitatedly around the lounge, for what I'm not sure, until I decided I had no other course of action but to stay put. Being in a strange flat in just your boxer shorts surrounded by three burly yet confused looking Moroccans and a girl who didn't appear to quite know where to look was … unusual and somewhat frightening.

'Hi,' I mumbled. They looked at each other, uttering some incomprehensible lingo until Laura appeared and dragged me away from the scene.

'So I guess you're wondering what happens now?' she remarked, drying her hair.

'Well I guess I ought to go back and see Bob and Ellie.' I didn't want to outstay my welcome, 'it is their weekend after all.'

'Well let's not get too hasty young man. We've got the whole day ahead of us.' She said 'young man' in what I can only describe as a protective way. It wasn't condescending or sarcastic, I quite liked it.

We spent the rest of the day swanning around London. It was as if we'd known each other for years. We went shopping, took in a movie, went for a meal and ended up back at her flat for more of the same. By the time I eventually got back to Bob's to pick up my car I was completely knackered but thoroughly, thoroughly happy. I didn't know if this was the end, we hadn't discussed it, but I didn't care. I didn't have the energy or inclination to go into the gory details with Bob. He knew something must have happened. I just hoped Ellie wasn't mad. I hadn't seen her since she left the club on the Friday night.

Chapter 20

I had a phone call from Jimmy on my mobile as I headed home. He wanted to meet me in the pub again. He seemed as bewildered as ever with the Maria situation, not really understanding what exactly someone like Maria, who from what he said sounded quite cultured and educated, saw in him. His self doubt was confirmed when I blundered in on the conversation he was having at the bar with Alan.

'But why do you think birds start getting the hots for me?'

'Errr, 'cus you look like a fat aids victim?' said Alan.

Jimmy scowled at him. 'Don't be a fucking tit all your life.' Alan however was having none of it and intended to make the most of his newly found outspokenness.

'Maybe it's because you look like an overweight Ewok in that fleece.'

'I'm warning you.'

I sniggered and ordered myself a pint.

'And you, just watch it,' Jimmy said, pointing his finger menacingly in my direction. I turned my initial childish laugh into a chesty cough in an attempt to save face. 'Can we just try and be sensible for a minute?'

'Since when have you wanted to be sensible about anything?' said Alan

'Since now,' Jimmy glanced round at our blank expressions. 'Alright?'

'Alright,' I said, trying to restore normal communication among the three of us, if there was such a thing. 'Do you want us to guess or do you think you know why women are attracted to you?'

'Well, I think I know why.'

'So enlighten us.'

'I reckon it's because I lark about. I make people laugh. I'm funny ain't I?'

Alan spat most of the beer he had in his mouth across the table and began to cackle, almost uncontrollably. 'What's so hilarious?'

'You! Since when have you been funny?'

'Well I dunno Alan,' I said, 'but you certainly seemed to find that amusing. Maybe he is funny.'

'OK wise guys, quit fucking about.'

'But that's what we do,' I said.

'What?'

'Fuck about. I tell you loads of stuff you couldn't give a toss about, Alan tells us about the latest signings and goings on at Bournemouth, which quite frankly, I couldn't give a fuck about, and you …'

'And me what?'

'You just take the piss out of both of us and …on a good night we sometimes get the opportunity to insult you back. This is what we do. This is where we're at. We just fanny about.'

'Well just for once can we knock fucking about on the head? I have something I need to speak about.' It had been surprising enough to find Jimmy wanting to speak frankly and openly the first time round. A second time was getting beyond a joke. Suddenly Alan decided to climb aboard the magical soppy roller coaster.

'Well maybe I've had things I've wanted to talk about in the past,' he said.

'Maybe I had things I wanted to get off my chest but didn't because I knew you'd just take the piss.'

'Awwh, Jesus, Alan! If the world had to stop every time you had a crisis we wouldn't have time to take a shit.'

'See you're doing it now and I haven't even said anything.'

'My heart pumps piss. Excuse me, but a rumour that Jason Brissett might be sold to Walsall isn't really earth shattering stuff is it?'

'It is to him,' I could see that I was getting caught between two stools; I wanted to hear what Jimmy had to say but I didn't want to see him walk all over Alan as normal.

'Yeah, that's just it … it is to me.'

'Well some saddo has got their priorities wrong haven't they?'

Alan just grunted.

'Fucking loser,' Jimmy muttered.

The conversation seemed to have hit a dead end. After a few moments' silence Alan opened his mouth once more. 'You just ought to watch your step. Mark my words, this is going to turn into Cass revisited and I'm not going through all that shit again.' Quite who Cass was I had no idea.

‘Shut it Alan, you know nothing, but then you’ve made not knowing fuck all into a fucking art form.’ Tempers were beginning to fray.

‘Ah, sod this. I’m off. I don’t have to put up with this shit.’

‘Alan just sit down and listen to what he has to say.’

‘Naah fuck it, he can sort out his own problems. As for you, if you ever want me to bore you rigid with useless information about Bournemouth, you know where I am.’ At that, Alan picked up his jacket and strolled, with shoulders hunched, towards the exit.

‘Yeah, that’s right, go off and see yer gay mate.’ Jimmy shouted after him. Alan didn’t look around but just continued his dignified retreat. ‘Fucking idiot,’ Jimmy mumbled.

‘Well, what do you expect, you’ve always got it in for him.’

‘Yeah well he fucking deserves it. You’re still here to help me out aren’t you mate?’

‘Hmm,’ I grumbled, ‘that’s probably because I’ve got ‘MUG’ stamped on me forehead. Anyways, who’s Cass?’

‘It’s a long story.’ Alan had obviously hit a nerve. Jimmy was more subdued.

‘Better get on with it then, eh?’

It turned out that a few years back, Jimmy had been engaged to this Cass and they had moved in together. From the brief synopsis Jimmy was prepared to give, it appeared he’d been really keen on her and she’d basically walked all over him and made his life a misery. Love being blind, Jimmy continued to bend over backwards for her until the day he came home early carrying a bunch of flowers only to find his beloved Cass in bed with another bloke. Jimmy went off the rails. This was possibly where the Stella story began. Basically the whole cock-up of a relationship had turned Jimmy into the shallow, untrusting, amoral individual now sat before me.

‘So you haven’t always been a selfish, inconsiderate arse then?’ Jimmy didn’t respond. It was clear this pondering on the past was doing him no good at all. ‘So are you going to give me the low down on Maria or not?’

Since the last time we had our little heart to heart, it appeared things had actually degenerated. He’d been out with Maria and a couple of her friends. They had wanted to meet the new man in Maria's life. Jimmy's role in this liaison would appear to have been a mainly listening-only basis. He heard about Paula's boyfriend (who was a 20 year old Italian model) and Lana's boyfriend (a DJ currently spinning his toons in Milan who'd also been involved in the last David Bowie tour). Maria on the other hand was dating an overweight builder from Bournemouth. You can understand Jimmy's concerns especially when it slipped out that Maria had poached two of her previous boyfriends from her 'friends'. I tried to point out that he'd done his own fair share of poaching in the past but this did nothing to allay his fears.

Our previous chat about why Jimmy thought women were attracted to him was also on his mind. In all seriousness, it probably was his larking about and gift of the gab that endeared him to members of the opposite sex. The problem was that he found being his normal lovable idiot self with Maria … well, inappropriate. What bothered him was that once you'd taken away his main attribute with regard to pulling birds, namely pratting about, what was there left to be attracted to? The fact her mates were dating international playboys and stud muffins did nothing to pacify his state of mind. A few pints later and Jimmy was in full flow.

'She's not like a normal girl,' he said.

'Errm, I'm not sure I'm with you.'

'Well,' his words were beginning to slur, 'most birds … no in actual fact, all the birds I've been out with …and all the birds I know that have been out with my mates …'

'You including Rebecca in this?'

'Yeah, well, didn't know her that well, but yeah. Like I was saying, most birds like to be treated special.'

'Don't we all?'

'Awh, don't be a ponce. Nah, I mean they like to be looked after, have someone there, feel safe.'

'I guess so.' I wasn't quite sure where this was leading. Neither was I quite sure who Jimmy had ever treated as 'special'.

'But no, not our Maria. She's got it all mate. Don't need nobody, totally independent.'

'And that's a problem is it?'

'Yes.'

'Why?'

'Cus I can't fucking handle it that's why. Blokes are supposed to take up the reins on things aren't they?'

'What is there to handle? She's obviously quite capable of looking out for herself. Surely that's easier isn't it?' This was obviously a bag of bollocks. Jimmy's problem wasn't that she could look after herself, just unease with his role in the relationship. He clearly felt undermined that he didn't hold all the cards with this little chestnut.

'Yeah, but what the fuck does she want with me? How the hell do I fit into all this?'

I've never seen Jimmy look so despondent (unless we count the time Bournemouth lost to Burnley in the Auto Windscreens Cup Final).

'I think you're selling yourself a bit short mate. I shouldn't get so down about it. Why don't you just talk to her?'

'That's the stupidest thing. I've tried to talk to her and any time I get close to saying something about how I feel or how I see things, she cuts me off short. For the first time in a long while I actually mean what I say rather than just doing it to get a bird into bed, and she won't even let me express myself.'

'Oh,' I'm sorry, I just couldn't think of anything else to say. Anyway, Jimmy was on his soapbox and I was pretty sure he wasn't quite ready to step down yet.

'She doesn't speak to me about that kind of thing. I never know how she feels or what she thinks. She always says that actions speak louder than words.'

This was turning into a severe case of boot on other foot.

'Well, what about trying that Greek theory or whatever it is? You get out of a relationship what you put into it. Why don't you buy her some flowers or something?'

'You're sounding like bloody Alan now,' he smirked. I guess he had a point. I'd somehow diverted into daytime TV psychiatry mode.

To top it all, Jimmy had actually confronted his Mum about his insecurities in the hope that she might be able to offer some words of wisdom.

'And do you know what she said?' he said.

'No, go on.'

'She said maybe she was just stringing me on until someone decent came along.'

Obviously this wasn't quite the response Jimmy had been looking for. I was in no position to say whether his Mum was right or wrong. All I knew was that Jimmy felt more and more unsure of himself and was increasingly disillusioned with the whole affair. He wasn't in control and felt he was being given the run around. Alan wasn't necessarily right in what he said about the repeat of the Cass situation. After all, who could tell at this stage? The worrying thing for Jimmy was Alan had openly said something that was already rattling around in the back of Jimmy's head. It seemed that Cass had more to do with this than met the eye.

Chapter 21

'The door to this house remains open' – Super Furry Animals.

Ellie rang during the week to thank me for coming to the party. I wasn't sure whether she was being sarcastic but she seemed genuinely pleased.

'Well of course I'd have come up. It was your engagement party for heavens' sake. As long as you both had a good night, that's the main thing.'

'By the sound of things we're not the only people to have had a good night.'

'No you're right, I think Mel and deep sea Ritchie enjoyed themselves too,' I knew precisely what she was getting at.

'Come on, tell me all the juicy gossip.' She wasn't being swayed off the point.

'Have you spoken to Laura then?'

'No, but it doesn't take Einstein to know that something must have happened. I never saw you all weekend.'

'Yeah I'm sorry about that.'

'Oh don't worry. We were in no fit state to do much anyway.

So come on, tell me what happened.'

'Who says anything happened? We just enjoyed each other's company.'

'Uh-uh, don't try and tell me you just held hands. I know what Laura's like.'

'Ellie I don't believe you,' I exclaimed. 'If you knew what Laura was like why the bloody hell didn't you warn me before I met her?'

'Ah-ha, so something did happen!'

'Yes. Happy now? It did. How I don't know. One minute she was in the club telling me how ridiculous it was two complete strangers could hit it off and the next thing I was in bed with her.'

'Connor, that's not like you,' she sounded quite shocked.

'No thanks to you I hasten to add. Thanks for introducing us,' I joked

'Well I guessed if it was going to happen, it was going to happen. I didn't want to get involved in Chinese whispers between the two of you.'

I wanted to get back to the point. 'So she does this sort of thing on a regular basis does she?'

'I'm assuming you shagged her,' she said casually. 'Let's just say that she's a tad more experienced than you.'

'No shit, Sherlock.'

'Don't get me wrong, she's a lovely girl but she's quite … she's had quite a few sexual partners shall we say.'

'I gathered she'd done it once or twice before.'

'You took precautions though?' After what had happened with Rebecca it should have been at the forefront of my mind, but I hadn't really given it that much thought. Thinking about it now though, I felt stupid.

'Errm, no,' I mumbled.

'No?' Ellie gasped.

'Well, I presume she did.'

'But you didn't figure on asking her.'

'She'd have said something if she wasn't. I presume she knows about the birds and the bees?'

I heard the doorbell ring in the background. 'Hang on,' said

Ellie. There were various rustling noises until eventually she came back on the line. 'It's Laura,' she said 'I'll call you back later.' She hung up.

I knew Ellie didn't want to be a go between but I was keen to discover what Laura thought about the weekend's events. I soon bored of staring at the handset, deciding to make myself a cup of coffee and have a smoke. The longer I had to wait, I figured, the more they must have to talk about. This was on the assumption they were talking about the weekend. They could have been talking about anything. As time went on though, I thought Ellie's delayed response signalled bad news. Maybe she'd just forgotten. The phone rang.

'What did she say?' I demanded impatiently.

'What did who say?' It was Laura.

'Sorry, I thought it would be someone else.'

'Ellie perhaps?'

'What makes you say that?' I asked defensively.

'Well you seemed to have had a bloody good chat about what happened.'

'How … how do you mean?'

'I don't believe you Connor. You told her we slept together. It didn't take you long did it.'

'I didn't … she just assumed … I didn't tell her anything.' I'd been rumbled. 'And yes, for your information, I am on the pill. How stupid do you think I am?'

'Hang on a sec, I never actually told Ellie we slept together. I only confirmed what she already suspected and she was the one rambling on about precautions. I never really thought about it to be honest, maybe I should have done but …'

'OK, OK,' she laughed, 'it's no big deal. I really enjoyed the time we spent together Connor.'

'Me too,' I suspected there was a fall coming.

'Maybe we could meet up again some time?' I was taken aback for a moment. I clammed up. I opened my mouth but nothing came out. 'That's if you'd like to,' she continued.

'Yeah sure, I'd like that,' I croaked, 'I'll have to let you know when I'm back up in London.'

'I was thinking of coming down to you,' she said. 'I could do with getting out of the Big Smoke for a bit.'

'Sounds good to me.'

'Next weekend any good?'

I couldn't believe my ears. 'Absolutely, no problem at all,' I tried not to sound too eager. 'I have only got a double bed though but I can sleep on the sofa….'

'God Connor, that was pathetic. I'm sure we can share a bed after what happened last weekend. Just don't go expecting a repeat performance.' I wasn't bothered either way. I was just looking forward to seeing her again. If anything did happen it would be a bonus.

Chapter 22

Although I thought it might do him good to get out, Jimmy decided that sulking on his own was preferable to watching Bournemouth play their midweek home fixture against Northampton. On the evidence of the first few minutes, I had to agree with him. Bournemouth's new season hadn't got off to the best of starts. I met up with Alan on the terraces and had the honour shaking hands with Terry. It was like meeting your mate's new girlfriend although I'm sure Alan wasn't seeking my approval. At least I hope he wasn't because I'm not sure I would have given it. Terry struck me as quite a timid character and I wondered if the story about him driving a bright yellow car was a myth created by Jimmy to do the chap down. He looked more like the type who passed his time (when he wasn't watching Bournemouth play) spotting planes and trains. He was dressed in a Bournemouth shirt, which wasn't unusual considering the surroundings, but it did look like it was long overdue a good wash. I imagined it would first require surgical removal from his bony torso. Even more worrying was the rest of Terry's attire. Whilst the rest of the crowd were sensibly wrapped in jumpers, coats, scarves and gloves, Terry wore nothing more than a thin retro tracksuit top, a wide brimmed burgundy West Indies cricketing hat and a pair of undersized Bournemouth football shorts. I stood on the far side of Alan from him. Even more surprising than Terry's dress sense however, was that Alan seemed more intent on discussing Jimmy's predicament than closely watching the action on the field.

'It strikes me Jimmy's getting fished in.' Admittedly Alan wasn't looking at me when he spoke. His gaze continued to survey the theatre of crud that was Dean Court.

'Of course he's being fished in. He loves it. Isn't that what it's all about, the not knowing, the wondering, getting the butterflies?' I said knowing, in this instance, I was talking absolute rubbish.

'No,' Alan said stubbornly, 'it's doing his bloody head in. He's making himself look an arse.'

'When has that ever stopped him from doing anything?'

'Yeah, but he's being treated like a mug.'

'We don't know that though do we? We're only going on the bits he tells us.'

'Which is mostly everything.'

'It works both ways though Alan.'

'Awh man, you haven't got a clue have you.'

'What the fuck is that supposed to mean?'

'The guy is getting walked all over. She's had him decorating her flat every night this week not to mention all the other crap he's had to put up with. He's been buying her flowers left right and centre, like you suggested,' he turned and looked at me, 'and it hasn't made an ounce of difference.'

'I didn't mean for him to buy her flowers *all* the time. It was just an idea.'

'But what is he getting in return? I can't see her decorating his house.'

'He lives with his parents.'

'My point is she's got him just where she wants him. He's not in control at all.'

'Alan, this control stuff is a load of old bollocks. Anybody in a relationship is just as in control as the other person. If someone's not happy they have just as much clout to fuck the other person off out of it as anybody else. Anyway, what 'other shit' he has to put up with?'

The conversation stalled for a moment whilst Bournemouth took a free kick in a dangerous position. As usual, it was a fuck up and a goal kick was awarded. When the conversation finally got back on track, Alan's 'other shit' was purely his opinion on the relationship in general. He did however seem to have gleaned some new information. Matt (Maria's ex) had been on the scene. Apparently they had been more friends than anything else, but he still seemed quite keen. Matt had turned up at Maria's flat during the day when she had been decorating. She'd moaned and groaned about how long it was taking her and Matt remarked that he could have done it much quicker. Jimmy got the arse about this for several reasons. Firstly, the fact that Matt had turned at all. Secondly, having worked his bollocks off after work and at weekends helping Maria to do the place up, he didn't really appreciate someone else coming in and saying they could have made a much better job in half the time. Thirdly, he was pissed off that Maria had challenged Matt to do some work in the next room to prove his point. Lastly, it also appeared that following their conversation Matt had managed to wheedle his way into changing the brake shoes on Maria's car.

'So now she's got two mugs on her case,' said Alan shaking his head in dismay. 'One runs around getting deals on paint and bits for the house, buying her flowers and helping her decorate. The other is sorting her car for frig all and painting her flat as well. Maybe she'll go back to Matt. It'll all end in tears.'

'Alan, that's bollocks. Jimmy's a big boy now.'

'You can say that again.'

'He knows what he's doing, and as I said, if he doesn't like it he can knock it on the head. As for Matt, if she or anybody else for that matter is going to go off with someone, it'll just happen. There is no point worrying about it. There is nothing anybody can do.'

'But he's a bit of a surf dude.'

'Who, Matt?'

'Yeah.'

'So what?'

'It seems most of Maria's mates and flings and ex's were surfies or hippies or something weird.'

'Your point being?'

'And she was out in Australia for 12 months. Imagine all the blokes she must have been with over there. Blonde beach bum hunks, tanned and toned in all the right places.'

'I'm still not with you, how does this affect the here and now?'

'Why the fuck after all that would you want to hang round with a fat idiot like Jimmy?' Alan gave a roaring vindictive laugh that really didn't become him. He might have found the nerve to stand up to Jimmy but that didn't give him licence to be malicious.

'Alan,' I said disbelievingly, 'we have no idea who she's been out with or what this Matt is like. He might be a big fat idiot as well who just happens to have considerably more balance and skill in the surfing department than Jimmy.'

'How many fat surfers do you know?'

He'd got me there. I didn't actually know any surfers but none of the ones I'd seen on TV had been the slightest bit overweight. It didn't mean however that Matt, or anybody else she happened to have dated, automatically fell into the stereotypical 'surfie' genre.

'Alan, you're just looking at the negative points.'

'Am I? Sorry, I would have chucked a few positives in too if I could have thought of any.' He began to roar with laughter once more. If he thought he was getting the better of me he had another think coming, although I was admittedly on a bit of a sticky wicket. Jimmy obviously wasn't too sure about the whole situation at the moment and bending over backwards for Maria was doing him in. But there had to be some good points …didn't there?

'Well, for starters …'

Luckily, Bournemouth were awarded a corner and so another interlude was called for while Alan half heartedly chanted 'Boscombe, back of the net'. The brief respite gave me the chance to gather my thoughts.

'Her friends are a positive point.'

'How does that work? Does having friends prove she can't be that obnoxious or do they give Jimmy the opportunity of coping off with one of them if it all goes tits up?'

'No, I mean she must be quite keen on him to introduce him

to her friends.'

'Big deal.'

'Ok, what about all the time they spend together? There's only one day in the last three weeks he hasn't seen her.'

'They've probably not got anything else better to do.'

'But she's trying to get her business up and running and move into her flat. I'd say she was pretty busy.'

'Exactly, so she's got him running around like a complete loon doing all her donkeywork. She's even got him looking into holidays to San Francisco.'

It was news to me but Alan may have shot himself in the foot on this one.

'So why would she do that if she didn't think there was a future?'

'There are three answers to that.'

'Which are?'

'Option one, it's a dangled carrot to make him think that there's a future whilst he works his nuts off decorating her flat.'

'Very sceptical Alan,' I said dismissively, 'besides, he's not doing all the decorating on his own. He's only helping her. You make it sound like she's stood over him with a whip.'

'Huh, he wishes.' Alan shouted before directing obscenities at the linesman. 'Second … she wants him to pay.'

'What's the third scenario?' I asked reluctantly.

'Third, less gloomy option,' Alan paused to take a swig of cola, 'she really does think there's a future in the relationship.' Quite how Alan was suddenly a world authority on such matters, never having had a girlfriend, I wasn't sure.

'But you don't think this is the case.'

'It's possible. Maybe she wants him to stick around for a bit longer to do some other chores. She might want a loft conversion doing or something.' Both Terry and Alan burst into laughter. I turned the corners of my mouth up into a half smile.

'You're enjoying this, aren't you Alan?'

'Damn right I am. After all the shit I've had to put up with it's about time he had a piece of his own medicine.'

Alan didn't seem to have grasped the concept of friendship. Well, not with Jimmy anyway. I guess under the circumstances it was understandable. Call me old fashioned but I felt Jimmy deserved a bit more support than that currently being offered by Alan. In fairness I don't think it was the constant ridiculing he'd had to endure that had made Alan chastise Jimmy in this way. This is what he wanted us to believe but even he wasn't that shallow. He was also not stupid enough to think Jimmy actually meant half the stuff he spouted. I think he just found the whole situation laughable. He knew all the down sides of the relationship, hadn't really got a feel for any good points and as far as he was concerned the whole thing was a complete waste of time. Why was Jimmy putting himself through all this? Why put up with all the heartache and insecurity? There was one easy solution. Dump the bitch.

'He's doing all the giving and she's doing all the taking. I just don't see why we're stood here having this conversation or why Jimmy's wasting his time worrying about the in and outs of his fucked up love life. He keeps telling her how he feels and doesn't get any feed back and in the mean time he's pandering to her every need.'

'So you think she should open up more and that would solve all the problems?'

'Yeah, at least he would know where he stands. She just keeps saying, actions speak louder than words …'

'That sounds like one of your clichés, maybe she is an idiot.'

'I just can't see what he gets out of all this. She never tells him how she feels.'

'Alan you know all that emotional bollocks means jack shit. All this admiration shite doesn't stand for anything. I've got piles of letters from Rebecca expressing every emotion under the sun. It doesn't mean anything now.'

'Sure it does, it's obviously how she was feeling.'

'Exactly, it's all just a snapshot in time. One brief moment in the grand scheme of things. Most of it's just a made up pile of shit anyway.'

'You've just got your fingers burnt and become a bitter and twisted old man.'

'Maybe.'

'Yeah maybe. Anyway, here's one for your old-fashioned

loving relationship scrapbook. Apparently Maria had a long-term boyfriend a couple of years back but then she went to Australia and found it hard to cope without sex.'

'She seems to have coped without sex with Jimmy for long enough.'

'Look shut up. So you know what she did?'

'No.'

'She rang her boyfriend and asked if she could shag a male prostitute to get it out of her system.'

'And did she?'

'No. They agreed they could shag people they picked up from nightclubs as long as they used a condom. Now does that sound like the sort of woman to be trusted in a long-term relationship? Doesn't quite fit in with your old fashioned loving scenario does it?'

No it didn't. 'Well at least she asked,' is all I could think to say in her defence.

There was no point in continuing this conversation. Although I hated to admit it, I was hedging more and more towards Alan's way of thinking. Jimmy, knock it on the head son.

Chapter 23

'Pussycat' – Mulu.

Laura was catching the Friday night train into Bournemouth station. I'd intended to tidy the house but time had crept up on me. The last few dirty saucepans and plates were shoved in the cupboard under the sink.

Considering the inclement weather I was surprised when Laura alighted the train wearing only a thin blouse, cropped denim jacket and a loose-fitting skirt which barely covered her arse. She skipped along the platform to greet me as if I were a long lost friend, throwing her arms around me and kissing me on the cheek.

'Oh it's so great to get out of London.' She looked straight into my eyes and smiled, 'and it's great to see you again Connor.'

'It's good to see you too.' My grin matched hers. We made our way to the car arm in arm and the nerves I had been expecting to kick in didn't materialise.

'Here we are then.' Opening the front door, I struggled through into the lounge with her bag dumping it by the side of the sofa. I was just about to ask if she wanted a drink when she grabbed me from behind, spun me round and pushed me backwards over the arm of the couch. Her jacket went flying across the lounge floor, she unbuttoned my jeans, yanking at them furiously and after a few heated, passionate kisses clambered on top of me. She meant business. It was like something out of a film. She unbuttoned her blouse and hitched up her already short skirt. She wasn't wearing any knickers. Needless to say it didn't take me long to arise to the occasion and we duly carried on where we'd left off. I wasn't used to the spontaneity or the seduction but found her attitude most refreshing. She just kind of went off on one. She was like a wild animal, screaming and moaning and throwing her head back. That's not meant to sound like I'm blowing my own trumpet, I'm sure with her track record I'm probably fighting relegation in the league table of sexual partners. I just mean that she completely and utterly enjoyed having sex. Her attitude allowed me to get on and enjoy it too. I wasn't looking at her and wondering how I was faring (was it good, was it bad, was she enjoying herself) I was just having exceptionally good lustful sex … repeatedly. For the first time in my life I had no inhibitions.

I did think of Rebecca on one occasion however, on the Saturday morning when a previous predicament came back to haunt me once more.

'Shit,' said Laura sharply whilst rummaging through her overnight bag.

'What's the matter?'

'My pill, I've forgotten to bloody bring 'em.' I went dizzy for a few seconds until Laura continued, 'Oh well, I'll just have to take it when I get home.' She sounded a bit despondent.

'Are you sure that's OK,' I asked naively, 'don't you have to take them at the same time every day?'

'Oh Connor,' she walked back into the bedroom, 'you're

such a sweet young man. I've got a stash of the morning-after jobbies back at the flat.' She stroked my hair reassuringly. 'They just make me feel awful when I take them.' I felt it was my fault. I felt guilty she was going to be ill over something we'd done. It sounded like this wasn't the first time this had happened though and she was obviously far more adept at dealing with the situation than Rebecca had been. I still wanted to put my mind at rest however.

'Just one thing,' I said reluctantly, not wanting to confirm I was quite as inept at this sort of thing as I appeared, 'is it not called the morning after pill because you're supposed to take it the morning after?'

'Nah,' she said with a dismissive laugh, 'don't worry young man, I'm not going to give birth just yet. You can take those things up to 48 hours afterwards,' she looked at me affectionately as if I were a cute little kid having just asked for a bag of his favourite sweets. 'I'll take one Sunday night when I get back, that'll cover us for the weekend. Don't look so worried.'

'I'm really sorry it'll make you feel ill.' I must have sounded like a lost and confused toddler. She seemed to find my stupidity endearing. I loved the way she took control of the situation without any fuss, just a big smile on her face.

The entire weekend revolved around drinking, smoking, sex and watching TV. We did go to the pub but after one drink we went back for more sex. I managed to show her the sights and sounds of the South Coast in the daytime. It only seemed fair really. She had wanted to get out of London after all. As much as I'd have liked to stay in bed all day with a nymphomaniac Kiwi, I was in need of a short break myself every now and then. We went out into the Purbecks on the Saturday and visited Lulworth Cove and Swanage. I enjoyed the whole experience. Laura made me feel good. She seemed to enjoy life so much. The sea air made her insatiable. We went to my parents for Sunday lunch after she expressed a particular interest in meeting them. I saw this as a good sign for the future. Why would she want to meet my parents unless she was keen for 'us' to go further? I approached the subject in the afternoon before she returned to London.

'Where do we go from here then?' I asked cautiously.

She looked deep into my eyes, 'I think you're gorgeous …' she said.

I smiled.

'…But I don't want a relationship at the moment.'

I frowned.

'We can't go headlong into a relationship when we live so far apart.'

I frowned again.

'Let's just carry on as we are and see what happens.'

I smiled again. There was a glimmer of hope. I couldn't see any problem with carrying on as we were, unless she wanted to see and shag other people as well. I wasn't too keen on that idea.

'If it's any consolation, I may not want a full blown relationship, but there's no-one else I'd rather be with, Connor.' She rubbed my nose with hers, grinning as she did so. Call me easily pleased but that was good enough for me.

Chapter 24

My planned Sunday night in with a cheesy smile on my face was interrupted by a knock at the door shortly after I'd dropped Laura at the station. It was the last person I wanted to see, Rebecca. She invited herself in, bold as brass and helped her self to a seat on the sofa. It looked like she'd just come back from a night out. I couldn't believe she'd gone to the trouble of dressing up for me. There was something about her that made me uneasy. Maybe I felt I had something to prove, that I was fine without her. Maybe I wasn't over her. Whatever, it made my hands clammy, my brow sweat profusely and gave me a particularly nervous demeanour.

'Just thought I'd pop round,' she said flippantly, dropping her bag in the middle of the lounge. She looked around the room quizzically. The place, despite Laura's antics, was fairly tidy. She looked surprised and I can't say I blamed her.

'Well it's good to see you.' I thought I ought to say something along these lines out of courtesy.

'Yes, you too.' She adopted an air of grandeur. I suddenly felt I had something to prove. She'd obviously 'just popped round' for a nosey and possibly a quick gloat but I didn't feel prepared for whatever she was about to dump on me. I knew very well she'd come to convince me she was getting on fine without me, was having a whale of a time in the process and was coping with life ten times better than I was. I didn't know how to react. She'd put me in this position before. I had two options. I could try and upstage her with bigger and better tales of excitement and fulfilment in true childish fashion. I didn't however want her to think I was lowering myself to her level with a 'my Dad's bigger than your Dad' style slanging match. The other option was to pretend I didn't really give a shit, lacked all interest in everything she said whilst divulging as little as possible about my own antics. The idea was to convey an air of mysticism about my new life. I'd tried this option before but hadn't quite perfected the act. First rule kids, give as little information away about yourself as possible.

'So what have you been up to?' This was a classic manoeuvre from the book of 'I couldn't give a toss'. By putting the ball in her court and then gently swaying my head from side to side, whilst momentarily gazing at other objects in the room, I gave the impression I wasn't really listening and didn't really care. In reality I became increasingly disheartened to hear about all the great places she'd been and all the blokes she'd shagged from Bovington army camp. 'All' is probably a slight exaggeration. It was actually three. This took her tally to four, which was still more than me. It made it worse somehow that she hadn't slept with anyone before me – having wanted to save herself for the right person - and now she was putting it about all over the barracks. This still didn't excuse what I was about to say.

'So you've turned into a bit of a slag then?' Rebecca smiled knowing she'd just scored fifty points for getting such a rise out of me.

'Well, you know what it's like,' she laughed.

'No actually, I don't know what it's like to be a squaddie mattress.' She smiled again, mentally marking up another fifty points. Would shouting about the fact that I'd been shagging the arse off Laura all weekend even the score? Probably not. I felt I needed a break from the proceedings and offered to make a drink. I asked if she wouldn't mind passing me the mug on the floor next to her as I was a bit short on crockery since she had cleared me out. Her expression changed to one of surprise and disgust when she spotted the lipstick marks around the rim. I'd inadvertently scored at least thirty points but it meant she had to go in for the kill. When we sat down with our coffee she rolled out the big guns.

Chapter 25

'I am the resurrection' – Stone Roses.

'Have you been away this year?' asked Rebecca uncharacteristically slurping her tea.

'On holiday you mean?' I played dumb.

'Yes,' she replied, 'on holiday.' I'd sussed her tactics. She'd obviously been somewhere spectacular on holiday. By asking me first, she'd have to listen to my crappy holiday for a couple of minutes whilst she coolly loaded and cocked her big guns. I'd have to reciprocate by asking the same question to her … and then, BAMM! her secret holiday destination would be revealed. She already had a smug grin on her face. It had to be somewhere spectacular, Barbados, maybe somewhere in South America. No, hang on, with a face that haughty it would have to be somewhere I'd always wanted to go, Canada or the Monaco Grand Prix maybe. The suspense was killing me but I couldn't think of anywhere in the world she might have been that would piss me off that much. I decided to play right into her hands.

'Oh, I just went to Greece for a couple of weeks,' I said casually. 'Have you been anywhere nice?'

'Yeah I went to France for a bit …'

See, France isn't that exotic. I can handle that.

'… in the summer …'

I hope this isn't going to be a complete letdown. Paris in the sunshine? Been there, done that.

'... to watch the World Cup.'

I froze, speechless. The colour drained from my cheeks. This had to be the cruellest of blows. After all the stress and heartache that had been caused by football during our relationship! Rebecca hated football because her Mum had said it was a waste of time watching silly little men kicking a pig's bladder around a field. *Match of the Day* on a Saturday night wasn't exactly banned but the aggro involved made watching it more trouble than it was worth. I just gave up trying in the end. Sometimes I'd get up early on the Sunday morning before she was awake to watch the repeat. Very occasionally I got to watch a match live at her parents' house. Her Dad knew nothing about football but I guess thought it was a good opportunity to bond with me and used to put it on if there was no-one else about. It wasn't long before we were hijacked by Rebecca and her Mum who instead of just turning the TV off or changing the channel would torture the hell out of me by saying the most ridiculous things. They used to grind me down by asking two or three times who was playing in which colour and why the man in the funny coloured shirt was allowed to pick up the ball. On one occasion I decided to stick it out for as long as possible in the hope they'd get bored and go off to do something else. Forty-five minutes of their brainless ramblings and giggling was as much as I could endure.

I had maintained Rebecca had no grounds for saying she detested football when she hadn't actually ever been to a match. With her agreement, I got three tickets for Euro 96 to see Scotland play Switzerland at Villa Park. I sold the other ticket to Bob. I'd obviously had the tickets for months in advance but it wasn't until the night before the game that Rebecca decided she didn't want to go. She had one of her tantrums. My main concern was to find someone to take her ticket as the match was being played on the same night England played Holland. Alan actually had tickets to go to Wembley and Jimmy wanted to watch the England game on the telly. Ellie, who'd always liked a bit of footy, said she'd go and so the three of us had the time of our lives whilst Rebecca sulked at home. We may not have seen England beat Holland 4-1 but we did witness Ally McCoist scoring Scotland's only goal of the Euro 96 Finals. Rebecca watched neither game and was doubly pissed off that Ellie had filled her boots; she was the only person who somehow made Rebecca jealous.

I eventually talked Rebecca into going to a pre-season friendly between Bournemouth and Southampton. I appreciate this was never going to be the greatest of exhibition matches but after the Euro 96 cock-up I wasn't in the mood to go out of my way. She said she enjoyed it but didn't want to go to any more matches and still felt the same when it came to watching it on the TV. No wonder I was so pissed off she'd been to see the World Cup Finals especially considering the problems we'd had in the lead up to the competition. On the night of the World Cup draw Rebecca and I had an almighty bust up. We'd meant to go round to my parents for a meal and Dad had timed it so we could watch the draw after we'd finished eating. When I told Rebecca this I was faced with, well, absolute raving lunacy; face down on the floor kicking her heels in the air to be precise, followed by running up to the bedroom in floods of tears and locking herself in. Normally I would have stayed to reason with her but by that stage I was so hacked off with being steamrollered all the time I decided to go to my parents on my own. They naturally asked where Rebecca was and I told them she was ill, which wasn't that far from the truth. I mean it was only the draw for God's sake. A ball was never even kicked. You just had to put up with an hour or so of cultural bollocks and then see a group of aged footballers pick a fart full of ping-pong balls from glorified goldfish bowls.

It suddenly crossed my mind that maybe this trip of hers wasn't such a big deal. The irony of Rebecca going to France while the World Cup was on wasn't really that bad, it just meant she had been watching it on a French TV in a French pub as opposed to being in England. The distinct disadvantage of going to France, a disadvantage that would have been wasted on

Rebecca, was that you wouldn't have had the pleasure of listening to Motty and Co. commentating on the games. No, on second thoughts this really wasn't a big deal at all.

'So where did you stay whilst you were over there?' I had regained my composure.

'Stay?' she replied, 'I didn't stay anywhere.'

'It was just a daytrip was it?' I sneered.

'No, I went over two or three times just to see the games,' she said confidently. I stiffened again and started to feel sick.

'You mean, you went to France just watch the games in a bar over there?' I said hopefully.

'No …' she said, 'well yeah, originally we did.'

'We?' I questioned.

'Yeah, work had spare seats on some of the flights so they gave them to our girls on the check-in desks.' I pictured a handful of blonde bimbos arriving in France. 'Like you said, we were only going to go to a pub to watch the games but it all happened so fast.'

'What … what did?' I braced myself.

'One minute we're sat in the departure lounge minding our own business and then we're chatting to Kriss Akabusi and Ulrika Jonsson on the plane ….' I suddenly went off *Shooting Stars*. She continued her story. 'We were wandering round airport arrivals wondering what to do when we got chatting to this limo driver. He had a couple of hours to kill until he had to take Mick Jagger to the game so he drove us round and showed us the sights.' I felt distinctly off-colour.

'Sounds great.' I gritted my teeth.

'So then we pile out of the limo at this swanky hotel where this guy's got to pick Mick up …' she was obviously already on first name terms with the Jaggers, 'and we thought we'd wander into the hotel lobby and stay there for a drink before deciding what to do.' I considered breaking her momentum by pretending to want the toilet but she was in full flow. Besides, I knew her story couldn't have involved actually going to the game because of the allocation of the tickets. It had been well documented that the French were being trés strict about letting anyone into the grounds without proof you were the person whose name was on the ticket. There was no way she could have got to see a match just by turning up. I sat back and let her carry on.

'So we were sat there minding our own business when we get talking to these German business people who are getting ready to see the match. To cut a long story short, these Germans had some spare tickets and they gave them to us.' Hah, this was to be her downfall. I could feel the muscles in my body relax. Her faux pas was going to be beautiful to watch.

'So did you get into the game then?' I said, coaxing her gently into my little trap.

'Oh yeah,' she replied indifferently. I could feel the corners of my mouth turning up.

'It's just that I thought you had to have a ticket with your name on it and prove you were that person with photographic I.D. to get into any of the matches.' I expected a dramatic u-turn in her fabricated story but she carried on regardless.

'Well yes, so did I,' she said. 'They didn't have the actual tickets, they had these receipt type things hung around their necks so all we had to do was say we hadn't got the actual ticket on us but we obviously had the receipt to prove it was all above board and that was that, we blagged our way in.' I slumped in my chair. I was utterly pissed off. Rebecca knew nothing about football. To tell her tale so confidently convinced me she wasn't talking out of her arse. I mustered the courage to ask which game she'd gone to see.

'Germany v Croatia,' she said smugly. Doubly pissed off that this was arguably the best game of the tournament I proceeded to test her on every aspect of the match. Unfortunately for me, she passed with flying colours.

'It was so easy, we did it all again.' I could feel one of the veins in my forehead throbbing. She'd also got into the England versus Argentina game. I don't know what pissed me off the most: the anti-football shit I'd had to endure whilst I'd been with her or the bare faced cheek she'd had to come around and brag about it when she knew full well I'd tried all means, fair and foul, to get a ticket to *any* of the World Cup games.

'David Beckham's got really lovely legs hasn't he?'

It could also have been that the whole experience was wasted on a complete and utter football philistine.

Chapter 26

Bob's impulsive stag break couldn't have come sooner. It was more of a pre-stag party really. I mean they'd only just announced their engagement and as far as I was aware they hadn't even set a date for the wedding but any excuse for a booze up was more than welcome.

I met Jimmy in the pub on the Friday night before we sailed on the early morning ferry from East Anglia to Holland the following day. He was keen for me to meet Maria before we left. I sensed tension from the moment I walked in. Maria was nothing like I'd expected. I don't know why because I hadn't really considered what she might have looked like. Although she was attractive she looked like she should have had her own horoscope column or owned an art studio or something. Her long, almost greasy looking black hair was tied back to reveal her plain, pale face. She spoke softly but I detected a very faint cockney drawl.

'Hello,' she said, leaning over to kiss me gently on both cheeks.

'Good to meet you at last,' I said genially. Jimmy looked uneasy and ushered us towards the bar. Maria made her way to the ladies.

'Is everything alright Jimmy?'

'Why?' he said defensively, 'why shouldn't it be?'

'I dunno, you just seem a little on edge.'

'Maria's suspicious about the stag weekend,' he muttered, shiftily looking over his shoulder.

'Suspicious?' I remarked, 'suspicious of what?'

'Well, y'know, lads on a boys' weekend in Amsterdam … I should have told you before you met her.'

'Told me what?'

'To keep a lid on Amsterdam. I told her we just having a few quiet drinks down in Newquay.'

'No wonder she's suspicious. Why the bloody hell did you

tell her we were going to Newquay? Newquay, Amsterdam, what's the flaming difference?'

'Connor you're such a prick sometimes. Have you ever been to Amsterdam?'

'No,' I said shaking my head, 'but I do know about the red light district if that's what you mean.'

'Red light district?' Maria had returned unnoticed. I looked over at Jimmy.

'Yes,' I said cautiously, 'we were talking about Amsterdam.' Jimmy rolled his eyes. 'I was thinking of going there for a short break,' I said, trying to escape from the hole I'd just dug.

'And you want to check out the red light district?' I got the impression Maria thought I was a pervert, which after what Alan had told me was a bit rich.

'No, Jimmy was just telling me about when he went.' Incriminating Jimmy was the only defence I could muster.

'So you've been to the red light area?' asked Maria.

'Well …' started Jimmy feeling his collar.

'And me,' she interrupted, 'it's amazing what you can get for a few Gilders.' The expression on her face intimated that there was more to her last statement than she was letting on. No, surely not. Jimmy looked nervously over the top of his pint glass before polishing off the contents.

'Shall we move on somewhere else?' he gasped. I still had nearly half my pint remaining but thought it best we go.

As we walked through Bournemouth gardens the atmosphere was tense. Jimmy and Maria hardly spoke a word. We approached *Oggies Bar* not a moment too soon. Maria and Jimmy went for the drinks whilst I bagged a table in the corner of the courtyard in front of the pub. I took the opportunity to do some people watching.

The temperature had dropped considerably and groups of people stood huddled around the outdoor heaters. A number of girls had obviously not listened to their respective mothers' advice and had failed to put a cardigan on. They were the most prominent (in more ways than one) victims of the night's chill. Others were struggling to master walking with any dignity. They should have known that alcohol, high-heeled shoes and an uneven block-paved courtyard didn't mix well. There had obviously been a run on *Burton's* attire. Hoards of spotty teenagers with untucked shirts leched over the aforementioned scantily clad girls. One lad was trying to flip cigarettes into his mouth whilst his mate was attempting to flick open the lid of his Zippo and light it in the same movement. I felt old.

I checked to see if Jimmy and Maria were on their way back. I was feeling self-conscious. Sat on my own, I was becoming increasingly pissed off with people asking me if the other seats were taken. A blonde haired girl stood with her back to me seemingly giving the kiss of life to a bloke … who looked a bit like Roger … and from the back, the girl looked very much like … Rebecca. She turned, looking me straight in the eye. I made a lame attempt to make out I hadn't seen them. I couldn't seem to get away from her at the moment. Seeing her snogging someone else made me feel queasy. It was all a bit … strange. The table was suddenly cast into shadow. I looked up to see Rebecca's brother towered over me.

'Alright?' he said chewing gum and looking along the line of tables. Billy was OK but he somehow always gave me an inferiority complex.

'Fine yeah, you?' I didn't quite know how to make my voice sound like I hadn't seen Rebecca or if I had, I didn't care, but I gave it a bloody good go.

'Who you up here with?' he asked, ignoring my question whilst adamantly avoiding my gaze.

'Just a couple of mates, you?'

'Keeping yourself busy?' His questions were delivered in a monotone and he hadn't looked me in the eye once. To make the effort to come over and talk and then act so uninterested struck me as odd. I got the impression that this was his way of threatening me, maybe warning me off.

'So so,' I said, my answers matching the passion of his questioning.

'Good. See you around.' He sauntered back across the courtyard and into a crowd leaving me wondering what the whole episode had been about.

Jimmy and Maria arrived with the drinks still not talking to one another. Rebecca kept looking at me to see if I was looking at her and I kept glancing at her to see if she was looking at me. I got drunk.

Chapter 27

'Party Hard' – Pulp.

By the time we arrived in Amsterdam I'd more or less caught up on the sleep lost on the Friday night out with Maria and Jimmy. I'd apparently been dropped home at about 1am although I had to take Jimmy's word on that as I was verging on the unconscious by that stage. He picked me up again about four hours later to drive to East Anglia and I was asleep by the time we arrived at Alan's. We then caught the ferry to Holland followed by the train to Amsterdam. Between the changes in modes of transport, I'd slept all the way. The ribbing I might have expected from not keeping up with the drinking on the boat wasn't forthcoming. Jimmy's mood was still low. I don't think he'd had much sleep himself whilst he attempted to convince Maria well into the early hours he was going to Newquay. I guessed given he'd left five missed calls on his mobile unanswered before we'd even got on the ferry that she wasn't having any of it.

On arriving in Amsterdam we made our way straight to the nearest bar. We had no time to waste. It was now early afternoon and we had to catch the train back to port at 1am. I still felt hung over but put on a brave face as I caught up with the who's who of the Amsterdam trip. Alan, Jimmy and Bob were the only people I knew. The others were all Bob's friends from London, seven of them in total, four married, two courting and one single. Needless to say the only people who were nervous about roaming the red light district were Alan, Jimmy (only because of Maria), the single guy and me.

We touched on some of the streets of ill repute when we made our way to another café. I couldn't quite get my head around the concept of a major European city being so diverse. Mothers wheeled pushchairs over quaint little hump backed bridges whilst cyclists on old-fashioned bikes weaved in and out of pedestrians. It would have been a picture postcard scene if it weren't for the fact that this tranquil ideal was surrounded by sex shops, sex museums and odd-looking people, mainly men wandering aimlessly through the streets, stoned off their faces or pissed as farts. Add some nubile women dancing in shop windows attempting to earn a living and the result, in my mind at least was an eclectic mix of … weirdness. I hadn't quite understood how 'in yer face' these women were going to be. If your heart desired (and most of the married hearts did) you could walk right up to the windows, face to face with these women and just watch them. Sad though it was, it just didn't feel right. I couldn't help wondering what they were thinking. Some looked happy and after a good time. Others looked sultry whilst a few of them exuded an air of vulnerability. I wasn't sure they wanted to be there at all. I think what made it worse for me was seeing the actions of the men in the street. They were shouting and screaming, banging on the windows, making obscene comments and gestures. I don't know who was sadder, them or me. A door opened half way up the street and a young man came tumbling out. His trousers were still around his knees, cramping his ability to regain his balance and he landed face first on the cobbles. For all the 'glamour' in the window there was no romance to be had there.

On eventually reaching the 'café' we asked to see the 'menu'. With the majority of us in high spirits we opted for the hash cakes. Munching them down as if we hadn't been fed for weeks we sat waiting for them to take effect … we got another round of drinks …nothing seemed to have happened. Some of Bob's mates got bored and ate the remaining cakes (Jimmy, Alan and the single guy hadn't eaten theirs). A couple of them started lighting up spliffs. The general consensus was that the hash cakes were crap.

'Err guys,' said Alan examining the wrappers the cakes had come in, 'it says here that …'

'The chocolate brownies are a waste of fucking money,' chirped one of the group. Steve was a self-confessed lout. There was a volley of laddish laughter from some of his loutish followers. Alan uncharacteristically continued un-phased.

'Err, no. It says here that no other narcotics should be consumed within twenty minutes of eating the cakes because that's how long they take to kick in.' We all looked at our watches. The cakes were ready to take effect.

'Don't be so fucking soft,' said Steve who had scoffed two hash cakes, downed a pint of lager and smoked half a joint in the last twenty minutes. He was the first to go to the toilets and chuck up. It couldn't have happened to a nicer bloke. Although throwing up had made him feel a whole lot better he'd still looked a complete cock in front of everybody else and his laddish charms became somewhat muted.

The rest of the evening seemed to turn into an episode of *Poirot*. As we toured the pubs, cafes and streets of Amsterdam an increasing number of the group added their names to the evening's casualty list. The cycle of feeling drunk, having the giggles, having the munchies, and feeling tired was staggered around the group. One by one we dropped like flies or disappeared into the red light district until it was time to catch the train. Other than getting accosted by a couple of pimps who thought I was taking a picture of them when I was actually trying to take a picture of Bob throwing his guts up over one of the bridges, I thought I'd lasted pretty damn well. I guess by sleeping for the majority of the way there I'd given everyone else a distinct head start. The problem was that by the time we got back to the train I was the only one who hadn't been sick. Whilst everyone else was fast asleep on the journey back to port, I was feeling as rough as a dog. At the station before we got off I finally chundered. Notices on the train warned that you shouldn't use the toilets whilst the train was in the station. I had little control over the timing of my needs on this occasion. The flap in the base of the latrine deposited the contents of my stomach onto the track. I turned round quickly as my body demanded that I go for a number two. I apologise to the passengers on the platform who may have witnessed a steaming pile of sick and poo as the train slowly departed up the tracks.

Chapter 28

It was bang on 6pm on the Sunday night when we finally got back to Jimmy's. I know this because I looked at my watch. I had been prompted to do so as Jimmy discovered the face of his watch was cracked.

'How did you manage that?' I asked.

'I have no idea,' he groaned. 'Oh well, it wasn't expensive. No need to worry.' I think he was too tired to fret about it. The weekend had taken its toll on both of us, mentally and physically, and the aroma of curry, which still hung in the air in Jimmy's flat, did nothing for my stomach. Jimmy however had more important things to worry about. A makeshift envelope that had obviously been hand posted through his door was lying on the mat and his answer machine glowed with the promise of new messages. He pressed play whilst tearing open the letter.

'You have … four new messages,' boomed the machine in an upper class English accent.

Saturday 17:12 - Maria in a stubbornly pissed off mood.
'Hi, it's Maria. I've just finished work. Just like to know when you get in seeing as how you're obviously not going to ring me to tell me when you are going to be back. Umm… and you didn't even ring me to tell me that you got there fine, so it would be nice to have a call when you get back please and by then you will have hopefully read my letter and you'll have some idea of how I've been feeling. OK? Thank you, bye.'

Sunday 13:56 – Maria clearly upset.
'Right, it's 2pm now and it's Maria. Um, I'm at the flat and I just thought I'd give you a ring. Umm … don't think you realise how upset I've been this weekend … been on tenterhooks ever since you left with loads of questions to ask you and it just makes me feel that if you cared you wouldn't have left me in such a mess this weekend. You know, when I get upset, I need to go out and kick my heels up and I've just been left at this flat with all this stuff going through my head while you're happily roaming around. These past couple of days have been killing me and if you'd been upset about the things you'd written in your letter you'd have sorted it all before you went away. Anyway, speak to you soon.'

Sunday 13:58 – Maria increasingly upset.
'This is just a continuation of the message I left a minute ago and just to let you know that I've just been sat here waiting for a decent explanation. As for all the flowers, CD's, paint, skirts and chocolate in the world. That shit means nothing to me. It's times like this when it counts. That's when it shows that you care and you obviously don't because you're off enjoying yourself and not even paying attention to me and why I'm upset. As for your letter saying that you wanted to make me happy, you'd not have treated me like this if your friends, who will always be there are more important. Anyhow, as I said, this is what I've said before, words will never win me over…'

Sunday 14:00 – Her upset turns to anger and hysteria.
'This is a continuation of the last message, umm … if you want to sort this mess out then come over as soon as you get my letter and get all these messages that I've been leaving you, umm … and if you don't come over and sort it out then I guess that's it cus I can't stand this non communication all the fucking time (she's now crying quite manically). OK, hopefully speak to you later, bye.'

'You have no more messages,' said the machine and a look of relief crossed Jimmy's face. We stood in silence for a while. I didn't quite know what to say.

'I suppose I ought to go round there,' said Jimmy sheepishly. You could see that his head was telling him he should go but his body remained firmly rooted to the spot. He didn't show me the letter and I didn't ask to see it. I figured I'd heard too much private information already. I didn't even know he'd written her a letter in the first place but I thought now wasn't the time to dwell on details. It was probably best to make my excuses and leave him to it.

'You will come to this party next week won't you?' said Jimmy hopefully as I made my escape.

'What party?' I was not in the mood for thinking about any more parties.

'They're having a bash at the health club where Maria's a member.' My face conveyed my lack of enthusiasm. 'They'll be loads of crumpet there,' he continued.

'We'll see,' I said nodding my head. 'I think you ought to concentrate on sorting out your shit with Maria first.' I turned and made my way down the communal hall.

'That's a date then,' he shouted after me. 'I'll give you a ring and let you know what time I'll be picking you up.' I think he was worried about going to the party with Maria on his own. With the way things were I guessed anything could happen in the next week so it wasn't worth making too many concrete plans. I waved my hand and continued on my way, dreaming of finally crawling into my own bed.

Chapter 29

'Giving up the Ghost' – DJ Shadow.

Although the Jimmy and Maria situation hadn't been wholly rectified they were at least still together by the end of the week. This meant that the party was still on although Jimmy had revoked his offer to come and pick me up. I thought it prudent to pick him up instead seeing as how he clearly wanted my moral support. There was of course the incentive of meeting toned, fit young ladies although it did cross my mind that these fit and athletic women would probably be attracted to other fit and athletic male members of the club. Nonetheless the scenery had the potential to be pleasing to the eye and having heard nothing from Laura I considered it to be the best proposal on offer.

On the way to the party Jimmy brought me up to date on the relationship. Unbeknown to him, Maria had gone through his clothes and wash bag on his return looking for damning evidence of misdemeanours Jimmy might have committed. Having found nothing and consumed with shame, she decided to tell Jimmy of her covert operation, which in turn muffled some of the ill feeling that had been apparent from the previous weekend.

'Apparently she was looking for condoms,' said Jimmy.

'Did she find any?'

Jimmy looked at me in astonishment. 'Of course she bloody

didn't. I can't remember a fat lot about the weekend but I think I'd have known if I shagged somebody.' There was a couple of seconds silence before he continued. 'That's not to say I went there with the intention of shagging anybody … because I didn't.' I didn't think for one minute he had. I'm not even sure he particularly enjoyed the weekend. He was too preoccupied with the consequences of his actions.

We met Maria on the grandiose stone steps leading to the entrance of the club. Balloons and banners adorned the fake granite pillars either side of the foyer. The club had recently been refurbished and this whole event was clearly a publicity stunt. It was more like a scene from a film premiere. Hoards of beautiful women, most of them middle aged, dressed in posh frocks and ball gowns, alighted from Mercedes, Audi's and BMW's eager to be photographed by a few of the local press who were covering the reopening. Luckily I'd made the effort but my baggy pinstriped trousers and semi smart shirt paled into insignificance compared to the rest of the fashion on display. A red Ferrari slid to a halt on the gravel service road where we were standing. A man in a designer suit got out of the car, adjusted his tie and smugly sauntered to the foot of the steps. There was a small mêlée as the photographers hurried around him to get the best shot. Flashbulbs lit up the night sky as the man repeatedly punched the air with clenched fists. I was trying to work out which film I'd seen him in. No, hang on; wasn't he was that chef bloke from *Ready, Steady, Cook*? He obviously thought a lot of himself whoever he was.

'He's the manager of the club,' whispered Maria. Jimmy and I looked at each other, our faces conveying the same thought, 'tosser'. I thought it best we made our way in.

There was champagne on hand in the reception. More beautiful people, presumably members of staff smartly dressed in plain mauve uniforms, handed out the glasses of bubbly. It all felt too overdramatic for a health club. As I sipped the free champagne making sure that my little finger wasn't sticking out, I noticed two of the hostesses nudging each other. I looked over to see a bespectacled blonde whispering behind her hand to another brunette. It took me a while to realise that the blonde was Stacey from next door. I gave Jimmy a nudge and took my drink into the bar.

I was one of the first in there. A band carried out a sound check towards the back of the adjoining restaurant. I interrupted the smarmy barman - dressed in dinner jacket and bow tie - from effeminately tickling the wine glasses with a cloth, to order a pint of lager. Jimmy and Maria were quick to follow me. The strained atmosphere between them, coupled with Stacey's presence made me feel that tonight wasn't going to be all I had hoped.

More and more people filtered in as the band started to play. They were surprisingly better than their appearance would have suggested. I relaxed as the evening wore on and the drink began to flow. Stacey caught my eye a couple of times but she seemed intent on avoiding me. I wasn't overly bothered. Jimmy and Maria even graced the dance floor for a fleeting jig. It was then that the brunette from reception approached me.

'So you must be Connor,' she sighed.

'Yep, that's me,' I said nervously, wondering where this encounter was leading.

'I've heard so much about you from Stacey.'

'I'm sure you have,' I took a swig from my bottle of beer. 'Look I'm not here to cause any trouble,' I continued, thinking I was going to be warned off. 'I didn't know Stacey was going to be here.'

'We work here,' she said as if I should have known.

'Well I didn't know that.'

'She's a bit upset you haven't gone over and said hello.'

'Why should I?'

'I know you guys haven't always seen eye to eye.' I raised my eyebrows. 'She's really sorry about what's happened.' I looked over to where she was stood, laughing and joking surrounded by dashing young men.

'She looks it,' I said.

'Don't be like that.' She put her hand on my shoulder. 'She really misses you.' I wasn't convinced. This had to be a wind up. 'Just go and speak to her.' She smiled and made her way back over to Stacey. A prod on the shoulder distracted me. I turned to see a tall slim girl beaming from ear to ear. Her height and make up made her look far more mature than her years. She must have been about sixteen.

'You're him aren't you?' she said excitedly.

'Who?' I asked, knowing that whoever she thought I was I was sure to disappoint her. She called to her friend who was looking just as excited from afar.

'Jen, don't be shy,' she giggled, 'come and say hello.' She looked back at me. 'It is you isn't it? What's his name …' she said to Jen, 'the footballer?'

'Lee Sharpe,' said Jen, blushing. I was confused on many fronts. I'd never considered I looked anything like Lee Sharpe. My Dad had sometimes remarked that I had Alan Shearer tendencies but that was because we both had receding hairlines. I wasn't sure how two teenage girls would have any idea who Lee Sharpe was. He wasn't the most prominent of footballers. More to the point, what he would be doing at a health club in Dorset?

'I'm not Lee Sharpe, no,' I said trying to let them down gently but it was if I'd opened my mouth and nothing had come out. They stood motionless, gawping at me. 'I'm sorry but I'm not Lee Sharpe,' I repeated.

'Well you sure do look like him,' said the first girl. Either she wasn't bothered that I wasn't who she thought I was or she didn't believe me. We stood there in silence whilst they looked me up and down. I glanced over at Stacey. She averted her eyes as soon as she noticed I was looking at her. She looked sad.

'Will you girls excuse me for a moment?' I assumed their continued silence meant that it was OK. I wandered over to Stacey who was dragged away from her group by the club manager as I approached. I opted to sit on the balcony on my own but found myself shadowed by my teenage following. There were three of them now.

'I'm Tina by the way,' said the tall girl. 'You don't mind if I sit with you?' she ushered her friends away.

'Not at all,' I said reluctantly. There was plenty of room on the three-seater cane sofa but Tina felt that she had to sit as close to me as possible. I moved along a fraction as inconspicuously as I could to give myself a bit more room.

'So what brings you here?' asked Tina, 'I haven't seen you before.'

'No I'm not a member, I've come with some friends.'

'Oh right,' she said shuffling closer to me once more. 'You really do look like Lee Sharpe.' Tina gazed deep into my eyes. Although she was attractive I couldn't help feeling uncomfortable being chatted up by a teenager. She didn't even appear pissed.

'If you'll excuse me, I've just got to pop to the loo,' I said making my excuses. Stacey walked past the window and gave me a look of disgust. I tried to catch up with her but by the time I got back inside she was lost within the crowds. I went to the toilet and lit a fag hoping Tina would get bored, wander off and annoy somebody else. Jimmy burst through the doors in a panic.

'There you are,' he said, 'I've been looking for you everywhere.'

'Why, what's up?' It was unlikely he was looking for me just for the sheer hell of it.

'Me and Maria are going to make a move.'

'What, now?'

'We've had a bit of a row.' I looked up at the heavens.

'What's the problem this time?'

'I made a bit of a joke and it didn't go down too well.'

'What have you said?'

'All I said was that she didn't find any condoms in my gear cus I'd hid them in my jacket pocket.'

'Very subtle,' I said.

'Things are a little fraught. I think it's best we go.'

'Yes I think it's best you do.'

'Will you be alright?'

'Yeah, I'll be fine.' I followed him out of the toilets only to be collared by Tina who'd been sat waiting outside.

'You've been a long time,' she said looking at her watch.

'I'll leave you to it,' said Jimmy grinning.

'Did I tell you I quite fancied Lee Sharpe?' said Tina. Before I could answer, Stacey bundled onto the scene.

'Why don't you just piss off,' she said aggressively to Tina. I was taken aback. She was normally so restrained. Tina wasn't having any of it.

'Why should I?' she replied 'Anyway, I'll report you for being abusive to club members.'

'I couldn't give a flying fuck,' said Stacey. She had an authoritarian look about her with her glasses on but Tina still stood her ground. I put my arm around Stacey and led her down the stairs to the patio outside. To my surprise, she wasn't drunk. 'She's been doing my head in all night,' said Stacey shaking her head. 'All I've wanted to do is speak to you.'

'Why?' I asked curiously, 'I didn't think you wanted anything to do with me.'

'I know, I know that's what you thought and when I saw you were here tonight I just wanted to say I was sorry. I've acted abysmally.'

'Apology …' before I could confirm my acceptance Stacey had pushed me up against a pile of timber presumably left over from the building works and we engaged in a passionate kiss. It was the first time I'd felt like she really meant it. On other occasions it had been like when we were kids and there didn't seem anything better to do than have a ruddy good snog. This time was different. I could feel it.

'I can't believe it,' she said gulping for air, 'I can't believe I've had this opportunity again.' I could only assume that the melodramatics of the club party had gone to her head. I enjoyed playing my part in the apparently real life movie scene however. We stood outside for nearly an hour, embracing and chatting and she really gave me the impression that she wanted to lead off from where it had all previously gone wrong. The club manager eventually caught up with us and called her back inside.

'Ring me tomorrow,' she said softly before kissing me gently on the cheek. Jimmy and Maria had gone, Stacey obviously had other business to sort out but I didn't feel like going home to bed. I decided to get pissed in the bar. The Lee Sharpe fan club didn't give me any hassle as I don't think Tina relished another dressing down. The drinks were flowing much more freely than when I'd first arrived and the live music seemed to get better and better as the night wore on. When they turned the lights off in the bar I guessed it was about time to catch a cab home.

Chapter 30

I'd just mustered enough energy to rise from my pit and make myself a black coffee when there was a knock at the door. Rebecca was stood on the front step smiling cheerily. I wasn't in the mood to do battle with her again and made every effort to block the doorway so she wasn't able to sneak past.

'Can I come in?' she asked.

'Depends what you want,' I said yawning.

'I just wanted a chat.'

'We had a chat the other day.'

'I wondered if we could have another one.'

'But I didn't enjoy the last one,' I said belligerently.

'Don't be like this,' she said mournfully, 'I just wanted to say I was sorry.' As that was an experience unlikely to be repeated, I stepped aside and let her through. 'I've acted like a fool,' she continued sitting herself down on the sofa. Apologies from members of the opposite sex were becoming a frequent occurrence.

'So come on, what's up?' I said more sympathetically.

For the first time in a long while, I saw a more vulnerable Becci. When all else failed she knew Connor would sit her down, make her a nice cup of tea and listen to all her woes. Why did I always do this to myself?

Her life was indeed a bit of a mess and in true Connor tradition it involved me. Becci was having an affair with Roger to try and get back at her new boyfriend because she suspected he was having an affair with someone else. Roger knew that Becci had a boyfriend but was as keen as mustard to get into her pants on a more permanent basis. She however wasn't too keen on Roger but he filled a short-term emotional hole so to speak. Becci's boyfriend, Dom, suspected that she was having an affair but for whatever reason didn't think it was with the prime candidate who was directly under his nose, namely Roger. Instead he suspected me. Becci's mother wouldn't let either Roger or Dom into her house as she said they were both a waste of space and not a patch on me. Her father was apparently of the same opinion, just less vocal about it. This only increased Dom's suspicions that her parents were protecting me. He spent most of his time burning around the streets of Bournemouth, upgrading his car stereo and becoming more and more physically violent with Becci whilst Roger hid like a big girl whenever Dom came sniffing around.

'So why are you here?' I asked sipping the dregs of tea from my mug.

'I realised Mum was right. Neither of them compares to you. They both just want me as an accessory, they don't really care for or love me … and I'm scared Connor. I want to get away from Dom before he hurts me badly but I'm too scared of what he might do.'

I could hear a mobile phone ringing inside Becci's bag. She stared at the display, her eyes like saucers. She began to shake but answered the phone nonetheless.

'I told you Dom, I'm at Jude and Harry's to see the baby.' People have often criticised me for thinking about things too much but there are times when it's an important thing to do. If I were in her position there's no way I would say I was with anybody else because the chances are Dom (going on what the bloke sounded like) would want to speak to them.

'Jude's just popped to the toilet actually.' I assumed I was right. He wanted to speak to her.

'Well, Harry's taken the dog for a walk.' Covering all angles is sometimes not as daft as it seems. Dom's voice was so loud I could hear him on the other end of the phone.

'You're fucking lying to me again aren't you bitch … you're with him.' He seemed very angry and sounded like he meant business. I suddenly felt very sombre. I just didn't know what to do. I didn't believe Becci deserved this. All through our relationship I'd like to think I'd been fairly laid back, and despite our footballing moments, we rarely argued. I certainly never called her a bitch. It felt kind of weird that my ex-girlfriend was having this conversation with her boyfriend in my lounge when I was nothing to do with the situation except it was me he suspected she was with. On this particular occasion he was right

I guess.

'Don't be so fucking stupid you twat, of course I'm not. Who do you think I am?'

I was even more surprised by Becci's response. Despite her obvious fear, her vocal performance was strong and cool. I'd also never heard her swear with such conviction before (if you discount the verbal abuse she fired into a girl in a nightclub who, unaware I was attached, was attempting to chat me up on the dance floor. Jude had saved the offending girl that night by bundling Becci out of the way marginally before she'd tried to smack her over the head with her shoe).

'You are so full of fucking shit,' raged Dom. I could see Becci was about to crack. She panicked. Part of me wanted to wade in whilst the other part thought it best not to get involved. As the saying goes, cometh the hour, cometh the man. Was I a man or a mouse?

'Oh, hang on. I think this is Harry coming back through the door now.' She took the phone away from her head momentarily and started to walk over to me gesturing for me to speak to Dom. I suddenly lost all ability to do anything with my body except wave my hands frantically in front of me. It was the international symbol for 'don't make me speak to him, I'll shit my pants'. Becci was feverishly thinking of something else to say.

'Oh, oh, it must have been the wind making the noise.' She'd made another error. There wasn't a breath of wind in the air. Maybe Harry and Jude had moved to Chicago.

'I'm coming round,' he shouted.

She finally did what I would have done very much earlier in the conversation.

'My … attry's … unning .. ow,' she stuttered, rubbing her hand all over the microphone to fain some kind of interference. She thumped the 'end call' button on the phone and grabbed me by the arm, dragging me out by the front door.

'You drive,' she said throwing me her car keys 'I knew you driving like a wanker would come in useful one day.'

I correctly presumed we were going to Harry and Jude's house. We quickly went over the points that we'd been discussing before Dom had phoned. I told her she had to get away from Dom. She asked if I would think about what she said about us getting back together. I said Dom was a complete arse and she would only be using me as a tool to get away from him. She said if that was the case she could have used Roger ages ago. I said Roger was a complete arse and that I'd only been reinstated onto the list of potential suitors because her mum had thought it was a good idea. She kissed me gently kissed me on the cheek as if to somehow confirm I was right and rang Harry and Jude to get the story straight before we arrived. My 'wanker-like' driving got us to their house in just over seven minutes. Considering Jude was supposedly on the toilet I can only assume that it must have been one hell of a dump. Rebecca gave me her mobile number and I left them to sort out their mess. Harry kindly dropped me back at the Health Club to pick up my car from the night before.

Chapter 31

'Satisfaction' – Wendy and Lisa.

I thought I'd give Ellie a ring in the afternoon. I flowered the conversation up to make it sound like I wasn't ringing just to find out whether she'd heard anything from Laura. I obviously didn't disguise my intent enough.

'Laura's on a course in Yorkshire,' blurted Ellie.

'What?' I was surprised she'd come straight out with it.

'Well that's why you've rung isn't it?'

'No, no.' I attempted to defend myself, 'I just rang to see how you are.'

'Oh Connor you're such a bad liar. Anyway, you're busy this weekend. A friend of a friend of Mel's is having a house party and I want you and Bob all to myself this time. No flouncing off with anyone, understood?'

'Is Ritchie going?'

'Who?

'Ritchie … the Jacques Cousteau of Clapham.'

'Oh that's all over and done with,' said Ellie dismissively. I smiled. 'Anyway, like I said, I want you all to myself this time you hear?'

'Loud and clear.' I wondered how I was going to balance my increasing number of social engagements. It was starting to get confusing. Another black coffee helped me weigh up my options.

Rebecca wasn't totally clear on her intentions but I got the impression she wanted to try and get things back on. Stacey also seemed keen to rekindle something from the pile of steaming crap that had gone before and Laura seemed happy to flit in and out of my life when it suited her. But which,if any, option should I pursue? I decided to consult the Canadian office. I logged onto the computer hoping Kristy was online to listen to my woes. Her advice was to get my arse over to Canada and forget about them all for a while. On the surface, it didn't seem to be such a bad option.

I'd spoken to Stacey earlier in the week and made my excuses for the weekend. She still seemed smitten and I thought not acting on her every whim as I'd done in the past might help keep it that way. I arranged to see her on Sunday night when I got back from London.

The house party was definitely the best option. I spent the Saturday evening watching the residents of Ellie's house parading round in various states of undress whilst they got ready. I gave up trying to watch the TV. The noise from numerous stereos playing a diverse range of music from various locations around the house made it impossible to hear yourself think.

The journey to the party involved me sitting smugly surrounded by beautiful women. I must have looked like the cat who'd got the cream. I had no idea where we were in London by the time we arrived at the house, only that we'd used a train, tube connections and a bus to get there. As we wandered into the house I guessed Mel's friend must also live in a house full of girls. These girls must have invited their girly friends. It was wall to wall totty with hardly a bloke in sight. I am usually the guy who stands in the kitchen all night at house parties, feeling completely overshadowed by the other competitive males who are either brilliant dancers or articulate conversationalists. While they glide around wooing the women, I generally sulk. The atmosphere here was completely different. There was an unspoken camaraderie between the men at the party; the women outnumbered us by about five to one. If you couldn't pull at a party like this it was your own bloody fault. Men greeted each other with wide cheesy grins, a sign acknowledging you were a member of the 'lucky bastard' club. Even Bob had to try hard to subdue his pleasure at being in such surroundings. We loaded our glasses with homemade punch and the night soon began to swing.

By about 11.30pm I'd danced (very badly of course) with my quota of five women, even managing to get one of their phone numbers. Not only was she stunning but she also gave me her work, home and friend's phone numbers in case I had any trouble getting hold of her. Everything was hunky dory until Bob approached, his face pale as a sheet. I could see his hand trembling as he filled his empty glass with the potent punch. Swigging it back in a couple of gulps, I'm not sure it had a chance to even touch the sides.

'You look like you've had enough of that stuff mate,' I said ironically.

'Yes, but you haven't seen who I've seen,' said Bob shakily. I ran a list through my mind of possible candidates but couldn't think of anybody who would concern me to any great extent. I looked at him with a blank expression.

'Jovana,' he said.

'Jovana eh?' I laughed. 'Fancy her being here. Strange eh? I wonder who she knows then?' Bob still looked petrified. 'She's no problem,' I said dismissively.

'You wouldn't say that if you'd been collared by her. She's shouting her mouth off about,' he paused for a moment whilst taking a drag of my cigarette which lay in the ashtray, 'that night.' Bob doesn't smoke.

'It wouldn't bother me,' I said frivolously, helping myself to another glass of punch.

'Yes but you're not going out with Ellie are you? You haven't had Ellie stood at the back of the sofa whilst Jovana explains to her friends how she stroked my scrotum.'

'Just calm down Bob, it was an accident. She thought it was my … scrotum, allegedly. Just tell Ellie what happened. She's a reasonable person. I'm sure she'll see the funny side of it when she realises it was all a mistake.'

'You must be joking. What's it going to look like if only now, when the beans have already been spilt, I decide to tell Ellie that a strange woman stayed round my flat.'

'OK, I'll speak to her then.'

'Didn't you just hear what I said! Anyway, I don't want you speaking to her. You'll fuck it up. You'll do more harm than good.'

'Thanks for your support mate, best I leave you to it,' I said defensively. I could see Jovana approaching. 'I suggest you make yourself scarce. I think your friend's looking for you.' Bob turned, took another drag from my cigarette and hid himself amongst the crowds. As Jovana drew nearer it crossed my mind that maybe she'd told her husband what had happened. Furthermore, maybe he was here. I considered doing a runner myself but it was too late, Ellie had closed ranks on me as well.

'Good evening Connor,' said Jovana.

'Oh you know him as well do you?' growled Ellie, her hands on her hips. 'I might have known you'd have something to do with it.'

'Yes, we had, how do you zay, an entertaining threesome,' Jovana smiled knowingly. A look of disgust crossed Ellie's face. I considered denying ever meeting Jovana but not having been party to any of the previous conversations I decided not to dig myself a potential hole.

'It was nothing like that,' I said to Ellie desperately, 'and as for you,' I turned to Jovana, 'you're not making things any easier.'

'You bet she isn't,' said Ellie defiantly.

'Look, why don't you find Bob and talk to him? This is nothing like it's being made out to be.' I could tell she wasn't convinced. 'You,' I said to Jovana, 'come with me.'

I led her away and left Ellie to confront Bob. 'What the hell are you doing here?' I asked.

'Aren't you pleazed to again zee me?' she slurred. She'd obviously had a bit to drink and I guessed that was the reason she was saying things without engaging her brain.

'That was Bob's girlfriend,' I said forcefully. Her eyes glazed over and she gave me a vacant grin. 'You could fuck everything up if you're not careful.'

'Oh comz on,' she purred, 'I'm only having a bit of fun, I don't mean any 'arm.'

'Well can you just watch what you're saying in future?' She nodded in an attempt at an apology. Her head was bowed but I could still see a grin on her face. 'You didn't answer my question anyway. How come you're here?'

'My friend's brother is a friend of the …' a puzzled look came over her face. I think she'd confused herself.

'OK, well it doesn't matter, just don't go saying anything else about me or Bob.' She nodded once again and we went to get her some water. Her bubbly persona seemed more forced than usual. I tried to dig a bit deeper, partly because I was curious and partly because it kept us both out of the way of Ellie and Bob. It appeared Vlad had become increasingly heavy handed and no matter what she tried to do to get away from him he always managed to catch up with her. I couldn't help feeling a little bit sorry. She may have seemed a little zany but I was sure she never meant any harm. A woman in her early thirties flounced over to where we were sat.

'We did it then,' she said to Jovana with a meek smile.

'This … my friend, Tiff,' said Jovana pointing to the woman. 'She invited me to the party to cheer me up.' I limply shook hands with her and smiled.

'I'm sorry, you did what exactly?' I enquired, wondering what her opening statement referred to.

'Oh, it's all kind of undercover,' she said laughing. 'We've been spreading gossip about this party for the last couple of weeks … but saying it's at another friend's house.'

'Why?' I asked, not sure I was following the logic.

'To throw Jove's ex off the scent of course. I just had a call on my mobile. He's turned up at the other address,' she said putting her hand on Jovana's shoulder. Her friend was trying to remain upbeat but it was obvious the constant hounding was taking its toll on Jovana.

'So is there a party at this other place?' I asked.

'No,' laughed Tiff bluntly.

'And this other friend, she's in on the deal, right?'

'Duh,' groaned Tiff with her pointed finger burrowing into the side of her head, 'what do you take us for, of course she is.' I resented the fact she'd mocked me when it seemed more appropriate, if you were trying to throw someone a bum steer, that you pick a friend's house where there actually was a party.

'And how long are you planning on keeping this bluffing up?' I asked.

'Not too much longer,' whispered Jovana, 'I can't take much more.'

'So what are you going to do?'

'That'd be telling,' whispered Tiff all-knowingly.

'I'm moving away. I'm going to move in with a friend. It's the only way to end this.'

'Or kill him,' said Tiff. I did a double take on her facial expression. I wasn't entirely sure she was joking.

So that was the plan. Jovana was going to run away to Southampton. Maybe I felt sorry for her, maybe it was the beers, but for some reason I gave her my telephone number.

'If it does all come off, you'll have to give me a ring. We'll have to meet up for a drink or something.' She smiled and nodded.

'I'd like zat,' she said faintly, 'we'll vait and zee what happens.'

Everything was black. My head felt heavy. I slowly forced my eyelids open, breaking the seal of gunk that had formed around my eyes. I was still in the living room, lying squashed up on the sofa next to Jovana. I remembered drinking copious amounts of alcohol and dancing in the living room. I think I snogged Jovana. No, that was a dream. Fumbling in the dark corners of my mind I realised I *had* snogged Jovana. Other than that, it was all a little hazy. I looked down. She was fully clothed. I was fully clothed. I looked at my watch. It slowly came into focus. It was

4.30am. The house was silent. I wandered around the ground floor but no one was to be seen. I followed my nose into the kitchen where a young woman was cooking breakfast.

'Who the fuck are you?' she said startled, dropping the frying pan back on the stove.

'I dunno,' I said wiping the sleep from my eyes 'who the fuck are you?'

'This is my fucking house.' Although neither of us had answered the question properly, I will admit I felt the more stupid.

'Oh,' I said humbly. 'I'm Connor, I came with …' I looked round half expecting to see at least one person from our group. 'I'm a friend of …' I stopped myself, realising that she probably wouldn't know who Ellie was. Even the person who invited us was a friend of a friend of Mel but it was all I had to go on, 'Mel?' I said timidly.

'Never heard of her,' said the woman turning back to the stove. 'It doesn't matter. You just gave me a fright. I thought everybody had gone home.' She turned back towards me and smiled sweetly.

'D'ya wanna bacon sandwich?' I took her up on her generous offer. I explained she shouldn't be alarmed if she found a strange woman on her sofa and asked her where the nearest taxi rank was. With my hands clasped tightly around the bacon sandwich for warmth I ventured into the chill morning air in the thin shirt I'd been wearing the night before. After walking for about ten minutes on the deserted back streets of Fulham (so I'd been informed), the directions given by my bacon butty friend brought me to a mini cab office. The room was no bigger than a downstairs toilet with an offcut of worktop in the far corner. It stank of body odour. I gently rapped the desk trying desperately to remember the name of Ellie's road. There was a flimsy partition wall at the back of the office. You could almost see it vibrating with the synchronised snoring from beyond. An Asian man, looking in worse condition than me, eventually emerged from the door behind the desk. It wasn't long before I realised his English wasn't so good. We agreed to drive in the general direction of Barnes until I recognised something or ran out of money. As we neared my fiscal limit I noticed *Threshers* on the corner. I reached into my pocket to pay the driver and discovered the added bonus of a solitary bent cigarette and a lighter. That would keep my mind off the cold as I weaved my way around the back roads to Ellie's.

Needless to say there was no movement at the house when I arrived. I considered banging on the door but didn't fancy incurring the wrath of a house full of sleep-deprived women. I looked at my watch. It was 5.15am and the bitter chill wasn't any easier to bear. Mel's bedroom was at the front of the house. I thought it better to disturb one person than to wake the entire house. I reached up and tapped lightly on the window. I waited for a while. There was no response. I repeated my actions until Mel's startled face peered at me from over the ledge.

'Oh it's you,' she said. My heart skipped a beat as I saw her face. This woman had had very little sleep, drunk like a fish the night before and still look absolutely stunning. I wouldn't have blamed myself for falling in love right there and then. 'What do you want?'

'What the bloody hell do you think I want,' I whispered. 'I want to get in. Open the front door for us.'

'No I can't be arsed,' she said rubbing her face.

'What?'

'There are strange people scattered all over the hall floor. I might tread on someone.' She may have been gorgeous but she certainly wasn't the most practical of people. 'You'll have to climb through the window,' she said.

I suddenly didn't want her to open the front door. I imagined showing my grand children pictures of Mel in years to come, embellishing the story of the morning I climbed through her bedroom window. Her window sill was particularly high and I needed her to help manhandle me into her room. After two or three attempts, with Mel seemingly determined to rip my shirt over my head, we eventually fell backwards onto her bed. I paused for a moment, my head having landed in her midriff albeit she did have her duvet wrapped round her. I made my apologies and brought myself to my feet. I suddenly realised my next problem.

'All my things are in Ellie's room,' I said quietly. 'Have you got another duvet?'

'What on earth for?'

'Well,' I stuttered, 'I just wondered if I could kip on your floor.'

'Don't be so silly,' she said straightening herself out. 'Just hop in with me, I won't bite.'

'What … what if?' I stammered.

'It doesn't matter what other people think, just get in, I'm tired.' I dithered for a moment, wondering if I should get in fully clothed. 'Just mind where you're putting your hands,' she giggled as she turned over, 'I haven't got any clothes on.' I'd had butterflies in my stomach before, but never in my groin. It seemed a waste to not even partly undress. I stripped off to my boxers and clambered into bed before she turned back over.

Needless to say I didn't get a wink of sleep. The rigid state I'd experienced at Laura's returned once more and I lay for the next few hours wondering what it would be like to give Mel a really big snog or to hold her in my arms. I mean I had kissed her and held her before but we'd only ever been larking about. Although nothing physically happened between us this time, our brief encounter ranked alongside the night I'd met Laura. The highlights included her head resting on my chest; the feel and smell of her hair on my face; her legs crossed over mine. At one point when she was snuggled up particularly close to me I'm sure I felt something I shouldn't have done on my leg.

I must have drifted off at some point. Ellie burst into the room bringing my brief slumber to an end.

'Does anyone know what happened …' she started.

Mel was already awake. 'He's here … with me,' she said, her grin anticipating the question. The look of disapproval on Ellie's face was clear to see. Two or three other faces peered round the edge of the door to witness our illicit bed sharing exploits. Mel wasn't phased at all. In fact, she seemed to be quite enjoying the attention and it was doing my street cred no harm either.

'What have I always told you Connor?' Ellie said angrily. The faces slowly disappeared back into the hallway.

'Always wash behind your ears?'

I could see Ellie wasn't in the mood for one of my whimsical retorts.

'Nothing … I didn't,' I started.

'Oh grow up Ellie for Christ's sakes,' said Mel leaping to my defence. 'We're not all children in this house you know. Some of us are adult enough to share a bed with a member of the opposite sex without giggling behind our hands.'

'Do you see me giggling?' barked Ellie.

'No,' said Mel reaching across me for her cigarettes on the bedside table. 'But it wouldn't hurt you to crack a smile every now and then. Lighten up a bit eh?' Considering the obvious atmosphere, I thought it best not to ask if everything had been sorted out from the night before with Bob. Ellie stormed off in a huff.

'Do you want any breakfast?' Mel slipped out from under the duvet briefly revealing herself in all her glory. I realised I should probably stop looking her up and down and give some kind of response.

'Yes please,' I said contentedly. Although my earlier bacon sandwich had filled a hole I quite liked the thought of Mel knocking me something up. She smiled, put her dressing gown on and headed for the kitchen.

Chapter 32

Although I felt like chancing my arm by offering to take Mel out for the day, I thought it best to leave. Ellie and Bob were still at each other's throats and I wanted to avoid any arguments. Bob was right; I'd probably do more harm than good. I received a text message from Laura on the way home. It was all about herself and how busy she'd been. I didn't bother to respond. I was more concerned about catching up on some sleep before the night's main event with Stacey.

I was woken at 5pm by a banging at the front door. It was Stacey. She stood on the front doorstep, dolled up to the nines.

'I'm not ready,' I blurted. She didn't respond, just continued to stare at me and sway from side to side. 'I didn't think we were going out 'till later?'

'We're not, I just thought I'd pop round and see you before I go out,' she said making her way into the lounge.

'Where are you going then?' I asked, scratching my head.

'I'm going clubbing with my mates. I wasn't sure what time you'd be back.'

'You knew I was coming back to see you.' I was beginning to wish I'd stayed in London and taken my chances with Mel. 'Anyway, I can come with you.'

'No,' she said sharply, her scowl slowly giving way to a false smile.

'Why not?'

'They're my friends. I'm going out with some of the folk from work, Andy, Dom …'

'Dom?' I said trying to remember where I'd heard that name before.

'Yeah Dom … and yes, before you ask, he is the guy who answered the door when you came round for your book.'

The energy was suddenly zapped from my legs as I realised it was a 'Dom' who was on the phone to Becci the day she was round at my house. It was an unusual name but surely it couldn't be the same person. I was torn between being angry she felt I couldn't go clubbing and petrified that this would be Becci's Dom.

'Has he got a girlfriend?' I asked cautiously.

'Who Dom? Yeah, a right snobby cow; really up herself. Why the interest in him anyway? You jealous?'

'No, just showing an interest.' Which is more than can be said for Stacey's interest in me. She'd turned on the television and made herself comfortable on the sofa. I really wanted to probe her further on this Dom character. Could he be one and the same person? The 'up herself snob' description was quite fitting for Becci but then again you could say that for a fair proportion of the female population out in Bournemouth on a Saturday night. And no, I'm not being sexist. As many blokes were as bad … just more pit bull than poodle.

Stacey's habit of changing our plans and popping in when

she felt like it became more and more frequent. I was kinda always there when she wanted me. I was sometimes honoured with a fleeting visit before she went out clubbing or a phone call at 3am when she'd come home. I was never allowed to tag along. It was a very strange set-up. She sent me very sweet text messages saying how much she cared and how understanding I was but at the end of the day she was too wrapped up in her friends and clubbing for anything of any substance to materialise. She had a phrase she used to sum us up. We were, in her opinion, 'date mates'. In my opinion this was a phrase that allowed her to blow hot and cold when it suited her. It made me angry that I let her get away with it. We had the odd day out here and there but I always felt we were just killing time until her next appointment.

It wasn't until I met Alan at the pub one evening that I put things into perspective. He was having a rough time of it. His Dad was in hospital after suffering a bad stroke. It had been touch and go for a while. Alan was solemn and reflective. It makes you reappraise what's important to you I guess. Jimmy hadn't been helping apparently. He'd continued to vent his relationship frustrations by picking on Alan.

'I think you need another drink,' I suggested. He nodded his head, half smiling. I returned to our table with two pints of lager and tried to change the subject.

'How's work going anyway?' I asked.

'Ah,' he said grimacing, 'that's what I wanted to talk to you about actually.' I got the distinct impression there was another tale of woe about to be dished up.

'Problems?'

'My boss has threatened to sack me,' said Alan. I screwed up my face in curiosity.

'Errm, and why would that be? What have you done?'

'Oh nothing,' said Alan shaking his head innocently, 'it's because I know you.'

'What?' I smirked. This was one of the funny conversations Alan had every once in a while which didn't actually mean anything. This time however he wasn't smiling back. He sipped his drink as if waiting for me to press him further. 'How does knowing me make your boss want to sack you?'

'I dunno,' he said shrugging his shoulders. I was becoming more confused.

'So,' I started, still wondering if this was a wind up, 'your boss knows me does he?'

'Well, he knows of you.'

'He's winding you up about wanting to sack you though, right? It's like an office joke or something,' I was trying to get to the bottom of this riddle.

'Oh no, he's deadly serious.' Alan still wasn't giving much away with his body language. He was emotionless. I trawled through my mind for anyone I might have upset in the last few months.

'So I've done something to upset him?'

'Oh yes, absolutely. He's not very happy at all.' This conversation was getting more infuriating by the second.

'For fuck's sakes Alan, who is your boss?' I asked impatiently.

'Dom Bradshaw,' he said. I froze. Alan paused for a second before continuing. 'Ring any bells?' This was the third Dom now.

'Well, maybe,' I said, trying to piece it all together. Seeing my confusion, Alan went on to explain that his boss was both the boyfriend of Becci and friend of Stacey. 'What …how?' Two questions wanted to come out at the same time. I tried again. 'How do you know all this?' I asked.

'They both pop into work to see him. I obviously recognised Becci and Stacey's your old next door neighbour isn't she? Didn't you used to knock about with her at school?'

'Hmmm,' I was still stunned by the way this bloody Dom kept popping his sizeable meaty head into my life.

'Anyway,' Alan explained, 'I've kinda been asked to give you a message.'

'Who? Hold on,' I was still trying to get my head round who knew who and how. 'What exactly have I done to upset him? How does he know you know me?'

'I got talking to Becci when she came in a while back. She'd been in a couple of times before but for some reason it wasn't until the other day that she decided to talk to me.'

'Right, go on.' I could feel myself getting angry. For the moment I wasn't entirely sure why.

'He took me to one side the next day and asked how I knew her. I explained that I knew her ex.' He paused.

'Yes … me,' I said impatiently. 'Go on.'

'Well, he just flew off the handle.'

'Dare I ask why?' I could feel the hairs on the back of my neck standing up.

'He said that you'd been pestering her, sending her texts and calling her on her mobile and that unless you stopped he was going to sack me. I really need that job right now.' His face conveyed his apprehension and distress.

'Alan…' I didn't really know where to start, 'he can't sack you for knowing me.' I took a large gulp of lager, 'and anyway, I haven't been pestering her at all. If anything, the silly cow's been pestering me.'

'Oh,' said Alan, oblivious to what I'd just said, 'and he said he was going to beat the shit out of you … and me, if you ever did it again.'

'Did he?' I snarled. I don't often get irate or react to situations in a hostile manner but all this going on behind my back had really got my dander up. Instead of panicking and worrying about the effect it all could have on either me, or more importantly Alan, I was consumed with rage. It was all untrue. Just who the fuck did this Dom think he was? Whether Becci had spun him some yarn or he was just being a bloody minded bully I wasn't too sure, but I was intent on finding out. I can't explain why I wasn't worried that he was a seemingly brainless thug. I think it was because Alan, who despite being Alan wouldn't hurt a fly, had been drawn into something that was nothing to do with him, or me for that matter. I got up from the table and made for the exit, leaving Alan rambling on about how much he didn't want to lose his job. I paced up and down the car park waiting for my mobile to connect with Becci's.

'Hello,' a voice answered timidly.

'Becci, it's Connor,' I said abruptly.

'Oh.'

'Now I don't know what the fuck is going on with that prick of a boyfriend of yours but you can tell him from me that I'm not fucking happy.'

'Oh,' she repeated.

'If he's got something to say to me then he's more than welcome to come and find me and say it to my face.'

'Errm why, what's been said?' She still sounded very coy.

'Look I don't know what's been going on or what you've told him but if he ever,' I paused as if to re-emphasise the point, '*ever* threatens my friends again he'd better live up to his word and … attempt to beat the crap out of me before I come and find him. He's more than welcome to come round my place any time he likes, but just leave my mates out of it. Alan's got enough on his plate as it is without your fucking boyfriend throwing his weight about.'

'I didn't … realise.'

'No, I'm sure you didn't,' I snorted. 'Just make sure you tell him, OK?' With that I hung up. I was shaking, not quite able to believe I'd had the bottle to phone and to say what I had without stammering or fucking it up. It wasn't male bravado; I was genuinely seething with rage. I took a few gulps of cold air and wandered back into the pub wondering about the consequences of my phone call.

After discussing our plans for the weekend and finishing up our drinks we decided to call it a night. Alan was still a bit shell-shocked but going out clubbing at the weekend would hopefully take his mind off things. I decided it was probably best, in the interests of us both, for me to cut all indirect links to this Dom character. I phoned Stacey on the way home and told her I didn't think it was a good idea we saw each other any more. It was something I should have done a long time before. She didn't seem particularly bothered.

Chapter 33

'Sound check' – Gorillaz.

The weekend couldn't have come sooner. I think we all needed a good night out. I'd had a word with Jimmy about giving Alan a break before we left. I didn't want any bitching between us. Jimmy was still in the doldrums with his relationship predicaments and I'm not sure he had the energy to keep up his piss-taking routine anyway. Alan was still in a flap about everything in his life, particularly his job, although from what he said Dom had been just as keen to avoid Alan, as he was to avoid Dom. Jovana, who was now staying at her friend's in Southampton had decided to come out of hiding and join us with some of her mates. She was in need of a good night out as much as the rest of us although I wasn't sure that meeting up with the triplet of miserable waifs and strays that trundled along to the *Empire* on Friday night was the best medicine for anybody.

Jimmy was probably in the worst frame of mind. That he'd agreed to drive was testament to that. Alan was intent on getting completely shit faced in the shortest possible time. He'd had four cans of Stella before Jimmy had even picked him up.

It was an evening of extremes. There was a foam party going on. Jimmy, worried that the foam would damage his suede shoes, sat on the balcony for the majority of the night, sipping diet coke. Alan on the other hand was permanently on the dance floor. I was glad he was enjoying himself and letting down what little amount of hair he had left. I tried to keep the casualty levels to a minimum by ushering him into small, uninhabited pockets of the floor so that his flailing arms inflicted the least amount of damage. It was usually only a matter of time before clubbers in a six-foot radius of Alan got pissed off being hit in the face by his arms or having foam vigorously rubbed into their hair. Maybe I was just jealous. I was a lot more conservative in my dancing approach, using the 'one dance fits all' rule while looking at the floor. The looking at the floor made me feel more secure. If I couldn't see everybody else laughing at me, then in my head they weren't there. There was the odd occasion where I would completely let go. I would transform myself into 'Lord of the Cheese'. This involved pulling silly faces and doing ridiculous dance routines. One of my favourites was throwing two imaginary balls into the air, one after the other, and then bouncing them off alternate shoulders, all in time with the music of course. Angela Rippon (does she still do *Come Dancing*?) wouldn't have known where to look. In my own mind, this routine seemed to go down well with friends and fellow punters because they thought, 'wow, he dances like a tit, but I bet if he was dancing properly he'd be really good'. In reality it probably just gave everybody else an ego boost, 'and I was worried about *my* dancing? Look at that prick over there'. There was to be no cheese tonight however. Alan, or rather the general public, needed looking after. My duties were brought to an end when Alan threw up. I helped him off the dance floor and propped him next to a less than impressed Jimmy. I watched the ensuing carnage from the balcony. The sick had originally formed a hole down through the foam for all to see. It wasn't long however until the contents of Alan's stomach became increasingly difficult for fellow clubbers to avoid as the foam gradually reformed over the top. Two girls slipped over in it. One of them burst into tears. She had every right to cry. I think I would have done if I'd had the misfortune of having Alan's regurgitated dinner up my back. Alan was oblivious to the mayhem he had caused. He just sat uncomfortably close to Jimmy with a silly grin and a vacant glare, his hair matted with sick where he'd tried to catch it in his hands and then proceeded to wipe his head. I was feeling a wee bit tipsy myself and witnessing Alan's antics hadn't helped. I had a walk round to find Jovana and attempted to clear my head in the process.

In contrast to Alan's carnage, I found her in the tranquillity of a quiet little alcove of the club, feverishly chatting to her friends. The arm gesticulation that accompanied the conversation resembled something very similar to Alan's dancing, just not quite as violent. Jovana smiled as I approached the table and her friends looked round to see who I was. Following brief introductions, they decided to hit the floor leaving Jovana and I to our own devices. She seemed a lot more relaxed. Whether the move had lifted the emotional weight from her shoulders I don't know but she wasn't flirty or forward and we had quite a serious conversation (despite my semi drunken state) about what we'd both been up to. Our dialogue wasn't strained or forced. There was the odd interruption from her friends who came back to pick up coats or drinks but the time just seemed to fly by, so much so that Jimmy appeared at the table wanting to go home.

'Come on, we're going,' he said sternly.

'Jimmy, this is Jovana,' I said. He just shrugged to indicate he couldn't care less if she were Mary Poppins. 'We can't go yet, we've only just got here,' I continued.

'Mate, it's one in the morning.' I looked at my watch in disbelief. He was right.

'Oh,' I said.

'Alan's been sick again and I want to get him home before any more comes up in my car.' I looked at Jovana who was pulling a face of disgust.

'Right, well, OK,' I said downing the last of my drink.

'It's OK, I can drop you home later if you like,' said Jovana. I looked at Jimmy and then back at Jovana.

'Errm, well if you don't mind.' I looked back at Jimmy who shrugged once more.

'Look, I don't fucking care as long as I get Alan home pronto and get some sleep. Just make your mind up.'

'I'll stay then,' I said.

'Fine, I'll catch you later,' said Jimmy hastily and with that he wandered back into a cloud of dry ice. I got another round in, we chatted a bit more and then decided to call it a night ourselves. Jovana's friends had all gone or were getting lifts by the time we made our way to the exit. The cold air hit me as we walked towards her car. I never quite understand why I always manage to feel twice as pissed outside as I do before I leave the club. Luckily we didn't have far to go but the bumpy ride in Jovana's beaten up purple Citreon 2CV (I think it had been sprayed that colour by somebody to try and hide the rust) mixed with her erratic driving, didn't do anything for my stomach.

‘Is zit OK if ize come in for coffee?’ she said as we neared my house. My mind didn’t register anything. I didn’t consider whether or not this was a come on. Nor did I worry about the state of my house. I just answered in the affirmative.

‘Nice plaze you got,’ she said as she wandered in behind me. Again, not being fully on the ball, I didn’t wonder whether she was being sarcastic or whether she was just happy to be in the warm after standing outside for a good few minutes whilst I fumbled with my keys. I wandered into the kitchen to put the kettle on. The house, luckily, was reasonably tidy, not that I was in any fit state to care.

I walked back into the lounge to find that she’d helped herself to the use of my stereo, which was now playing *Blur* at a very low volume as she reclined on the sofa with a small plastic bag.

‘You vant some?’ she asked nonchalantly, thrusting the bag filled with what looked like sherbet in my general direction.

‘What is it?’ I asked putting two mugs of coffee down on the table.

‘Just try some.’

‘OK,’ I said naively.

‘Just lick your finger and dip it in,’ she insisted. I followed her instructions. It didn’t taste great but for some reason I wanted more. ‘Just imazine you are cleaning your teez with it.’ Again, I followed her instructions and sat down beside her on the sofa. The atmosphere was fairly relaxed. We chatted, listened to music, watched a video and the more the night went on, the more tired I became. I started to feel quite sick and the room began to spin violently. Although tired, I just couldn’t go to sleep. In contrast, Jovana seemed full of energy which made me wearier still. I can remember her helping me upstairs, getting me undressed and into bed. I remember her getting undressed and climbing into bed with me. It must have been early morning by then. She’d had to shut the curtains to keep the light out. I felt completely useless. I had no control over my body, I was really ill. I can only liken it to the moments when you come round from a general anaesthetic, albeit this lasted for hours on end. Eventually I nodded off to sleep.

The alarm clock by the side of the bed confirmed that I hadn't been asleep very long. It was 8am. There was no sign of Jovana. I hobbled over to the window. Through the curtains and my half-open eyes I could see that her car had gone. I breathed a sigh of relief and stumbled into the bathroom. My reflection in the mirror wasn't a pretty sight. I was pasty white and my mouth felt dry yet slimy. My eyes opened fractionally wider when I realised I had what looked like red and purple bite marks over my neck and shoulders. I felt unclean. The tap whined as I attempted to splash myself with cold water. Nausea still constricted my stomach and I felt cold and hot at the same time. Picking a T-shirt up off the bathroom floor, I carefully made my way downstairs and into the kitchen. Despite the dryness in my throat, I didn't feel like anything to drink. I certainly didn't want anything to eat. There was a note propped up on the kitchen side.

'Connor, thanks for a great evening. I'll come back round tonight after I've been home and sorted a few things out, Jovana'. I didn't have any energy to worry about the note. I wandered back into the lounge and realising I probably didn't have strength enough to make it back up the stairs, I turned on the television and collapsed on the sofa.

The dull thudding in the corner of my mind got louder and louder until it felt like someone was hitting me round the head with a blunt object. I opened my eyes but could see nothing. The noise continued. The light from the television was the only thing illuminating the room. The noise was relentless. I shakily rose to my feet. Someone was at the door.

Chapter 34

It hadn't actually occurred to me to wonder who was there. I just wanted the noise to stop. Luckily for me it was Alan.

'Where the fuck have you been?' he demanded, bursting into the lounge. 'You look like shit.'

'Thanks.' I lifted my hand to the corners of my mouth. My lips felt as if they had been glued together.

'This is the second time I've been round. I've been banging

on the door for ages. What the fuck you been up to?' I relayed the previous night's events, much to Alan's disgust. She's been giving you speed, you … you prat,' he started. 'Look at you, you're shaking … your shirt is wringing wet.' He was right. I was a complete mess.

'How was your night anyway?' I croaked, trying in my embarrassment to change the subject.

'Don't fucking worry about me,' he said leading me back over to the sofa. I clocked the phone out of the corner of my eye. I had messages. 'That's probably me,' said Alan following my glare. 'I've been trying to call you all day. Didn't you hear it ring?' I shook my head and lay back out on the sofa. I was shaking. Alan disappeared upstairs.

'You got home OK?' I asked.

'No, you both fucking left me. Well, Jimmy did. I spoke to him earlier, he reckons he couldn't find me and assumed I'd gone already.'

'Oh,' I gurgled. Alan reappeared with my duvet. Considering the state he'd been in the night before, he was looking remarkably well.

'I spent the night round the back of a shop underneath some boxes. I tell ya, my mouth felt like the inside of Ghandi's sandal this morning.' I momentarily wondered if a sandal technically had an inside, but I understood the point he was trying to make. My mouth felt like both his sandals after he'd trodden in some dog poo. 'I walked home just as it was getting …' he paused. 'What?' he said, seeing the sudden panic in my eyes.

'The note,' I screeched.

'What note?'

'The note from Jovana, she's coming back round.' I scrunched myself up into the corner of the sofa clutching the duvet tightly under my chin. Alan looked at the ceiling in disbelief.

'Oh god,' he cussed despairingly, 'well just don't let the silly cow in.'

'No, you've got to stay here,' I said despairingly, 'you've got to stay here with me, I can't face her on my own.'

'Well you won't need to face her if you don't open the door.

Anyway, I need some sleep. I suggest you do the same.'

'What time is it?' I asked.

'Just gone six.'

'Fucking hell,' I screamed, 'I've been asleep all fucking day.'

'Look, I've really got to go. I just wanted to make sure you were alright.'

'I'm not alright,' I yelped like a big girl. 'I can't face her again, look at me.' A bead of sweat trickled down between my eyes and onto the end of my nose.

'She probably won't come. If she does … don't let her in. I'll ring you later to make sure you're alright. I've really gotta go get some sleep man.' He ran me a glass of water. 'Drink that, you'll be fine.' He made his way to the front door.

I was still shaking and sweating. The more I shook, the more I panicked. Realising I'd only had a pot noodle and a cheese sandwich in the last 36 hours I thought it wise to eat something. My stomach churned as I scanned the contents of my fridge. It was as much as I could do to moisten my lips with the water. I ambled round the house as best I could making sure all the lights were off and the curtains drawn just in case Jovana decided to make the promised return visit.

I was smoking a cigarette and watching *Match of the Day* with the volume turned down when there was another knock at the door. I froze and tried to blank the noise out of my mind. Just as before, it got louder and louder until suddenly it stopped. There was silence. I remained motionless, barely daring to breath. A few minutes later the banging started again. This time louder still. Maybe it was Alan. He knew I was in after all. My thoughts were almost immediately proved wrong.

'Open zee door Connor.' Jovana was shouting through the letterbox. I remained still in the hope she would go away. 'I know you're in zair. I can see the television iz on.' I wondered if she could hear my heart pounding from where she was. It sounded deafening to me. I could have left the T.V. on and gone out for all she knew. I remained defiant. 'I can see ze T.V. through ze crack in the curtains, and you're smoking. I can see the end glowing red.' I'd been rumbled.

Against my better judgement, I opened the door. She

bounded in, seemingly full of energy, which immediately made me feel worse. She skipped into the kitchen as if I wasn't there and put the kettle on. It wasn't long before she produced her bag of sherbet and settled down on the sofa. Something told me it was going to be a long night. I felt powerless. She talked and talked. It was as much as I could do not to be sick. I didn't have the inclination to ask her, or rather, confront her about the bag of sherbet or the marks on my shoulders. She didn't ask how I was or comment how awful I looked. The format of the evening pretty much followed that of the previous night. She picked various films she wanted to watch and CD's she wanted to listen to and then talked over the top of them. It was like a bad dream. The longer the night went on, the more I became convinced she had no intention of leaving. She seemed quite relaxed although her eyes were wild yet vacant. I noticed that when she went to take a drink, her hands also shook quite violently. Being too nice has always been one of my downfalls. Whereas most people would have told her to fuck off, probably before she'd even set foot in the door, I was confined to listening to her anecdotes which quite frankly made me even more concerned than before. It transpired that she had quite a, how do I put it, dysfunctional family. She had two brothers. One was in prison having been charged with grievous bodily harm whilst the other lived at home with their mother after recently being acquitted of attempted murder. She also had a son called Chris. He was eight years old and spent the weekends with Boris, his biological father. It sounded very much like the kind of dysfunctional family you didn't want to get on the wrong side of.

As we reached the early hours once more she must have seen my struggle to stay awake. As before, she helped me upstairs, stripped me naked and put me to bed. It wasn't long before she joined me, entwining her naked flesh with mine. There was no chance of me becoming aroused even if I'd have wanted to. I left her to kiss and nibble my body whilst I concentrated on drifting off to sleep.

I woke the next morning feeling a lot better. The shaking had all but gone. Jovana was nowhere to be seen. I rose to my feet and threw on whatever clothes were nearest to me. I peered carefully through the curtains. Her car had disappeared. There was no trace of a note this time. I breathed a sigh of relief and decided I could probably force down some breakfast cereal. The sudden ringing of the phone made me jump. I dropped the box of cornflakes. It was becoming increasingly worrying that I panicked every time there was a knock at the door or the phone rang. This was my own home. I should feel safe. It wasn't as if my life was in danger. The answer machine informed me it was Ellie. I rang her straight back.

'Hello stranger,' she started, 'long time no speak. How come you didn't answer the phone?'

'I was just wrestling with a box of cereal,' I answered innocently. Ellie laughed.

'OK, so you haven't got any dodgy women there then?' I didn't answer. 'It was a joke,' she continued.

'Oh, right,' I laughed nervously. It was probably best not to mention anything about Jovana. I hadn't actually spoken to either her or Bob since the episode at the party.

'Are you OK?' she asked. 'You seem a little distant.'

'No … yeah, I'm fine. How's everything with you?' I tried to change the subject. 'How's Bob?'

'Don't ask,' she replied, 'we're still not speaking.'

'Still? You guys are supposed to be engaged.' It was obviously one of those times when Ellie had dug her heels in. She could be a stubborn little cow when she wanted to be.

'Anyway, I didn't ring to talk about that. I just rang to see how you are.' I took this as an invitation to pour out all my troubles and woes of the last few weeks.

'Aren't you a bit fragile for that sort of carry on?' she remarked. Although she was probably bang on the mark, having one of your best friends describe you as 'fragile' was not the most endearing or flattering of observations. I was actually a little bit hurt. I took it to mean that I couldn't cope.

'How do you mean?' I asked. Ellie just laughed.

'Well for starters, Becci just seems to pop round when she feels like it while her boyfriend is making threats to beat you and poor Alan to a pulp. Stacey is leading you a merry dance and now you're hanging around with this older woman who gives you drugs.' I didn't let her know that the strange woman who'd been at the house had been Jovana. I changed the names to protect the not-so-innocent.

When she summarised it like that, yes I suppose things could have been better. She failed to mention Laura, but with things as they were I didn't really feel like adding her into the equation and complicating the issue.

I decided to consult the Canadian office once more. She wasn't online but had sent me an email. She had two weeks holiday to take, was planning to come to England and wanted to meet up whilst she was in London. The airline fares she'd come up with seemed unbelievable. It would be good to see Kristy for real, but I had a better idea. Why didn't I take her up on her previous offer and go to Canada? Although travelling to another continent to meet another strange woman wasn't possibly the sanest of ideas, I couldn't see how it could be any worse than being at home. I put my thoughts into my emailed reply. I needed time to let the dust settle and running away to Canada seemed the ideal way to let things die down.

Chapter 35

'The Distance' – Cake.

For £265 I was able to book a return flight to Toronto. Kristy was to pick me up from the airport and I was to stay with her and her parents for two whole weeks. She seemed very excited at the prospect. Having never ventured outside Europe before, I was also looking forward to the experience. I decided, however, to make a contingency plan just in case anything untoward happened. You hear so many horror stories of people who have met on the Internet. I made sure I had access to plenty of money. At least I knew she was a woman (I assumed she was from our telephone conversations) but whether the photographs she had sent me were actually her and whether she was 26 years old, I had yet to find out. From our discussions, she didn't appear to be a mentalist, but as long as I had money, I could escape should the need arise.

The only thing left to do was to try and make my peace with people before my departure. I saw it as a kind of catalyst to the dust settling process. First up was Rebecca. She saved me the bother of contacting her by popping in for one of her Sunday morning visits. I hadn't spoken to her since my outburst on the phone. Dom hadn't beaten me up and as far as I was aware Alan hadn't been given the sack but now I assumed, was the time for me to receive the rough end of Rebecca's tongue … so to speak. I was pleasantly surprised to find she'd actually come round to apologise. She claimed she didn't know Dom had been threatening Alan (or me indirectly) and that she hadn't said anything to suggest to him I was pestering her.

'He's just a bully who likes throwing his weight about,' she said.

'Well, I'd rather not get involved. You can't keep popping round like this whenever you feel like it.' I was firm yet calm. I'd done my quota of shouting as far as this issue was concerned.

'I know, I know, I just wanted to explain. Dom is a shit bag. He's been seeing someone else but suspects that I am too.'

'Becci,' I said rolling my eyes, 'you've already told me all this.'

'Yes, I know. I'm sorry that you and Alan have got caught in the crossfire.'

'But why would he think you're having an affair with me?'

'I don't know,' she said. I wasn't sure I believed her. 'He's paranoid about you. Everywhere we go he asks if I've been there before … with you. Normally I have and this makes him angry.'

'Well I can't help that,' I laughed. She smiled, yet looked like she was about to cry.

'Mum keeps mentioning you in conversations whenever she and Dom are unlucky enough to meet.'

'I think you just need to make a decision. Whatever you do, I don't think staying with Dom is doing you any good.'

'I don't know what to do.' A single tear tracked down her right cheek.

'Well Roger can't be worse than Dom,' I laughed, trying to lighten the mood. 'Why don't you give him a chance?' I can't say I went a bundle on either of them, but Roger seemed the lesser of the two evils.

'I think that's just it. He's too nice.' Please refer to previous passages regarding nice guys versus complete bastards. Although some guys can be *too* nice, I didn't put Roger in this category. He was what I considered 'false' nice. The smarmy, white toothed type more slippery than a greased eel. Falling between two stools, they weren't genuinely nice but then they weren't out and out bastards either.

I digress. Rebecca had to sort out what she wanted. I think she knew she was better off without Dom but was afraid of what he might do if she tried to call it a day. Roger was just a get out clause, an excuse to move on, but she wasn't sure she really wanted him either. Whilst sympathising, I explained I didn't want to be a pawn in any of her games. She acknowledged that and said she'd be in touch when she'd sorted her mess out. We hugged on the doorstep, she dried her eyes and left.

Next on my hit list was Laura. I hadn't heard from her what with all her courses and my fucked up social calendar. She was still difficult to get hold of but when I eventually tracked her down she was as bubbly as ever. After briefly explaining what I was up to she said that she wouldn't be able to come down and see me before I left but wished me all the best for my travels.

'I want to be the first person you see when you get home,' she said. 'The first weekend you're back, I'm coming down to see you, it's been far too long.' I wasn't sure I believed a word she said but I'd said my piece and the ball was firmly in her court. I wasn't going to do any chasing when I returned home to dear old Blighty in the hope that only serious candidates would apply.

Stacey, although I wasn't intending to speak to her, had heard I was going to Canada. She rang me shortly before I was due to leave. She wanted to clear the air and we agreed to meet in a secluded pub of her choice in the country. Unbeknown to me, but probably not to her, this secluded pub was home to various local rock bands on a Friday night. She greeted me in the car park with a kiss on the cheek before leading me inside. I was then introduced to three of her friends whose names were inaudible over the din of some spotty teenage thrash collective.

After surviving the crush at the bar we, along with her friends, made our way to a quieter part of the premises. I stooped under the low beams as we searched for a table, slightly disgruntled our private chat had been hijacked by a harem of her mates. I slowly sipped my pint, assuming that the conversation would eventually swing my way. I began to drink with more haste as I realised that Stacey, despite having invited me here for this chat, didn't seem to have any intention of actually talking to me. Until I could make my excuses and push off home, I began planning my packing, mentally listing everything I needed to sort out before I left for foreign shores. Ten minutes later, and still not having spoken a word to Stacey, I left. I gulped the last dregs from my glass and made my excuses. Being there had been a complete waste of time and I did wonder if she'd done this on purpose to make some kind of point. Quite what the point was, I didn't know or care. I left all the same. It wasn't until I was opening my car door that I heard Stacey's footsteps hurrying towards me.

'Hey, wait up,' she panted. I turned round but said nothing. I opened the car door. 'Why you running off so soon?' she asked.

'I thought you wanted to talk,' I said belligerently.

'I do, I do,' she said 'it's just difficult with everybody else around.'

'Stacey, you've blanked me all night,' I said defiantly.

'I wanted to speak to you, it's just hard sometimes.'

'I'm not sure inviting all your mates has made it particularly easy, no. I'd have been better off staying at home and getting on with my final preparations. Anyway, I'm here now and you've got me all to yourself. Say whatever it is you have to say.'

'OK,' she said. The mood changed. 'OK, I don't want you to go. I think you're lovely, you make me feel special and protected and I don't want you to go.' Whatever you might think, it was an emotional plea. 'There, I've said it now,' she finished, finally catching her breath.

'Why haven't you told me any of this earlier?' I asked slightly less hostile.

'Well,' she said looking around as if to find someone to help her out with her answer, 'I dunno, but I'm telling you now.' I honestly didn't know what to do. 'Give me a hug,' she said with large dopey puppy dog eyes. For the first time in my life I felt someone tremble in my arms. I'd like to think it was genuine but my pessimistic nature put it down to the cold. My view was further strengthened by the fact that she wouldn't let go. It was warmer to cuddle up to me than face the chilly conditions on her own. I hated her for this. This is what she did. Lure me into her 'butter wouldn't melt, little girl lost' routine only to make me feel like a doormat. It would have been much easier to have had a shit night, say bollocks to it and headed home. That way it would have been sorted. 'Just stay safe and we'll sort this when you get back,' she whispered in my ear. I couldn't think of a credible response. 'I don't want to let you go,'. Although my heart saying 'well don't then,' my mind was telling me to get into the car. I broke off our less than brief encounter, not wanting to get sucked into Stacey's part-time fairytale world but agreed we'd talk when I returned. The problem with Stacey, as far as I could see, was that she couldn't make her mind up what she wanted. She either gave me the cold shoulder, too preoccupied with herself, her friends and having a good time (to the exclusion of me) or turned into the sweetest girl you'd ever have the pleasure of meeting. My 'making peace' agenda had not gone according to plan.

The only cast member of my female social circus I didn't contact was Jovana. Having spoken to Stacey and Laura and managed to finalise … well, nothing at all, I thought it best that Jovana remain out of the equation. I didn't want to give her the opportunity of also bestowing on me the 'we'll see how things are when you get back' routine. I was hoping she'd be too preoccupied with prison visits and babysitters. Now that she'd had her fun with me I just prayed it would all die a death (hopefully a peaceful one; I think I'd like this one would go in its sleep).

The upshot of it all seemed to be that everyone felt we had something special although nobody wanted to be with me exclusively. I consoled myself with the thought I wasn't sure I wanted to be with any of them anyway. The only thing to challenge this feeling was the receipt of two text messages from

Stacey before I packed my bags for North America.

'Miss u! More than u think / know. Sorry gnite babe'.

This was followed by,

'Perhaps when u get back we can go out & maybe try again (if u like) very hard this evening mixed emotions & feelings. I miss u so much! It was so nice t c u & 2 b held by u. Have a nice holiday. I'll think of u every day. Missing u already! Fingers crossed everything will work out & it will b cool babe. I care too'.

I didn't respond, left for Canada deciding that I'd deal with all the loose ends when I returned. I wasn't sure if I was any better off now than when I'd started the peace making process. There still seemed more questions than answers.

Chapter 36

Day 1

After a nine-hour flight, I arrived in Canada to find Kristy looked exactly like her photograph. She had blonde, shoulder-length hair, a slightly podgy face and an infectious grin. I think her facial expressions were over-accentuated on account of her nervousness. I on the other hand was fairly relaxed, but then I had the advantage of being worn out from a long flight and downing more than the occasional beer. I did have the disadvantage however of not having had a cigarette for nine hours. I sniffed out the stale smoke towards the nearest designated smoking area feverishly riffling through various pockets of my luggage to find my 'bitch sticks' as Kristy called them. Needless to say, she didn't smoke.

'Don't laugh at my car,' she said as we made our way into the multi-storey.

'Why would I do that?' She could have come and picked me up in a dumper truck for all I cared, I was just appreciative of her hospitality. We eventually reached a beaten up old Ford

Mustang. It was black in colour (apart where it had been dented) with a two-litre engine (considered particularly small in Canada). I decided not to tell her I had a 1.4 litre Vauxhall Astra.

'It's a bit small and quite old, but I love it,' she said beaming from ear to ear. I got the impression we were going to have a good few days. She appeared very genuine and full of fun. Everything was going to be OK. The mustang by the way went like shit off a shovel.

We drove for what seemed a relatively short time. It was certainly over an hour but the very professional running commentary from Kristy about places along the way coupled with a brief history of Kitchener, the place where she lived, certainly made the time fly despite my tiredness. Founded by Mennonites and German farmers, Kitchener was named after the British Field Marshal (the inhabitants deciding during the First World War that, despite being of German descent, they would change the name from Berlin, which had been their original choice back in 1826). I was to spend the next couple of weeks surrounded by a population sixty percent of whom had German ancestry. Luckily there wasn't a beach or a sun lounger in sight. This was Canada, land of cornfields, prairies and errm, more cornfields. The countryside soon gave way to industry as we approached her hometown. The traditional German *Vorsprung durch Technik* had obviously taken its toll on the landscape. Kristy seemed to know a lot about the history of the place. I guessed she must have had German ancestors herself.

'My Grandmother is Hungarian and my Grandfather was French,' she said. I was more confused than ever. I nodded and smiled and left it at that.

On reaching her house, I leaned out of the car window to check the wing mirror as we reversed up her drive. She pressed the wrong button on the electric window controls. Instead of winding her window down, she wound my window up. My head became trapped between glass and doorframe. I first viewed her family and friends (many hundreds it seemed had turned up as part of my welcome party) from a ninety-degree angle as they ran excitedly from the house to greet me. I muttered 'hello' as best I could as they congregated around the passenger door.

The excitement was obviously too much for some of them; they tried to open the car door while my head was still stuck. Luckily Kristy stopped laughing in time to press the correct button to free my head but this didn't prevent my momentum from sending me crashing onto the driveway. I looked up at the smiling faces above and gave an embarrassed smile. It wasn't the most majestic of entrances. Before I had chance to draw breath I was lifted to my feet and introduced to everybody: Her mother was gaunt with an icy cold glare (it must have been the Eastern European in her); her Dad was the exact opposite, a real life Fred Flintstone with a big personality; sisters, friends, grandparents all wanted a piece of the new arrival. I felt like a celebrity. Everybody wanted to shake my hand, ruffle my hair or hear me say things in an English accent. The circus had arrived in town.

I'd lost count of how many hours I'd been awake. Other than a couple of catnaps on the plane I figured I hadn't had any sleep for nearly a whole day. After only a brief respite for some food however, I was coerced into going clubbing with the excitable rabble. I changed, had a shower and in my trance-like state, we all made our way to the local watering holes. Lots of questions, lots of cheering, kissing and hugging, a couple of dedications and plenty of beer followed. The only beer available seemed to be *Coors*. It tasted like shit but I was too tired and grateful to worry about it. The female members of the group seemed particularly keen on my arrival but were reluctant to speak to me when Kristy was around.

'Snog him,' shouted one of the guys in the group pushing one of the girls up close to me. 'It's obvious you're dying to.' The girl sheepishly looked at me.

'I can't,' she said reluctantly.

'Yes you can,' I enthused, exaggeratedly puckering my lips, 'go on, snog me.'

'I can't,' she replied, 'Kristy would kill me.'

'What's it got to do with her? Go on, snog him!' repeated the guy.

'She's been so looking forward to you coming over, I wouldn't want to …' she broke off, spying Kristy returning with more beers and made her way back into the crowd. The guy and I exchanged confused glances before grabbing another drink from Kristy and jumping up and down like idiots. It was a long yet enjoyable night.

Day 2

I don't remember much about getting home. I only made it as far as the front garden. That much I'm sure of: I awoke face down on the lawn. Kristy filled in the gaps over brunch. I got one of those sinking feelings where segments of your drunken mind are pieced together by someone else. Having collapsed half way home and insisting that I was more than happy to sleep on the sidewalk, it was as much as Kristy could do to get me to the house. Getting me inside had been a bridge too far.

Whilst on the subject of bridges we spent the day touring the local area and the Elora Gorge. This involved visiting a 'kissing' bridge, which is one of those wooden enclosed things that you sometimes see on the television. Apparently these were built because horses are buggers when it comes to crossing water and so by enclosing the sides the horses of yesteryear were oblivious to the fact they were being duped. Kristy certainly knew her stuff although she didn't know why they were ultimately known as 'kissing' bridges. I imagined it was because you could have a bloody good snog in them without being seen. Who could say? Answers on a postcard please.

In the evening Kristy took me to an ice hockey game. I guess it was the Canadian equivalent of Bournemouth versus someone else crap. Their minor league status did nothing to calm the pace of the game and actually increased the number of bloody good scraps. The fact that the ice was speckled with blood by the time the game finished was testimony to my view that there had been more fighting than hockey. I think most people left the arena without knowing the final score. It was just an excuse to see a load of college kids beat the crap out of each other. Having seen it first hand, I can thoroughly recommend it. The score? I have no idea.

Day 3

Drove to Toronto for the day. We had a coffee at Wayne Gretzgy's (not his house, the restaurant he owns) and ventured up the CN tower. The latter took longer than expected due to the time I needed to pluck up sufficient courage to walk on the glass floor. Egged on by Kristy I had to pluck up even more courage to lie down on the glass whilst she took my photo. I wasn't down there long until some smart-arse shouted, 'is that a crack in the glass?' I haven't moved so fast in my life! After reaching the safety of the solid floor and witnessing everybody else pointing and laughing I decided that it was probably best we made tracks. We moved on to the Sky Dome where we had a guided tour of the stadium ahead of the Toronto Blue Jays hosting the New York Yankees. Kristy's Dad had somehow managed to get tickets for the game in row four. The view was fantastic and although my knowledge of baseball was fairly limited, the atmosphere was terrific. The stadium had a retractable roof and the second biggest video screen in the world (the Japs had since built a bigger one). There was even a hotel built into the side of the stadium but unfortunately I wasn't able to see anyone in any of the rooms. Apparently it was a regular occurrence for couples to rent out the rooms when there was a big game on (and I imagined that they probably didn't get much bigger than playing the Yankees) and go at it like rabbits in their hotel window for the benefit of the crowd. The whole mood was unusual enough anyway without seeing people shagging the arse off one another. Opposing fans sat side by side and you could buy alcohol inside the ground. You didn't have to get out of your seat to get anything either. Just clicking your fingers was enough to attract the attention of one of the stadium's vendors and get yourself a beer. It was all very civilised and a far cry from an away game at Millwall.

Day 4

Once again we were up bright and early. Our destination this time was a cottage (a large bungalow in fact) near Lake Heron owned by Kristy's parents. Kristy and I made our own way there, giving us a head start on the others. This allowed me time to explore before the rest of the family descended upon us. Fields surrounded the cottage, which was a couple of minutes' walk from the lake itself. I soon discovered that other family members had cottages in the same area as once again a crowd of excited friends and relatives greeted me. The most hostile reception was from Kristy's cousin, Dan. I imagine Dan was in his mid-thirties. Short, but built like a brick shit house he seemed uncomfortable, maybe even jealous of the attention I was receiving. He greeted me with a morose expression, the corners of his mouth only beginning to contort upwards when the bones in my hand began to crack from the handshake he gave me. Kristy had already told me she thought he was a bully. Her postulation was clearly correct as he attempted to make me look as small as possible in front of my adoring public. We went on a boat trip; he tried to push me overboard. We walked along the shore; he tried to push me in the lake. When it came to the baseball I really didn't need his help to look pathetic but that didn't stop him lending me a stubby-fingered Canadian hand. I've always been pretty good at sport. My hand-eye coordination is respectable enough to allow me to muddle my way through most sporting trials. My throwing however is abysmal. I throw like a girl. No, actually that's an insult to girls. I can only describe it as throwing with my wrist instead of my arm. No matter how much ridicule I received or how many times people have tried to show me, both at school and in later life, I just can't do it. Dan took every opportunity to hurl the ball at me as fast and hard as he could which severely damaged my catching ability. Even wearing an ill fitting catcher's glove, the constant pounding made my hand more and more painful. I stuck at it, not wanting to look like a wuss in front of everybody or give Dan the satisfaction of thinking that he'd won. I began to wince every time I caught the ball. People called for Dan to stop.

'No, I'm, I'm ok,' I joked after an hour or so of play. I must have lasted about another ten minutes before an involuntary yelp of pain escaped my lips. Dan sneered at me from across the field and the game was called to a halt. My hand was so swollen it was as much as I could do to get the glove off. My injury just meant that I had more people swarming around me murmuring about what a prick Dan was. He seemed happy to have got one over on me.

'You British wusses,' he mocked before walking over to the barbeque for the latest offerings.

It was getting late and a damn sight colder by the time the barbeque finished. We walked down to the lake to witness the stunning sunset whilst Kristy's Dad started a campfire. On our return we huddled around the glowing coals for warmth, toasting marshmallows and exchanging stories. The tales became more and more exaggerated as people's alcohol-to-blood ratio increased. I got up from the log we were sitting on to stand further away. As well as being too hot, the fire was beginning to hypnotise me. Dan, seemingly not content with the humiliation to date, lurched forward in an attempt to push me into the fire. The fire worshippers gasped. Having committed his body weight to the act, Dan was helpless to stop himself as I sidestepped. He lurched forward, frantically waving his arms before landing on his knees in the embers on the edge of the fire. The gasp turned into laughter as Dan sprang to his feet with scorch marked jeans. The spectacle was made funnier as Dan repeatedly hit himself on the forehead to extinguish what he thought were flames on his singed eyebrows.

'I told him not to be such a hot head,' I chuckled as I walked to the kitchen to top up on marshmallows.

Chapter 37

'Ghost Town' – The Specials.

Day 5

Kristy, her two sisters and I slept in a chalet at the bottom of the extensive garden. My initial research, from the night before, showed that Canadian women were relaxed when it came to the issue of farting. I'd been brought up to believe that women didn't fart. My mum had never done so. Only one of my girlfriends had ever admitted to having farted and that was only because I'd heard her. Even then, I could only liken it to the sound of a puncture on the smallest bike in the world. Kristy's sisters however would have put Jimmy or Alan to shame. Not only did their flatulence reverberate around the chalet, they really did smell like something had crawled up their arses and died. The mixture of alcohol and the pungent smog which filled the cramped makeshift dorm, ensured I got a good night's sleep at least.

The following morning the hinges on the door creaked as I forced them back as far as they would go. I took a gulp of clean Canadian air and wondered what the day would have in store. Thankfully, it was a much needed lazy one. Kristy had a bit of a hangover so we just toured the local area, had a spot of lunch and made our way back to Kitchener in the afternoon. I was more than happy to watch telly and play board games in the evening. It had been a hectic schedule so far.

Day 6

Our next excursion, to Niagara, could only be described as eye-opening. This was one of those occasions where reality was completely different from preconceived ideas. I had expected spectacular falls in the middle of nowhere. Whilst the falls were undoubtedly magnificent, I wasn't expecting to be able to drive alongside them or to be greeted by the Canadian equivalent of Blackpool in the form of Clifton Hill. This was allegedly the honeymoon capital of the world. Every hotel seemed to have 'honeymoon' somewhere in the title. I personally would have described it as the 'haunted house' capital of the world. If I'd been aware of this before our arrival I probably wouldn't have bothered going. It didn't matter that these mock haunted establishments looked tacky from the outside, I've always had a phobia about them. It can be the least scary ghost train at the most crappy of fairs, it doesn't matter, I hate anything where there is the potential for me to be frightened. Films are the same. I remember getting so anxious about watching *First Blood* as a kid (not knowing what it was about, the title alone scared me) that I made myself ill even before the feature had started. Yes, I know I'm a big girl's blouse but then maybe I wasn't actually scared of being scared. Maybe I was scared of looking stupid in front of other people by jumping or shrieking like an idiot when all that had happened was a very fake plastic figure had mechanically lurched from a cardboard coffin. I don't want people pointing and shouting 'ha ha you jumped then' when there's a loud bang during a tense moment. Yeah, I think I'm just petrified of making myself look a prat, which I'm quite capable of doing on my own without the help of mechanical mannequins. If I were to go into a haunted house or watch a film on my own, I'm sure I'd be fine.

Gingerly looking at the various establishments lining Clifton Hill, I realised this theory was absolute bollocks. There was no way I was going in any of them on my own. In conclusion, I *am* a big scaredy-cat but I had an advantage now though. Being in my mid-twenties, I didn't have to go in haunted houses. It was something teenagers and small kids did. I was well within my rights as an adult to decline without repercussions from peer pressure. There were plenty of other tacky places to go in any case. They all looked tedious but not in the least bit scary, although the person who'd conceived the *Believe it or not* museum must have wanted their head testing. Who would want to come to arguably the finest falls in the world and look at cows with eight legs or shrunken heads? That aside, there were waxwork museums, fortune-tellers and casinos. I could even have my picture taken to make it look like I was going over the falls in a barrel if I so desired. All would be a complete waste of time, granted, but at least it would save me the indignity of venturing inside a haunted house.

After a distant glimpse of the falls on the drive past we decided to find somewhere to stay. The fact that the majority of the hotels had 'honeymoon' in the title worried me on two levels. Firstly, it conjured up images I'd rather not have associated with any potential honeymoon of mine (assuming that I ever got round to having one). Secondly, it meant that we were unlikely to find a room with separate beds. Having traipsed around various establishments unable to find anywhere that had any rooms available (let alone rooms with twin beds) we explored the sleazy areas of Clifton Hill. We ended up with a single room in a two-storey prefab. The lack of curtains was unfortunate given that all the other apartments were only assessable via the high level walkway that ran directly outside our window. From this walkway you could touch the walls of the fried chicken restaurant next door. At least the extractor fan from the fast food outlet masked the immediate smells from inside our room. The lights didn't work. I'll rephrase that. There wasn't a bulb in the fixture. There was a double bed that was marginally more comfortable than lying on a sheet of plywood. Other than that, it was the kind of place any couple would wish to spend their dream honeymoon. We decided to get something to eat, provided it wasn't chicken. Unfortunately for me the place we chose was directly opposite *The House of Frankenstein*. This was probably the first time Kristy had any inklings of my phobia.

'Are you OK?' she asked as I feverishly glanced from my food to the haunted house.

'Yes, yes, I'm fine,' I frowned.

'Why do you keep looking over the road then?'

'I just can't concentrate with that thing there.'

'This is the House of Frankenstein,' blared the public address system in an over-exaggerated horror movie voiceover type way. I continued to listen with a pained expression on my face. 'Scared? You will be …in fact you'll be terrified … in the House of Frankenstein (cue clapping thunder)'.

'And that bothers you?' she sniggered.

'Well, no.' Another deep voiced loop began. 'Well, yes,' I said glancing over at the twelve-foot high model of Frankenstein's head (or should I say Frankenstein's monster's head), which protruded from the top of the building. In true Clifton Hill style, he was munching on a cheeseburger.

'What, that?' laughed Kristy.

'Look, I've just got this thing about haunted houses.'

'Oh we've got to go in one, please, please I love them.' She may well have liked them but I guessed she loved them all the more for knowing that they made me very uneasy.

I stuck to my resolve, even after the constant 'please, please, please' routine that a toddler might use on a parent to get his favourite sweets. Then Kristy decided to play the gender card. This involved making me feel weak and cowardly (which I undoubtedly was) by suggesting I was a useless excuse for a man (harsh, but possibly fair) because she, being female, was perfectly happy and keen to go into a haunted house. I however, notionally the hunter, the fearless man prepared to laugh in the face of danger, was too lily-livered to accept the challenge. She wore me down. It's something about a woman questioning your masculinity which makes you do things you'd otherwise avoid. I managed to play down in my own mind that I'd actually given in to Kristy by suggesting to myself that this could be good therapy. I would face my fears and get over my phobia. I was after all a fully-grown adult. I had nothing to be scared of. Kristy would be with me and it was all make believe. I just had to remember that. What was the worst that could happen? It was only a few minutes of my life. I therefore gave in to Kristy on one condition; we got it over and done with. I didn't want to be wandering around all night thinking about it. We shook on it and finished our meals.

Not content with the fact I'd reluctantly given in to her demands she decided to undertake a mini poll of public opinion on the scariest haunted house in Niagara. This, allegedly from more than one source, was a place called *Screamers*. The name alone made me uncomfortable. It wasn't a tacky sounding *House of Frankenstein* or *Day of the Damned*. These guys meant business. They were intent on scaring the living shit out of you and were going to enjoy every blood-curdling minute.

We walked into the reception area, which didn't do anything to allay my fears. The guys behind the desk weren't dressed in Dracula costumes; there weren't any gruesome models of zombies with gory flesh wounds and there was a distinct lack of scary music. The foyer was plain black and the assistants were pleasant and well dressed in their *Screamers* attire. There was a board behind the desk with a monthly total of how many people had entered along with how many had actually 'survived'. Kristy laughed heartily at these alleged statistics.

'Awh, come on. How bad can it be?' she kept saying. I was more concerned with what they meant by 'survived'. Did people actually die in there? It was explained to us that if at any point we were too scared to continue we were at liberty to shout 'screamers' three times. The lights would then go up and the assistants would rescue us. Kristy burst into fits of laughter once more. The assistant's face didn't crack. This was all part of the act, right? The statistics behind them were just a fiction to make out it was really scary, right? I had to do this. I took several slow deep breaths as I paid my entrance fee and repeated my mantras in my head. I am an adult. It's all fake. Nothing in here is real. It's only a few minutes of my life. I looked at my watch and made my way over to the curtain that shrouded the entrance. It was 9.20pm. I was ready. I could do this. I just had to get round this place as quickly as possible. Run if necessary. I took one last deep breath and reached for the curtain.

'Whoa, whoa, whoa,' shouted one of the guys. 'You can't go in until the green light comes on.' I looked to my left to see a set of traffic lights, which were clearly on red. 'Just remember to follow the red LED's to get out.' I nodded solemnly. Why were we waiting? What red LED's? Kristy clung onto me from behind. I noticed a poster on the wall. Quick skim-reading revealed that I shouldn't go in if I had either a heart condition or was pregnant. I unfortunately couldn't exclude myself from partaking on either of these grounds. I read on further.

'You should not enter Screamers if you have a fear of the dark or are offended by things, human or otherwise touching you.' I was scared. I lost concentration and my mantras were all but forgotten.

'I don't want anything fucking touching …' I managed to utter in panic before a buzzer sounder, the light went green and Kristy thrust me through the curtain into complete darkness. I froze, forgetting my initial strategy of going as fast as I could. I cautiously shuffled Kristy in front of me and we crept gingerly into the dark. I had my eyes shut for the majority of the time. Quite what advantage this was I wasn't sure as we couldn't have seen our hands in front of our faces if we'd wanted to. We didn't know where we were going or what lay before us. All I knew was that whatever it was, Kristy would get there first. The long anxious periods of murky silence made my imagination work overtime. Where were noises coming from? Was that angry dog barking really within a couple of feet of us? Was a hot wet tongue really licking my arm? We eventually reached a dead end. I knew this, Kristy told me.

'It's a dead end,' she said.

'What?' I said feverishly. 'It can't be.'

'Well it is.'

'We must have taken a wrong turning.'

'How can we have taken a wrong turning,' she said, 'we've followed the lights.' I looked warily around me. There were no LED's to follow, just total darkness. The conversation became increasingly frantic.

'OK, OK, we'll make our way back. Keep your right hand on the wall so we know where we are.' I'd seen it done in a film I think.

'You touch the wall.' Kristy started to laugh nervously.

'I'm not touching the fucking wall,' I whispered. Needless to say it was our only option. We assiduously made our way slowly back down the gloomy corridor, tentatively touching the walls, only to find another dead end. We retraced our steps once more and arrived at the same blind alley we'd started at. 'I'm gonna shout screamers,' I said in a panic.

'No you're not,' said Kristy harshly, 'there has to be a way out.'

'Yeah by shouting screamers and them getting us out.'

'We're going to do this.' I had to give her credit. She was determined which was more than could be said for me.

'I can't do it any more.' A faint red light started to flicker in front of us. It gave me a moment's hope. 'There, there, follow the light,' I shouted, propelling Kristy forward as quickly as I could. It was like trying to move a stubborn mule.

'What light?' said Kristy. It had gone out.

'There,' I whispered as another started to glisten about twelve feet to the right of the previous one. It went out again before I could angle Kristy's head around to look in its general direction. 'I'm going to shout screamers,' I repeated.

'No you're not,' said Kristy turning to put her hand over my mouth.

'Mmmph,' I gave a muffled shriek as I felt hot breath on the back of my neck accompanied by a faint gasp.

'What?' said Kristy removing her hand.

'There's, there's somebody in here with us,' I blurted.

'Don't be ridiculous,' said Kristy, before letting out a high-pitched scream.

'What, what?' I said fervidly.

'Something just poked me in the ribs.' The only comforting factor in all this was that she was starting to get as freaked out as me.

'Right, that's it! I'm gonna shout …' I started, before a dim light revealed a man swinging lifelessly upside down from the ceiling in front of us. The light also showed that what was once a dead end had now been transformed into a continuous corridor, well for the next twenty feet or so at least. We scrambled underneath the suspended victim and headed down the passage to the sound of heavy footsteps behind us. It went dark again. It was silent. I could feel my heart pounding ten to the dozen. We stopped.

'Why have we stopped?' I asked. 'Keep moving.'

'I can't, I think we ought to …' Before Kristy could finish, a bright light flashed on to reveal a guy ambling up the hallway behind us. He was wearing a hockey mask and wielding an axe. Needless to say, I became anxious.

'Move, move,' I shouted as we plunged back into darkness once more.

'I'm not going forwards, I dunno what's there,' screamed Kristy.

'Well I'm not going backwards; there's a madman with an axe. NOW SHIFT!' Forcing her reluctantly up the corridor we encountered runaway trains, flashes of light and things hanging from the ceiling. Increasingly frantic, we made our way through a series of twists and turns in the dark whilst being poked, prodded and serenaded by the *Halloween* theme tune. I pushed Kristy harder and harder as the bloke apparently gained on us. It seemed never-ending until, with us both emitting blood curdling screams, we stumbled through another curtain and back into reception. A group of around eight young adults stood staring at us open mouthed. We stopped screaming. The assistant, now sporting an arrogant grin, had just about enough time to congratulate us and hand us each a small piece of card before I burst out of the exit for some much needed fresh air. I looked at my watch. It was just gone 9.40pm. We'd been in there over twenty fucking minutes. I bent over and rested on my knees. Kristy wandered out behind me looking at the card she'd been handed. She was marginally calmer than I was.

'Your card's a different colour to mine,' I said. 'What is it anyway?'

'I think it's some kind of certificate,' she said squinting, her eyes adjusting to the bright lights of Clifton Hill. 'It says, 'you survived Screamers. You are truly a brave soul.' I picked my yellow card from out of my pocket. 'Why what does yours say?' I looked down and read from the card.

'You survived Screamers but only because someone else led the way.' Kristy burst into fits of laughter.

'Man, they must have been able to see everything in there,' she squealed gasping for air. 'They must have infrared or something. They saw you go in first to start with.' She was obviously proud of the recognition. I groaned and put my card back in my pocket. My phobia had been far from cured.

Chapter 38

Day 7

Day seven started awkwardly. Living the haunted house nightmare had resulted in me getting very drunk. We toured the many bars of Clifton Hill before retiring to our makeshift honeymoon home a little worse for wear. Having woken up in a state of undress next to Kristy, who only had her knickers on, I began to piece together the events of the previous night. We'd snogged, instigated by me and then I must have gone to sleep. I ran through it again in my mind. Nothing much could have happened. We'd both been in a sorry state. The atmosphere was strained but I decided not to mention anything unless she did.

That was the day I saw Niagara in all its glory. From road level the water seemed to slide over in great solid sheets. From the Maid of the Mist tour below, the spray from the falls was so dense it was as much as you could do to see the edge of the boat. Both aspects were awe-inspiring. The excitement became more intense as we ventured further down the river and took a jet boat ride. I never knew anybody could get so wet wearing full waterproofs. We had a fantastic day, although there was still an awkward silence on the ride home.

Day 8

The mood seemed more amenable. We chatted freely on yet another long drive down to Windsor on the Canadian/American border. Kristy was due to enrol at college and was a bit stressed to say the least. We finally arrived at the apartment which would be Kristy's full-time home when she started the course. It was early afternoon by the time we got there. We dumped our things and made our way to the college.

The rest of the afternoon was spent trudging from department to department, standing in queues and sitting in rooms waiting to be called. The establishment itself was remarkably like the American colleges I'd seen on the telly. The grandiose stone exterior surrounded by wide leafy walkways gave way to an interior not dissimilar to anything you'd find in a British educational institution. I tried my best to be typically English whilst giving the impression that I too was enrolling for a course. Other students who had noticed my overstated accent, approached me whilst we were waiting. Most of them wanted to know what I was doing in Canada and what course I would be studying. My story was that I had come to study in Canada to broaden my horizons and study English.

'They do study English here?' I whispered to Kristy.

'Yes,' she giggled, holding her paperwork over her mouth.

'Well I hope we can get together when term starts,' said one of the girls. 'I presume you're staying locally.'

'Oh absolutely,' I said, wondering how many plums I

currently had in my mouth.

'Here's my phone number.' She hurriedly scribbled her phone number on a scrap of paper. 'I'm sorry, I didn't catch your name.'

'Hugh,' I said confidently, firmly shaking her hand. Each time it came to Kristy's turn to be called I made my way outside and found a quiet shady spot to have a smoke, away from the skateboarders and idiots on roller blades.

Kristy, having unburdened herself of the enrolment process decided that it was about time I was brought down a peg or two. My punishment for being cheeky for most of the day was a trip to the cinema to watch the *Blair Witch Project*. Having recently been put through the *Screamers* experience I decided it was best to sink three pints of lager before we went in. In hindsight, I'd like to make two points. Firstly, whilst being marginally pissed may increase my ability to speak to members of the opposite sex, I'm unconvinced it makes me any less anxious at the prospect of watching a horror movie. Secondly, having watched the film some months later completely sober I realised that it isn't actually scary in any shape or form.

'It's a true story you know,' said Kristy, utterly convinced as we left the cinema.

'You can't be serious,' I mocked hoping that she was messing around.

'No really,' she continued gravely. 'They found those film canisters in the woods.' I sank another couple of beers when we got back to the apartment and decided to sleep with the light on, partly because it helped to stop the room spin and partly so I could keep a watchful eye on anyone who might be planning on attacking me with a pile of twigs/raffia work.

Day 9

Seeing as we were so close to the States it seemed a shame not to take the short trip over the Ambassador Bridge into Detroit. There was nothing in particular I wanted to do there. I just wanted to say I'd been. Armed with my passport, Kristy reluctantly agreed to drive over the border (Canadians are big fans of the Americans, eh?) I was happy and relaxed until we reached American customs. Kristy wound her window down as we approached.

'I fucking hate Americans,' she muttered under her breath. I, on the other hand wasn't too fussed either way. After the welcome I'd had in Canada I was sure the Americans would have no problem with allowing me to drive around Detroit for an hour especially considering the close alliance between our respective governments.

'Hello,' said Kristy smiling politely.

'Where ya from?' said one of the officers sternly as he chewed on a piece of gum.

'I'm from Canada,' said Kristy showing her passport. The officer scrutinised the document and then looked at me.

'And where's he from?'

'He's from England,' said Kristy.

'What's the matter, ain't the boy gotta tongue in his head?' sneered the officer.

'Yes, but you asked me …' Kristy growled before I jumped in.

'Hello,' I said politely, 'I'm from England.'

'What is the purpose of your visit sir?' asked the officer, chewing more frantically.

'Well, I'm staying in Canada and I just thought …'

'I didn't ask you what you thought or where you were staying,' barked the officer, leaning forward. The welcome was more hostile than I'd imagined.

'I just thought …' I started. The officer raised his eyebrows, reminding me that I wasn't supposed to think. 'We were just going to drive around Detroit for a bit to say that I'd been.' I cringed at how ridiculous this must have sounded.

'I see,' said the officer with a sigh.

'Do you have a visa?' I gave Kristy a look of dread. She hadn't mentioned anything about needing a visa.

'I, I didn't realise …' I stuttered.

'Do … you … have … a … visa?' repeated the officer in a raised voice. 'Yes or no?' I realised it was probably best to answer the question as briefly as possible.

'No,' I replied through gritted teeth. The longer I spoke to this chap, the more I agitated I became.

'Well,' he laughed patronisingly, 'how the HELL did you think you were going to get into the United States, son?'

'I didn't realise I needed one.'

'Speak up boy I can't hear ya.' This was rapidly turning into some kind of boot camp drill.

'I have my passport,' I said hopefully. I say hopefully but I wasn't entirely sure I wanted to venture over the border any more. The officer ordered me out of the car and led me to a hut where I was given some forms to fill in.

'This one has to be completed front and back,' he bellowed, pointing to the first document. 'Just fill out the front of this one.' He handed me another piece of paper. 'I repeat, do not fill out the back of this form. Do you understand?' I nodded and sat down to fill them in. The forms were fairly straightforward. The first just asked me my name, address, passport details and the like. The other was a series of questions where I had to tick yes or no. Quite who was going to tick 'yes' to whether or not they were carrying any narcotics or had been involved with any terrorism organisations I wasn't sure. I completed the forms and went back to the desk.

'Do you understand English?' said the man behind the counter. I was disconcerted that this question was coming from an American.

'Yep,' I replied flippantly, 'I *am* English.'

'Then why the hell didn't you fill in the forms like you were asked?' He grabbed the papers, not actually having looked at them in any detail, and proceeded to tear them up into tiny pieces. I kept a lid on my anger and duly filled in the forms in the same way as I'd done before. This time, the man did actually have the courtesy to look at them before passing comment. The problem now was that I needed to pay for my visa in American dollars. Needless to say I didn't have the correct currency and the process, once again ground to a halt. A woman intervened and explained that I could exchange some money with her but that it needed to be a minimum of twenty dollars. After an hour at customs, the red tape was finally cut and we made our way into Detroit. It wasn't worth the aggravation. The highlight of the thirty-minute drive was seeing some steam coming out of the manholes in the road like I'd seen in the movies. We made our way back to Canada.

Canadian customs officials, as I'd experienced at the airport, were much more chipper than their American counterparts. Everything seemed to be going smoothly until he asked to see my passport. The man shuffled into his booth and remerged some time later.

'Is there a problem?' frowned Kristy.

'No, no problem at all Ma'am,' he said, 'it's just I noticed the young man's passport hadn't been stamped when he arrived in Toronto.' I had visions of me going through some prolonged ordeal to prove that I *had* actually arrived from England and that Kristy wasn't trying to smuggle me in from the States. My fears were soon dispelled. 'It's just I know most people like their passport stamped when they've been away from home,' he continued jovially, 'so I've done it for you. You both have a nice day now.' He politely saluted us as we started our journey back to Kitchener.

Chapter 39

'Trouble' – Coldplay.

Day 10

The wind down towards my return to England started. The morning consisted of some last minute shopping and developing numerous reels of holiday snaps. (It's considerably cheaper over there you know). I bought a tie to go with one of my smarter shirts in anticipation of the wedding of a family friend we were attending in the afternoon. The ceremony was much the same as any British equivalent. You know the drill: the congregation coughed, fidgeted and cried its way through the service. Tanya, a friend of Kristy's sister caught my eye. She was tall and slim with a dark complexion. This seemed to rile Kristy but I wasn't aware how much until we went to the post ceremony bash.

I tried to speak to Tanya several times but Kristy would keep popping up and interrupting. I'd go to the bar with Tanya and Kristy would be behind us. I sat down at the table with Tanya and Kristy would join us. She would then take over the conversation, raving about the wonderful week we'd had whilst trying to get as close to me as possible. I initially avoided Kristy's numerous invitations to dance, pissed off that she was trying to muscle in all the time. I didn't want Tanya thinking Kristy and I were 'together'. My avoidance tactics worked well until …

'So are we going to dance then?' she asked candidly.

'Well, I've just got to go to the bar and …'

'You don't want to dance with me do you?' You've got to hand it to her, she was quick on the uptake.

'No, it's not that, I just …'

'You've been funny with me ever since Niagara.'

'No, I haven't, it's …'

'I've never been kissed like you kissed me in Niagara. I know there's something between us yet you won't even dance with me.' She started to cry. I began to feel increasingly nervous. I'd got myself into yet another mess.

'Kristy, don't, don't cry. I don't know …'

'You're just like all other men,' she blurted, 'you lead me on, we could … can have something good together and yet you just don't get it do you?' I must admit she was right, I didn't. I failed to see how a simple snog in Niagara was deemed the basis of any serious relationship especially given the fact I was bound eastward on a nine-hour flight the following day. Before I had the chance to reply, Kristy ran off into the crowds. I went to the toilet.

I emerged some time later to be confronted by her mother.

'Where's Kristy?' she enquired sternly.

'I… I dunno,' I stuttered.

'Hell right you don't know,' she bellowed. 'She's run off somewhere. Nobody can find her.' I looked at the floor. I presumed that she'd seen Kristy and was aggrieved I'd made her daughter cry.

'Now look here Mister, I don't know what baggage you came here with, but you should have left it the hell at home.' I could feel myself bubbling up inside. I'd left England behind, albeit temporarily, to get away from all this crap and now it was happening here. I looked her straight in the eye.

'Yes, I've got baggage, but I didn't bring any of it with me to Canada. I came here to get away from it all and haven't once thought about or mentioned any crap I may or may not have to deal with when I go home tomorrow.' A red mist was descending. 'That's exactly what I intend to do … deal with it when I get back. Now maybe you should ask your daughter precisely why she's crying …'

'Cus you won't dance with her,' she interrupted.

'And people usually cry when other people won't dance with them do they?' We were almost nose-to-nose by this point. 'I suggest you get the whole story from Kristy and then assess whether or not she's overreacting.'

'Over reacting!' she shouted. I thought the blood vessel in her forehead was about to pop. 'That's my Kristy you're talking about.' Kristy's Dad saved me from this no-win argument. He ushered her away before gesturing me towards the reception. I thought it best to follow his instructions and made my way to a vacant stool at the bar. I rubbed my head in disbelief, waiting for the other half of the parental bollocking. It wasn't long before he came, perched next to me and ordered us a couple of beers.

'Don't worry about it,' he said putting his hand on my shoulder. 'Kristy's had a thing for you for a while. She thought you guys would get on.'

'We do get on.'

'You know what I mean.'

'I just thought we'd be good friends. I didn't come here looking for anything.'

'I know. I could tell the moment you arrived. It's not your fault. You weren't aware of the hysteria surrounding your visit. I told them not to get too excited, but try having your voice heard in an all female house. I know what happened in Niagara.' I looked at him aghast.

'If I'd known Kristy felt so strongly I would have never have let my guard down.'

'Feeble excuse,' he tutted. 'You're not getting out of it that easily. I am her father after all. I'm just saying it's not *all* your fault.' We clinked glasses. 'I just wanted to say this'll all die down in time and it's been a pleasure having you around. I wish you all the best for the future Connor.'

'Thank you,' I said humbly.

'Don't worry, I'll speak to Kristy. Will you just do me one favour?'

'Yes of course.'

'Dance with my daughter. It'd mean the world to her.' I nodded although I suspected it might just make everything ten times worse. In the circumstances however, I guessed it was the least I could do after seemingly making a pig's ear of everything once more.

Kristy was eventually tracked down and yes I did dance with her. I had been stupid. It seemed that yet again I'd fucked everything up. The only thing I'd accomplished by coming to Canada was to increase the number of people upset with me. I kept myself to myself for the rest of the evening and stuck to the coke. I didn't want to make a bigger fool of myself than I already had. I decided to leave Tanya well alone.

Day 11

I lay in bed as long as possible. I packed very slowly, declined anything to eat and like a coward, stayed in my room. The eventual farewells from Kristy's Mum and Dad were similar and yet completely different at the same time.

'You give my regards to Ollie Cromwell y'hear?' shouted her Dad. 'And if you see Robin Hood,' he continued, 'tell him to stop futzing around in those green tights.' There wasn't a hint of a smile on his face. This was known as dry humour. Similarly Kristy's Mum's face had no intention of cracking. Her arms were folded, and her gaze was cold and steely. I lifted up my holdall intending to say,

'I've got all my baggage with me now and I'm taking it back

with me so you needn't worry.' This actually came out as 'Thanks very much for having me, I've had a wonderful time,' before I sheepishly climbed into the car with Kristy. The drive back to the airport was in total contrast to the outbound trip. Not a word was spoken until we were minutes from our destination. Kristy wanted to come into the airport and see me off. I just wanted to get away as quickly as possible. Kristy became more and more flustered as we drove around and around trying to find somewhere to park.

'Time's running on,' I said.

'Fine, fine,' she snivelled, 'I'll just drive you to the drop off zone.' It all seemed a bit sad it had to end like this after we'd had such a great time. The wedding episode had put the kibosh on our 'friends larking about' pretence. Kristy seemed to get out of the car before it had even come to a complete stop.

'Don't I even get a hug?' She burst into floods of tears. My half-hearted embrace was reciprocated with a bear hug. It was all a bit embarrassing and after wanting to come to Canada to escape from England, I now wanted to return to Blighty as quickly as possible. 'I've put a note in your bag,' she sobbed. 'Read it when you get home.' I nodded, kissed her gently on the cheek in an attempt to end this rather awkward situation. It just made her cry more and tighten her grip on me.

'I'm going to have to go,' I wheezed, gasping for air. As she stood there, puffy eyed and red faced, I realised I was more than capable of fucking up any situation anywhere in the world. I had the Midas touch in reverse. Whether it was my naivety or my ineptitude in dealing with situations, anything I touched seemed to turn to shit. My talent knew no bounds.

Chapter 40

I think the saying goes, 'out of the frying pan, into the fire'. Which was an apt description of my trip to Canada. It could just as easily have been used for my return home. After a handful of hours' sleep I was awoken by a frantic knocking at my door. It was Jovana. She looked wild and, well, shit scared.

'Can I come in?' she blurted, bustling her way past me. I

wondered why it was people always managed to catch me off guard and barge their way into *my* house. I considered having a portcullis installed, rubbed my eyes and sighed. This was the last thing I needed. I could tell from Jovana's melodramatic entrance that I was probably better off not knowing what was going on. I thought it rude not to ask the question however.

'What's up now Jovana?' I asked, throwing my arms in the air with despair.

'I justz need to stay 'ere for a bit,' she said feverishly peering through the curtains. I stared at her, my arms folded, my body language demanding an explanation.

'It'z my husband,' she said, 'he's following me.' It transpired Jovana had met up with a hairdresser in Southampton. Everything had been running smoothly until the previous weekend when Jovana had stayed over with Vlad. They'd spent the night together playing happy families. Vlad was suspicious that she was seeing somebody else, which of course she was. Seeing as how Jovana had told Vlad that we had seen each other, he assumed that this other person was me. Thinking he still had a chance of reconciling with Jovana, he was adamant that nobody was going to stand in his way. In an attempt to protect the hairdresser and under the assumption she was being followed, Jovana had made her way to my house. Do you ever get that feeling of déjà vu? It seemed to me that this whole episode had Becci, Dom and Roger plastered all over it. I was too exasperated and jetlagged to take it all seriously. I didn't believe, even if her story was true, that Vlad would have followed her down to the South coast early in the morning in order to protect his interests.

'I'm back off up to bed,' I said. 'Stay as long as you like, just shut the door on your way out.'

'You don't care about me?' she screamed.

'Jovana, you've abandoned your car half way across my front lawn. Don't you think that if he was following you we'd have had a knock at the door by now?' She shrugged her shoulders. 'I find it hard to believe that you'd choose to come here and incriminate me. Why not keep on driving and save a confrontation on my doorstep? I'm off to bed,' I repeated. I was just getting settled under the duvet when I heard Jovana clomping up the stairs. She burst into the bedroom and crossed the room to peer nervously through the curtains. I groaned and turned over, pulling the duvet over my head. After a few moments, Jovana broke the silence.

'Can I get into bed wiz you?' she purred.

'Yeah whatever,' I said sarcastically, gazing over the duvet to see what she was up to. She lifted her top off over her head and moved round to the side of the bed.

'Whoa, whoa, whoa,' I repeated, snatching the duvet around my chin and kicking my way over to the opposite side. I realised I'd back peddled too far when I fell into a heap on the floor. I emerged from under the duvet to see a gob smacked Jovana, stood in her bra, staring at me. 'Look, I don't wanna get involved in anything that might be going on.' Jovana looked sheepishly at the floor. 'I suggest you leave.'

'But …' she retorted. The red mist was becoming worryingly familiar.

'What part of 'fuck off' don't you understand? I'm sick of all this shit. I've had a fucking gut full. Just go.' I pointed authoritatively towards the door. Jovana begrudgingly put her top back on and sloped off downstairs. She slammed the front door and I heard her car rev off into the distance. I breathed a sigh of relief and attempted to get back to sleep.

The next confrontation with my past came in the form of two answer machine messages later that week. The first was from Ellie. She was still at loggerheads with Bob and wanted me to go up to London at the weekend to accompany her out on the piss. The other was from Laura. She hoped I'd had a good trip to Canada and wanted to come down for the weekend. I had to make a decision as to whom I was going to see. It seemed appropriate in the current climate to keep things as simple as possible. Friends were more important at times like this. I didn't respond to Laura's message, deciding to catch up with Ellie. I thought it best not to mention anything to Bob. I didn't want to be seen to be taking sides.

Ellie and I went out for the day on Saturday. We did some

shopping and grabbed a bite to eat. More importantly, we chatted like we used to at school. We were joined at the hip back then. The opportunity to spend quality time together was rare these days and it made a refreshing change. Ellie seemed particularly relaxed considering she wasn't on speaking terms with her fiancée. I assumed that hearing about my crap existence made her feel considerably better about her own predicament. She wanted to know all the gossip from Canada and gave an unsurprised snigger when I told her about the holiday's conclusion.

'What have I told you about meeting strangers off the internet,' she laughed, 'you must have known it was going to happen.'

'No, I swear I didn't. I wouldn't have gone otherwise. I went there to get away from all the shit flying around here.'

'Oh Connor,' she said ruffling my hair, 'you do have a tendency to go into these things with your eyes shut don't you?' Ellie was not averse to being patronising every once in a while but she had a valid point on this occasion. I went on to tell her about the message I'd had from Laura.

'Hmm, that's a bit off,' she sighed.

'What do you mean by that?'

'Well, it's not very fair is it?'

'Eh?' I looked at her blankly.

'You don't know do you,' she continued.

'Know what?'

'Laura's ex-boyfriend has moved back in with her. He's been living there since before you left for Canada.'

'But … ' I hesitated for a moment, 'that doesn't mean that there's anything going on …' I looked at Ellie's expression, 'does it?'

'They've been sleeping in the same bed so draw your own conclusion.'

'Yes, but there isn't another bed for him to stay in.'

'For God's sake Connor, they're trying to patch things up. Ask yourself why she hasn't told you her ex has moved in.'

'Errm, cus I was in Canada?'

'Oh,' she sighed, 'you can be so infuriating sometimes. She's merely trying to keep you both hanging on.' Ellie shook her head in dismay.

We decided to get pissed in the evening. In principle, I didn't see a problem, but Ellie's suggestion we had a competition to see who could snog the most people worried me. Ignoring the obvious fact I was going to lose, I was more concerned with Ellie wanting to hold such a contest in the first place. If Bob got to hear of it, I'd feel guilty by association. On the other hand, spending an evening getting fresh with rubbish male strangers might just make her realise Bob was the one for her. Yes, she'd realise she ought to cut him some slack. Whatever the consequences, Ellie wasn't going to listen to me in any event. If she wanted to go out and pull men, then pulling men is what she'd do.

We were three sheets to the wind by the time we joined the queue for the *Clapham Grand*. After a few drinks with the girls in town and not much to eat, it hadn't taken either of us long to get into the swing of things. We were the only ones who thought it would be a good idea to go on to a club and consume more alcohol. Just for the record, at this point, neither of us had racked up any points regarding our snogging wager. It stayed that way well into the night, too preoccupied with cheesy dancing, spinning each other around and propping each other up to worry about anything else. The presence of the resident 'Dr Glitz and the Flirtations' meant you could pretty much do anything you liked on the dance floor without looking out of place. There had been a few men sniffing about during the brief moments I'd left her on her own to go to the bar but Ellie didn't seem interested. I began to think that maybe she was missing Bob after all. I maintained this view until late in the evening when Ellie kissed me. By saying Ellie kissed *me*, I'm not shirking my part in the proceedings, I just hadn't been expecting it. We'd been dancing particularly closely granted, and yes Ellie had a sultry look in her eye but I still didn't expect her to actually kiss me. We swayed from side to side and looked deep into each other's eyes until we were almost nose-to-nose. I thought she was larking about. It was as much as I could do to not laugh. We stared at each other for ages. The longer it went on, the more uneasy I became. The impression she was messing around began to diminish, and more worryingly, I started to wish she would kiss me. When she finally planted her lips softly onto mine I didn't know how to react. I hoped it was purely the alcohol I'd consumed that made it feel so right. Nonetheless I was confused. I pushed her away.

'What about the house rules?' I said. 'I'm not supposed to kiss anybody from the house, you know that.'

'Fuck the house rules,' she said softly and our lips engaged once more. The kiss became increasingly intense. Ellie's hands began to wander down my body to the front of my trousers. Suddenly, she pulled away sharply. Still giving me *the look*, she backed away and disappeared into the crowd. Momentarily rooted to the spot, I realised I had to look for her. She wasn't to be found. I waited until there were only a handful of people left in the club, searching every nook and cranny and the surrounding streets immediately outside. There was no sign of her. I made my way back to the house to find her curled up in bed. I breathed a sigh of relief and settled down for the night. Belle was away for the weekend, so I had her bed. As I lay there running over the evening's events in my head, the door to my room was gently pushed open. Ellie stood in her nightgown, staring at me.

'What?' I whispered hastily. Ellie didn't move. She still had that look in her eye. It was as if she was sleepwalking. 'What is it Ellie?' I said. My heart began to push against the inside of my ribcage. Ellie continued to stare at me until she slowly shook her head from side to side and glided back to her room as elegantly as she'd arrived. I wasn't sure what it all meant or whether I was supposed to follow her. I thought it probably best I stay put, tried to get some sleep and confronted the situation the following morning.

'I don't know what you're talking about,' she laughed when I recalled some of the proceedings of the previous night.

'You don't remember any of it?' I asked sceptically.

'Errm,' she gave a thoughtful look, 'nope.'

'You must remember the kiss in the nightclub.'

'Did we kiss?' she giggled. 'I'm so sorry I must have been more drunk than I thought.' I ignored the implication Ellie would need to be completely off her tits to kiss me.

'You don't remember us kissing?' I said in disbelief.

'No, sorry,' the thoughtful expression on her face seemed half-hearted. 'Oh God, don't tell anybody,' she laughed.

I was more confused than ever. I invented a fictitious call on my mobile, requiring me to return home post haste, and left.

The more I thought things over on the way home the more despondent I became. I hadn't heard from Stacey since her emotional outburst before I'd left for Canada. Jovana was as mad and unpredictable as ever. Laura had moved in with her ex after telling me she wasn't looking for anyone else. I'd been to Canada and managed to hurt Kristy's feelings and now on my return to England I'd snogged my best mate's fiancée. I was the common denominator in a catalogue of fuck ups. I tried not to think about Bob's reaction if he found anything out.

Chapter 41

'Moving' – Supergrass.

Returning to my empty house, I felt the lowest I'd felt for a very long time. Since splitting with Rebecca I'd tried to get back on my feet but it had got me no-where. Had I actually gone backwards?

With my trip to London unexpectedly cut short I had to think of something to fill the rest of my Sunday. I didn't feel like venturing out anywhere so decided to see who was lurking online. You'd have thought I'd have learned my lesson. I hadn't. Having met a car park stripper and a nutter from North America, I now found myself conversing with other randoms, mainly female. I got carried away with one girl in particular. Her name was Nicola, a very forward young lady from Arizona. Her picture, if indeed it was her, gave the impression she was as forward as her text led me to believe. I don't mean she looked like a slapper, just foxy. Online conversations seem to revolve around one or both parties moaning about their current predicaments. It wasn't any different with Nicola and me. We gave each other a brief history of out recent shit until the conversation turned to New Year celebrations. Nicola was bound for Las Vegas. All expenses, including those of respective partners, were to be paid by her company. Her problem was that she didn't have a partner to take with her.

'I'll go with you,' I joked. There was a long pause while we each pondered the realisation that there was actually no reason why I couldn't accompany her. I know this sounds ridiculous. Here was a girl whom I didn't know from Adam. I didn't even know if it was her in the photo. I just figured that going to meet a complete stranger to welcome in 1999 in Las Vegas sounded much more interesting than anything I was likely to do in this country. Sure, it might be a complete disaster (refer to Canadian adventure) but it would be a hell of a story in any event, even if I was sat in a bar somewhere on my own in Arizona having discovered Nicola was actually Nicholas, a gay man in his mid-fifties. I made my usual mistake of getting too excited about something far too early.

After logging off, I took some time out to think. What would this New Year hold? In light of the Bob and Ellie situation, there was every possibility it was going to be as crap as normal but out of this negativity came a glimmer of hope. If things could turn so pear-shaped so quickly, surely they could come good again just as fast? What harm was there in going to Arizona? What did I have to lose? I checked the flight costs. Half-hoping it would be far too expensive, I was surprised to learn that a return flight would cost less than £300. Despite the low price, the fact I subsequently spoke to Nicola a couple of times on the phone and the receipt of some more eye pleasing photos of her, the trip remained a pipedream.

I'm wouldn't say I 'm an impulsive person. I generally have to weigh up all the pros and cons of any and all of the options on the table in front of me before making a concrete decision. I can't even buy a sandwich from the shop without checking the fat content and sell by dates on various packets. On the rare occasions I am spontaneous however, I become consumed by it. I tend to do things that I wouldn't normally dream of doing. It just happens. I remember once going to a Paul McKenna show in Bournemouth. In order to choose his ten victims from the audience he played some hypnotic music and talked over the echoed microphone in his deep soothing voice. The lights went down and we were told to close our eyes. The idea was that we forced our hands together and tried to imagine them being stuck to each other. 'Feel the glue oozing through your fingers,' I remember him saying. It went on for a few minutes until we were sharply told to stop. Anyone who couldn't part their hands was instructed to come up to the stage. My parents sniggered and placed their hands by their side whilst mine remained firmly stuck together like shit to a blanket. I'd like to point out that I was sceptical before I went to the show. I wasn't convinced that hypnotism actually worked. I was also easily embarrassed. I would do anything to avoid having the spotlight on me. Taking this into account, quite why I shot up out of my chair and rapidly made my way to the stage remains unclear to me to this day. With my hands magically stuck together at arms' length in front of me, I marched to the steps leading to Paul McKenna. I think it was the combination of seeing Ellie sat on the stage with her hands also clamped (I wasn't aware she was attending the show) and the dazzling lighting which forced the glue to fail. It was too late by then. I was there, stood in front of thousands of people holding my hands limply together. I hid at the back with the rest of the morons, expecting to be lynched for being a fraud. Mr McKenna glided in and out of the congregation of believers. Eventually, he came round to me and shot me a puzzled expression. He sharply tapped me on the shoulder to indicate I was dismissed. I slithered back to my seat.

Just as I'd unexplainably acted against my better judgement on that occasion, it happened again, mid-morning during my tea break. Admittedly it wasn't the most spontaneous of notions. I'd spoken to Nicola and had had a few days to ponder how great it would be if I had the bollocks to do it. However, it was an instant decision that morning. I hadn't come into work thinking I was going to book the flight and considering myself a sensible, rational and logical human being it wasn't the type of decision I would normally have taken. You might assume other factors had come into play, but no one had egged me on or suggested it was an opportunity not to be missed; I hadn't had a particularly bad morning at work; nobody had pissed me off any more than normal. I just picked up the phone and booked a flight to Phoenix. I wanted to tell Nicola straight away. Thinking it best I didn't ring the States from the phone at work, I ran down to the phone box. It was much further than I'd anticipated. Things never seem very far away in the car do they? The light drizzle turned into a heavy downpour and I was completely soaked by the time I dialled the number. The phone rang and rang until eventually someone picked up the receiver at the other end. There was a grunt. I suddenly realised it was about 5.30am there. This didn't do anything to dampen my excitement.

'I've done it, I've done it,' I shouted down the phone. It took a while for my enthusiasm to be reciprocated. Nicola took time to wake up and then a bit more time to realise who she was talking to. Once she'd grasped what the hell I was going on about and that I wasn't winding her up she became more hysterical than me, well as hysterical as you can be when you're half asleep.

This was going to be a New Year with a difference. I wasn't going to be freezing cold and soaked to the skin in Swanage. Nor was I going to be stood on my own viewing the New Year's celebrations from the corner of somebody's kitchen. Shit or bust, it was going to be an experience.

Bob rang in the evening. He still hadn't heard from Ellie. This was both good and bad news. Bad news for Bob but at least Ellie hadn't spilt the beans about our coming together. I felt sorry for him. Ellie, despite being my long-term friend, was acting like an obstinate git. Bob hadn't done anything wrong, nothing had happened with Jovana or anybody else but she'd formulated in her own mind that Bob was guilty and that was that. He was downhearted to say the least.

'Will you speak to her?' he croaked, holding back the tears. How the hell was I supposed to respond to that? After what had happened she was hardly going to listen to me. 'She'll listen to you,' he continued. Denying Bob my help wasn't an option.

Telling him 'yes, but….' and going on to explain what had happened wasn't really the best plan either. I had no choice than to agree to help. I just had to think how I was going to approach it.

'You've done what?' yelled Ellie. It was immediately clear she wasn't taken with the idea of me venturing to Arizona. Using the subject in the hope I could swing the conversation onto Bob was proving more difficult than I thought. Appalled by my actions and in the throws of getting ready to go out, the best I could do was to organise an audience with her at the weekend … to discuss what a silly boy I'd been. If I couldn't get around to mentioning Bob over a whole weekend, there was something wrong.

Chapter 42

The days leading up to the weekend only served as a brief reprieve from the verbal onslaught I was to receive from Ellie.

'Why should this girl trust you anyway?' she bawled, apparently unconcerned for my safety.

'I'm a trustworthy guy.'

'Well I wouldn't trust you,' she scowled, 'you're a womaniser.'

'Come on Ellie,' I said throwing my hands in the air in disbelief, 'you of all people know that's not true. You've always said I was the perfect gent. How can I be a womanising scumbag *and* a perfect gentleman? Make your mind up.'

'I think you *are* the perfect gentleman and you try very hard to win over a girl's heart.' I knew there was a 'but' coming. 'The problem is that if you don't instantly succeed you give up and move onto the next one.' She gasped for air. 'That's what makes you look like a womaniser. By the time the girl has fallen for you, you've moved on and find yourself in another pile of shit.' I got the feeling we were straying off the point slightly. This wasn't about Arizona. This was about me in general. Considering Ellie's own situation with Bob, I thought it a little harsh.

'I think my problem is when I start to feel someone

becoming attached to me I panic. In the beginning I want them to dote on me, and then when they come round to the idea I just lose it.' I stopped and thought about what I'd just said. 'Anyway, where do my bunch of female reprobates fit into your synopsis? I didn't get anywhere with any of them.'

Ellie remained unphased. It was as if she had her speech all mapped out and nobody was going to throw her off course. She should have become a politician. She could be one of those annoying smart-arse people who had an answer for everything.

'Yeah, well, that's because you start off too intense.' I wasn't sure I appreciated a summary from Ellie about how crap I was in relationships. I could have stayed in Dorset, quite easily worked that one out for myself and saved myself the bother. 'I'm sure you've spun this poor girl in America a wonderful yarn. Mark my words, you'll do the same with her as you do with everybody else. Maybe if you took a step back and went with the flow you might get on a bit better. Just relax a bit.'

I heeded her last piece of advice and stopped myself from throttling her. Although she was hardly an expert in relationships herself it was tough that the majority of what she was saying was true.

'Yeah I suppose I do try too hard and it puts people off but that's hardly got anything to do with Nicola. I'm not going to Las Vegas to get hitched and move in with her.' Ellie pouted as if to suggest she wouldn't have been surprised. I carried on regardless. 'The reverse psychology thing just doesn't work for me anyway. If I try the standoffish bastard routine, turning up late and never calling it just results in me never hearing from them again.' I looked down at my shoes. 'I don't make a very convincing bastard in any case.'

'Oh Connor, You're a great guy, just very impatient and indecisive. It's so simple if you didn't get so wound up all the time. Geez, how come I can't figure out the men I date as easily? It's so unfair.'

'No, it's just that I'm rubbish and easy to figure out,' I shrugged. 'Hang on, though - if I'm so easy to figure out why do I have so many problems?'

Once again, Ellie had an answer lined up. 'No, your women

can't figure you out and that's when the shit hits the fan. I'll excuse them though. They haven't known you as long as I have. Anyway, who says you are rubbish?' Ellie smiled, 'I think you're great.'

'Well you're in the minority I'd guess.' I changed the subject before I spent too long wallowing in self-pity. I thought it was time to drop Bob's name into the conversation.

'I'm going to call him,' she said sheepishly. 'I've been so stupid.' I raised my eyebrows and frowned to acknowledge my agreement.

'You guys are great together. You really need to sort this whole mess out.'

'I've been stubborn,' she said sombrely.

'You have, yes,' I grinned.

'I'll call him tomorrow.'

'Good,' I sighed. Mission accomplished. The conversation turned horribly back onto me.

'Anyway, what are you going to do?' she asked.

'I have absolutely no idea.' Ellie then proceeded to remount her moral high horse and preach to me about the ways of women. According to the book of Ellie I needed to pick one hypothetical girl and make it clear to the others that we were just friends. I should stop trying to win everybody's heart and stop being a big girl's blouse. When I challenged her theory by asking what happened to leaving my options open we then moved onto option two. In this scenario I should tell all of the prospective suitors that I wasn't looking for a relationship, just companionship and sex. On balance I think I preferred option one. It sounded less complicated and more likely to work in practice than its rival.

'The trouble is have you got one to pick?' she said, 'they all sound pretty rubbish.'

'I have one in mind,' I said.

'Who, who?' shouted Ellie, excitedly jabbing me in the ribs. I shook my head.

'Don't tell me it's Nicola. You don't even know her.'

'No, it's not Nicola,' I said quietly.

'What you going to do about Arizona?'

'I don't know.'

'Can you cancel the ticket?' she said feverishly.

'Did I say I wasn't going?'

'But what about *the one*?'

'I don't think she's interested anyway.'

'Connor,' crooned Ellie, 'how do you know if you don't try? Who is it?' I refused to comment yet again. The conversation was beginning to do my head in. Ellie was going to ring Bob. My peace mission had succeeded. Anything else was superfluous. It was time to get pissed.

The house was full so there was a severe lack of beds for guests. Some of the girls had invited their friends over so even the sofas were taken. I eventually wedged myself in the hall in an uncompromising position. My feet were stuffed diagonally into the cupboard under the stairs so that I didn't protrude into the thoroughfare any more than was necessary. It also made me less liable to get kicked. Despite this precaution I woke up with a throbbing head. This wasn't due to being booted. It was more a mixture of the alcohol from the night before and the fact that the phone had been ringing constantly since around 6.30am. I estimated it must have rung about fifteen times by the time Mel got around to answering it at about 8am.

'No, I'm sorry, this isn't the chemist,' she said politely. The majority of the house had been disturbed by the phone by now and had decided to get up. Considering the ever-increasing amount of sleepy eyed human traffic that was trundling past my head I decided to do the same. We had breakfast and watched crap Sunday morning telly and still the phone kept ringing. Nobody could understand why we were getting so many calls for the chemist until around 10.30am. Mel choked on her mug of coffee.

'Oh,' she spluttered. 'I think I may have made a slight mistake.' The rest of us looked at her bemused whilst she hastily trawled through the local paper.

'What is it?' asked Ellie.

'I've just had a horrible thought,' said Mel, her eyes widening as she become conscious that her horrible thought was a reality. She gently put the newspaper down on the coffee table. Mel, the journalist had been in charge of putting the emergency chemist phone numbers in Saturday's paper. 'I must have had a funny five minutes. I've put our number in.' There was silence for a moment until the whole room burst into laughter.

Ellie rang me later that week to say everything was back on with Bob. I breathed a sigh of relief.

'We're going away for New Year as planned,' she said.

'Oh, great,' I said, 'anywhere nice?'

'Yes, we're off to Ireland,' she said triumphantly. Ellie had obviously not been too humble in her approach to Bob. I knew full well he'd been hankering towards going to Barcelona but Ellie had obviously got her way. 'You gonna come?' she asked innocently.

'Ellie, you know I'm going to the States,' I groaned.

'Don't be so silly. Why would you want to spend New Year with a complete stranger when you could spend it with your friends?'

'Errm, cus I've paid for it?' I retorted.

'Can't you get a refund?'

'Nope,' I hadn't checked but I was pretty sure I couldn't.

'Connor, can I be honest with you? Don't get mad …'

'Go on,' I hissed.

'You're an idiot.'

'Why thank you,' I was at my sarcastic best.

'Well you are.'

'Why, because I booked a flight to Arizona when there was nothing else on offer other than staying in on my own?' There was silence at the other end of the phone. 'I suppose I could forfeit hundreds of pounds and play Captain Gooseberry with you and Bob.'

'It's not just us going,' she said.

'Who else then?'

'Bob's going to ask Alan and Terry if they want to go …'

'Hmm, both in couples in one way or another.'

' … and some of the girls from the house might come along.' I paused for a second. 'Ah, so now you might be interested. Come on, who is it?'

'Who's what?' Luckily Ellie couldn't see me blushing.

'The one.'

'I'm not saying,' I suspected she'd go mental.

'It's Belle isn't it,' she gasped.

'No.'

'It is, it is,' she laughed excitedly, 'I knew it was.' This conversation of 'oh yes it is, oh no it isn't' went on for quite a while until I got so pissed off with Ellie heckling me that I blurted it out.

'It's Mel.'

'You're joking,' she laughed but soon stopped when she realised that maybe I wasn't. I remained silent and awaited the barrage of insults. It didn't take long. 'She's way too good for you.' It was hurtful but not unexpected.

'Thanks mate,' I said sarcastically.

'She'd chew you up and spit you out before you knew what hit you.' Normally I'd have been offended by Ellie's bluntness but for once I stood my ground.

'That might be so, but you told me to pick one and if I had to pick one, it would be her.'

'But …'

'But nothing. It's not whether you or anybody else thinks she's too good for me. You never mentioned anything about making do with second best. You asked me to pick. I pick her.'

'Yeah, but she won't …'

'And what makes you so sure?'

'She uses men who wear flash suits and drive sports cars. Men with money Connor.'

'Maybe she uses them cus she ultimately doesn't want an egotistical wanker?'

'Oh Connor you're so naïve.' I hated it when Ellie was patronising.

'No Ellie, what's the point in setting your sights lower so you're less likely to be knocked back? If I am, so be it, I'll move on, her loss.' Ellie changed her plan of attack.

'OK,' she conceded, 'but Mel wont be in Arizona will she.'

'Why, is she going to be in Ireland?' I hoped the answer was 'no'. Not because I didn't want to see her, I just didn't want to make things any more complicated than they already were. The reality was that Mel hadn't decided whether she was going yet. Although she fancied the idea, she'd partly committed to a friend who was staying in London. The jury was still out.

I must admit that the trip sounded very pleasant. Ellie had rented a cottage in Northern Ireland for Christmas and New Year. It slept six officially and anybody else would have to make do with the sofa or the floor. The rules according to Ellie were that she would accept a maximum of eight on a first come first served basis. The cost of the accommodation would be split among whoever went and we were to make our own way there. In the lead up to Christmas, the infamous eight changed on a daily basis. Ellie and Bob were obviously definitely going. Alan was going with Terry and Jimmy was going with Maria. I would have made seven but didn't want to commit in case Mel didn't want to be number eight. Timing was all-important. If anyone else expressed an interest then I'd be buggered. If I was the last one in it would mean Mel couldn't go. It was a nightmare. I was torn between Arizona and Ireland. I rang Ellie numerous times to get an update. This was about the fifth time this week.

'She's not going to think much of you if you go to Arizona for a mucky few days,' said Ellie referring to Mel.

'She'll still be here when I get back,'

'What if she goes to Ireland though and you decide to go through with Arizona?' She had a point. I don't think I'd have liked to have been in the States knowing Mel was in Ireland in an isolated cottage being single. It was infuriating. I had to make a decision.

'Is Mel likely to go?' I asked.

'Connor, for the millionth time, she's still undecided.'

'Well maybe she should make *her* mind up.'

'Maybe she would if you made yours up.'

'What's that supposed to mean?' I asked.

'Connor,' she whispered, 'she's keen.'

'You what?' I smiled.

'It's all the girls have talked about for the last few days.'

'You told her?' I asked half offended.

'I may have let it slip,' she sniggered. 'Anyway, that doesn't matter. If you must know, Mel's not going to go to Ireland unless she definitely knows you're going.'

'Why …' I started.

'But even then,' Ellie interrupted, 'she's not 100% sure if she can wriggle out of what she's already planned.' This didn't make anything any clearer or easier. There were a few moments' silence as I tried to weigh up the options. If I went to America, I'd spend New Year with a stranger. She could be a cracker and we could have a fantastic time in Las Vegas. She could on the other hand, turn out to be a minger. New Year might be more miserable than usual and I could fuck up any chances I had with Mel. If I went to Ireland, I'd lose my flight money to the States and Mel might not even go. I would however get to spend the New Year with my friends and there was a chance that Mel would turn up. Time was running out. I needed to sort a flight if I was going to Ireland and let Nicola know I'd changed my mind. Ireland was the safest option and possibly the most rewarding.

'OK, I'll go.' I could sense Ellie smirking on the other end of the phone. 'On one condition,' I said adamantly.

'Hmm, go on,' said Ellie.

'I'm number seven, right?'

'Yep.'

'I'll go if you cap the numbers. I don't want anyone else taking the number eight spot other than Mel. If Mel doesn't go we'll just have to share the cost of the cottage among seven instead of eight.' I was surprised that Ellie agreed but then she'd budgeted on the cost being split six ways in any case.

I decided to ring Nicola and tell her the news on a night that I could arrange a pre-Christmas drink with the boys down the pub. That way I could get pissed after receiving an earful 'Earful' was an understatement. She started off by saying she was hurt, upset and I'd let her down. That kind of response was expected and I took it on the chin. Then she went a bit cuckoo. I didn't expect her to say she considered me to be her boyfriend and ask how we were ever supposed to know if we were meant for one another. She started to cry uncontrollably and yelled down the phone.

‘I loved you Connor, how could you do this to me?’ I tried to explain we hadn’t actually met and maybe she was overreacting a bit but this just seemed to infuriate her more.

‘How can you say that?’ she screamed. ‘I just knew you were the one for me and now you’ve taken that away from me.’ Ironically, the fact that she went a little mad made the ordeal easier to stomach. It only went to prove I’d made the right decision. I now could look forward to Ireland.

‘How you getting there then?’ I asked Alan. I knew Ellie and Bob were spending nearly the entire Christmas period over there. They were going on the ferry and driving over. I was flying from Bournemouth to Dublin the day after Boxing Day but I wasn’t sure about the others.

‘Oh, didn’t you know, I’m not going,’ said Alan. My eyes flickered between Alan and Jimmy to see if this was a wind up. Nobody smiled.

‘He’s not going,’ repeated Jimmy. For some reason Alan had only just realised that if he went to the cottage for New Year he’d actually miss two Bournemouth games. As it stood at the moment I was going with two couples.

‘Belle and Dan are going instead,’ said Alan. Make that three couples. I wasn’t sure who Dan was but I guessed that Belle had acquired a partner.

‘Any news on Mel?’ I enquired. Alan and Jimmy nudged each other and grinned like two little schoolboys. I didn’t know whether to be more worried that they were acting like children or that there appeared to be some new found alliance between them. ‘So are you going to tell me?’

‘Dunno mate,’ said Jimmy, ‘but you’ll have done well for yourself if you manage to pull that one off.’

‘Hmm,’ I said thoughtfully. There was a pause before Alan blurted out one of his worrying conversational tangents.

‘Is it lucky or unlucky if a black cat crosses your path?’ he mulled. I looked at Jimmy and waited for the verbal onslaught. It didn’t come.

‘It depends on whether you trip over it or not,’ said Jimmy dryly.

‘I think it’s unlucky,’ I said anticipating a wave of belated expletives from Jimmy.

'Oh,' said Alan and the table went quiet. I looked at Jimmy. He was just leant back in his chair, exhaling cigarette smoke through his nose. I got the impression there was some sort of private joke going on that I wasn't aware of.

'Why Alan?' I said forcing the conversation, 'has one crossed your path?'

'No,' he said forcing a handful of crisps into his mouth, 'I had a dream about one.' I couldn't believe Jimmy wasn't going to seize on this.

'So it's a hypothetical black cat?' said Jimmy.

'Well, yes … and no. I just wondered if dreaming about one and actually seeing one amounted to the same thing.' I looked at Jimmy who seemed to be scratching his chin in thought. 'Now I come to think about it,' Alan continued 'it might have had a dab of white on its chin.' The table fell silent again. I decided that it was up to me to ask what the fuck Alan was going on about.

'Am I the only one who's a bit scared by this conversation?' I said shaking my head.

'What do you mean?' said Alan.

'Why are we having a conversation about a black cat which may not have actually been black and in reality, didn't actually ever cross your path?'

'Connor's right,' chirped Jimmy, 'I think it has to be jet black.' I was more confused than when we'd started. 'Anyway, I think it's about time you stopped dreaming about cats and started dreaming about pussy.'

'Why, is that good luck?' said Alan. I held my head in my hands.

'No,' chuckled Jimmy, 'but it's a start.' I didn't stick around long enough to get to the bottom of the black cat chronicles. I was guessing Alan suspected, for good or bad, it was some kind of omen for Bournemouth's form over the Christmas period. I made my way home and left Jimmy and Alan to tell respective stories about how great Maria and Terry were. I suppose I should have been grateful that the needle had gone from among us. Jimmy, I assumed, was settled with Maria and distinctly more mellow about everything and Alan didn't feel that he had to 'belong' anymore. The only one who seemed confused about everything was me. Living an ultimately single life interspersed with crap liaisons didn't seem to be the way forward somehow.

Chapter 43

'Where do I stand?' – The Montrose Avenue.

I always end up undertaking last minute Christmas shopping. I could possibly tolerate the crowds if I knew what I was looking for but I find myself, every year, jostling my way aimlessly through the throng of fellow shoppers getting more and more pissed off. It doesn't help that I stack the pressure on myself by insisting I buy unique and well thought out gifts. The trick is to buy people things that even they don't know they want, unusual yet appropriate. Seeing someone's indifferent face as they unwrap a CD or a box of chocolates fills me with dread.

This year I was less in the mood than normal. The closer it got to leaving for Ireland the more anxious I became. Whilst everyone else was excited about packing their gear and having a wonderful time, I was still wondering if Mel had made a decision. Two days before Ellie and Bob left, I thought I'd ring her.

'So,' I said

'So,' she echoed.

'Have you decided?' I held my breath.

'Yes.' she said. My stomach began to churn. After all the waiting I wasn't sure I wanted to know. 'I'm afraid I'm going to have to stay in London.'

'I see,' I murmured. There was a pause.

'Don't be like this Connor, you know I want to come to Ireland with you.'

'Well come then,' I said.

'I can't. I promised I'd stay with my friend and now she's split up with her boyfriend I feel as though I've got to stay.' I wondered if there was any truth in this at all. See, if I was Mel and I felt that strongly I would have suggested that her friend came with us (I'm sure Ellie could have accommodated one more) or asked if I'd like to spend New Year in London instead. Nothing was forthcoming.

'OK,' I said, 'well, I'll be in Ireland if you change your mind.'

'Connor, you're so sweet. Never say never babe.' I wasn't convinced. I gave it up as a bad job.

Ellie and Bob were leaving for Ireland the day before Christmas Eve. Jimmy and Maria were going up to London to join them on the drive to Holyhead. From there, they were catching the ferry to Dun Laoghaire and driving up to the North. Quite what Belle's arrangements were I wasn't sure. I was more engrossed in doing the rounds before I left from Bournemouth airport the day after Boxing Day. I went to my grandparents' in the Midlands for a couple of days and spent Christmas Day with my parents. Our traditional pre-Rebecca festive arrangements were reinstated. This involved opening our presents in the morning, Christmas dinner with all the trimmings and then a lazy afternoon watching telly and playing board games. This year was slightly different as Dad had been taking guitar lessons and proceeded to play *Jingle Bells*, very badly, over and over again until thankfully Mum said that maybe it was time to put the guitar away. Dad took 'putting the guitar away' to mean 'play another song'. We then had to listen to his own festive interpretation of *Wild Thing*. Mum eventually took the guitar off him. She fell asleep on the sofa in the afternoon whilst Dad and I settled down for a PlayStation marathon. It was an enjoyable day but I couldn't help wondering what the others were up to in Ireland.

I spent Boxing Day sorting through my presents. I assumed that my parents had bought me a guitar so that Dad and I could collaborate on a *Jingle Bells* duet the following year. I was sure we could pull it off. It's amazing how appreciative a captive audience can be. The deodorant and shower gel combination packs went in the bathroom (I'd three this year which was a record I think) whilst the boxer shorts and ties were neatly dispatched into the wardrobe. I packed in the afternoon, continually changing my mind as to what I should actually take. It's quite worrying how long simple tasks can last when you could faff for England. The decorations would be easy enough to take down when I got back. I hadn't made much of an effort. I didn't see the point. I was the only bugger who was going to see them in any case. A handful of cards lined the window sill, the largest of them being from the dealership where I'd bought my car. A piece of gold tinsel hung loosely around the light fitting and the tree stood bare in the corner of the room. I had decorated it but made the mistake of putting the lights and the rest of the ornaments on before checking that the lights actually worked. Needless to say they didn't, so I took the lights off to see if I could figure out what was wrong, which messed up the rest of the tree so I ended up taking everything off. The broken lights, tinsel and baubles remained in a heap at the base of the tree with a shallow covering of discarded pine needles.

Dad gave me a lift to the airport the following day. I checked my bag in and sat with him in the lounge as we waited for my flight. We didn't say much. I spent most of my time staring into space, or so I thought.

'Will you stop it?' said Dad.

'Eh?'

'Stop glancing at your phone, it's not going to increase the chances of her calling.'

'Oh, sorry,' I grunted. Admittedly I wasn't the best of company.

'Why don't you just ring the girl?' he said. I shrugged. 'Go and see her then.'

'Dad, I'm just about to get on a flight to Dublin.'

'Go and get your bags and come home,' he said sympathetically.

'I can't. I've made my decision. I've already cancelled Arizona. I'm going to Ireland.'

'OK, OK,' he said putting his hand on my shoulder. My flight was eventually called. 'I'll see you in a few days,' I said and made my way to the gate.

The coach journey from Dublin to Eniskillen was longer than the flight. I wasn't complaining though; the scenery was fantastic. Ellie and Bob came to pick me up from the coach station and we made our way to the cottage. Ellie had been right; it was in the middle of nowhere. The weather was cold and grey, which gave the place an eerie feel. They'd obviously had a lot of rain. Boggy fields surrounded the single storey stone cottage. Jimmy had the fire going and was snuggled on the sofa, which was to be my eventual bed, with Maria. I stopped in my tracks for a moment. I'd never seen Jimmy cuddled up with anyone before. It was only slightly less distressing than seeing Alan in the same position.

'You alright mate?' said Jimmy climbing to his feet and shaking my hand.

'Yes … fine thanks,'

'Good, good, do y'wanna drink?' he asked enthusiastically. I accepted, firstly due to the novelty factor of Jimmy actually asking, and secondly to allow him to demonstrate to Maria that he was actually house trained. I glanced round the room hoping to see Mel's face peeping around a doorway. It didn't materialise.

Considering the resource limitations, they'd made a damn sight better job of festively decorating the cottage than I'd made at home. I knelt down by the tree and unpacked the presents I'd brought with me. I wasn't sure if anyone had got me anything but I thought it better to come prepared just in case. Judging by piles of already opened presents, I was due to receive … fuck all.

'We may as well open them now,' said Bob scrabbling down on his hands and knees.

'Well,' I said reluctantly, 'it might be best we wait 'til Belle gets here. Then everyone will …'

'Why don't we open them on New Year's Eve?' said Ellie hastily.

'Yes, that sounds good,' said Maria mechanically. I think I was in on the female wavelength thing; it was embarrassing to open the presents now knowing that they had nothing to give me in return. If we opened them on New Year's Eve they would all have time to pick up something from the local shops. I wouldn't imagine the area was riddled with designer gift outlets but I suppose chocolates and more deodorant was better than bugger all.

It was a relaxing and very pleasant few days. Nobody got up

very early, which suited me fine as I was on the sofa. There wasn't much left of the mornings by the time everybody had queued for the bathroom and had a spot of breakfast. The afternoons weren't much busier, either spent down at the pub or around the fire. When the weather was a bit brighter (i.e. not raining) we ventured out. The scenery was breathtaking and the atmosphere relaxed. The local people were very friendly and I wasn't ever made to feel uncomfortable by being the only singleton. It was just what the doctor ordered.

Belle and Dan arrived on the day before New Year's Eve. They'd brought the car over in the same manner as the others. It was well into the afternoon by the time they'd unpacked and settled in. There was a general consensus that we'd explore the area immediately surrounding the cottage before it got dark. Bob and I vetoed the decision. We'd already had a vigorous muddy walk on one of the afternoons it had been raining when nobody else was willing to venture out. We opted instead for a drive to Eniskillen to find a pub for a quiet drink. If Maria hadn't been so adamant about wanting to go on the walk I think Jimmy would have joined us. We left the others to their ramble.

Bob insisted we take a detour into Southern Ireland on the way. You could mostly travel between North and South without knowing you'd crossed the border. The improved quality of the road surface was the only way you could tell you were back in Northern Ireland. The only blemish on the surroundings was the redundant border control towers. It sent a shiver up my spine just to look at them and think about how it must have been. There were still outbreaks of violence of course. I guess my perspective, as an Englishman living in England and only seeing the carnage from wild acts of terrorism on the news, was different from the people who actually lived there day in and day out. As we walked up the main road in Eniskillen reflecting on the past few days, I stopped in my tracks and put my hand across Bob's chest.

'What?' he said. He followed my gaze to a lightly smoking rubbish bin hanging on a lamppost about fifty yards in front of us. 'Let's go back,' he said worriedly, 'we passed a pub on the way down.' I looked feverishly up and down the road to see who was about. There were kids playing in the street and a couple of mums pushing pushchairs but no one had seemed to notice the bin, now bellowing smoke. 'Come on,' said Bob.

'Wait here,' I said jogging nervously towards the bin and into the adjacent shop.

'Wot will I getcha?' asked the guy behind the desk.

'It's the bin,' I gasped. 'I just thought I ought to tell someone.' The man seemed unimpressed by my increasingly hysterical behaviour. He slowly leaned over the counter to see flames licking out from its top.

'Dah,' he reached under the desk. 'It's juss dose bluddy kids,' he said, making his way out of the shop with a fire extinguisher. He seemed very sure but this didn't stop me from cringing as he sprayed water onto the flames. For all I knew he could have set something off and taken half the shop with him, me included. I peered through my fingers, relieved to see the man returning to the counter. 'Dare always throwing bluddy fag ends in dat bin,' he said shaking his head. 'Now, wot was it d'ya wanted?' I thought it best I bought a packet of cigarettes and made my way sheepishly out of the shop.

Chapter 44

'Your face,' laughed Bob as we eventually sat down with our pints of Guinness.

'I don't know what you're smiling at. I seem to remember you wanting to head in the opposite direction,' I retorted. In hindsight, why anyone would want to bomb a corner shop I don't know. I guess we were possibly more paranoid than the locals.

'Ah well, apart from the bomb scare it's been a good break eh?' chuckled Bob.

'Yes, very nice,' I sighed contentedly.

'Tomorrow should be a good crack too,' said Bob, 'eve of a new year and all.'

'Hmm,' I pondered, getting a twinge of my seasonal blues.

'Do you know what your problem is?' said Bob sensing my reflective mood.

'Enlighten me,' I said sarcastically.

'You spend too much time thinking about the past instead of working towards the future. You always get worse this time of year.' I nodded knowingly.

'I'm not sure I have that much to look forward to,' I said feeling deflated.

'And you're always so bloody pessimistic,' Bob laughed.

'A cynic is just a person who doesn't want to be disappointed again,' I said.

'A cynic is just a miserable git waiting for something crap to happen. Snap out of it mate. OK, you might not have concrete plans to look forward to but take a look at what you've got.' I gave him a bemused look. 'Geez Connor, you have your health, a good job, good friends, your own home, nice car … '

'And no girlfriend,' I interrupted.

'See there you go again,' he continued. 'Why do you always have to be so negative?'

'Because Bob, I'm no better off than I was twelve months ago.'

'I dunno how you can say that. The world is your oyster. Things could have been a lot worse you know. You kept the house; you weren't married; kids weren't involved.' I shuddered at the thought. 'You're free to do what you want.'

'Any old time?' I quipped. 'Wasn't that a song?'

'Connor, I'm being serious. Why don't you just enjoy being single and stop beating yourself up about everything.'

'That's easy for you to say,' I ranted, 'you have Ellie.'

'You'll find somebody too if you just take a step back and stop looking so damn hard.'

'Hang about …' Bob raised his finger and gave me a look that told me he hadn't finished his speech yet.

'Stop looking for things to go wrong; just deal with things as they arise; stop comparing everything to something that might have happened in the past and stop worrying about things which may or may not happen in the future.' I wasn't sure if I was supposed to be taking notes. I was actually quite offended. Was I really that irritating and transparent? 'And stop sulking when people are trying to help you,' he concluded with a smile.

'So in summary,' I joked, 'I've got to stop doing lots of things.'

'Yep,' said Bob nodding firmly. I wondered if it was knowing you'd found true happiness which made you view everything through rose coloured spectacles. That wasn't fair on Bob. A lot of what he said was true. I did spend too much time wallowing in self-pity and I reflected it was probably best I took onboard at least some of what Bob had said, for my own sanity if nothing else.

After Bob got his little pep talk out of the way we reverted to our 'two blokes sitting in a pub talking bollocks' routine until we had to ring Ellie and Jimmy to come and pick us up and retrieve the car. After a few more drinks back at the cottage, the sofa seemed especially comfy. I slept like a log.

It was a good job really. I opened my eyes the next morning to find myself being poked and prodded by the rest of the group.

'Come on lazy bones, get up,' said Ellie.

'What's the rush?' I questioned rubbing my eyes and yawning.

'It's the New Year,' said Ellie putting on the television.

'No,' I said patronisingly, 'It's the morning of New Year's Eve.'

'It's my New Year mate,' said Dan. The penny dropped as I turned to see him patriotically wearing an Australian rugby shirt.

'Are you really Australian?' I said naively. I had noticed the strange accent but as he wasn't particularly annoying I'd assumed he was from East Anglia.

'Duh,' said Ellie thumping her fist on her forehead. I blushed and made my way to the kitchen where I assumed they had acquired the punch they were holding.

'Quickly,' shouted Ellie from the lounge, 'you haven't got much time.' Celebrating the Australian New Year in the middle of the morning drinking punch whilst wrapped in a duvet didn't seem nearly as depressing as normal. We spent all day watching the telly and celebrating the New Year from all the different time zones all over the world. We were in various states of consciousness by the time it got to the evening.

'We haven't opened our presents,' slurred Ellie at about 11pm. I glanced round the room. The inebriated bodies didn't appear to give a shit about any presents. People seemed more content to save what little energy they had left for midnight. Ellie was the liveliest of the bunch, but then she'd had a nap in the afternoon. 'Chop chop,' she shouted clapping her hands and eventually finding her feet. I did my Father Christmas bit and foraged under the tree, carefully handing out the presents one by one. They were all last minute gifts, nothing particularly exciting but I guessed it was the thought that counted. I'd got a PlayStation game for Bob and a book on yoga for Ellie. She'd been on about taking it up for years. Not knowing Dan too well I thought it best to buy a joint present for him and Belle. They seemed to like the *Shine* CD's I'd got them. Maria was a tough one to buy for as well. I opted for a scarf. She seemed the arty scarf type.

Jimmy was last to open his, which was surprising seeing as he had the smallest gift. His eyes lit up as he could see I'd bought him a watch.

'I got you that to replace the one you broke in …' I faded out as I saw Jimmy's face turn white with horror. Maria was obviously still unaware we'd ever been to Amsterdam.

'Broke in where?' said Ellie. I panicked.

'*Sainsbury's*,' I blurted.

'*Sainsbury's*?' said Maria.

'You broke your watch in *Sainsbury's*?' said Bob. 'How on earth did you manage that?'

'I put my hand …' started Jimmy.

'He got his hand caught on one of the freezer doors. It was quite funny at the time.'

'You were with him?' asked Maria.

'Yeah,' we both said.

'Since when have you two ever gone shopping together?' said Bob.

'Well …' began Jimmy again.

'We only popped in for a can of drink and a sandwich, didn't we Jimmy?' I said. He nodded vigorously.

'Why were you delving in the freezers then?' This was

turning into an inquisition.

'What?' I mumbled.

'You said you broke it on the freezers.'

'No, I meant …' I started, trying desperately to think of something plausible.

'He meant the refrigerated whatnots,' Jimmy laughed nervously, 'not the actual freezers.'

'Yeah, I meant …' I started, trying to reinforce Jimmy's previous statement before Maria interrupted me.

'Why did you tell me you broke it at work?' she said.

'At work?' said Jimmy stalling for time.

'You heard me,' said Maria folding her arms.

'Oh, no … that was my other watch,' Jimmy laughed.

'So anyway, do you like it?' I asked him pointing at the box, trying to get off the subject of his previous watch.

'Yeah, yeah, it's great mate, thanks very much.'

'You're welcome,' I smiled. Bob eventually broke the silence that followed.

'Drink anyone?' he said cheerily. I was first to accept. Being on your mettle was far too sobering. The tension subsided as we got on with the more serious matter of drinking. It only then occurred to me that I hadn't actually received a present from anyone.

'Oh, I almost forgot.' said Ellie handing me a brightly decorated parcel. 'Here's your present from us.'

'It's a joint effort. We've all chipped in,' said Bob, 'including the girls back at the house.' I've never been one who's able to just unwrap a present. I have to tease myself first and try and guess. The problem is I'm normally right. You can then see the disappointment on the faces of the givers as you confidently speculate on the contents. You can't just come out with wild guesses though. It might look as though you were reeling off random items in the hope that one of them might be correct. It is much better to talk through your deductions as you go along and then present your conclusive answer. It's an art form. My prowess is legendary. I should stop doing it really because it just pisses people off, but I can't help myself.

'OK,' I said rubbing my chin as if I were contemplating

defusing a bomb. 'It's the size of a shoe box … but it's not shoes … too light.' I looked up to see everybody grinning at me. This was a tough one. I shook the box gently. There was no hint of any movement inside. It felt very much like an empty box; there wasn't any weight to it at all. I was stumped.

'Open it,' said Ellie excitedly.

'Yeah, get on with it or we'll be here 'til next bleeding New Year,' smirked Jimmy. I bowed to public opinion and hoped nobody noticed I didn't have a clue. I tore the wrapping off to reveal an Adidas shoebox. I opened the box to reveal … nothing, nothing except tattered bits of white tissue paper. I looked up at the group and shrugged.

'It's taped to the bottom,' said Jimmy and as I delved through the paper once more I could see an envelope stuck to the base of the box. I feverishly ripped it open to find a wedge of *Moss Bros* vouchers. 'That's so you can treat yourself to a new suit,' said Jimmy.

'Yeah, we don't want you turning up to our wedding in that awful *Miami Vice* number you usually wear,' chuckled Ellie, her laughter echoed by the rest of the group. The vouchers were wrapped in a note from Mel which simply read,

'Looking forward to seeing you in your suit. Have a great New Year and sorry I can't be there.'

'I think she might just take you as her partner if you scrub up alright,' said Bob. Again, there were playful murmurs from the others.

'Stranger things have happened Bob,' I said smiling, 'stranger things have happened.'

'And that's to remind you what great friends you have,' said Ellie. I delved down into the envelope to find a picture of all of us stood outside the cottage. 'Who says you haven't come anywhere in the last twelve months?'

'Thanks,' I said looking up at the others, half choked. 'I really appreciate this.'

'I hate to break this up,' said Jimmy, 'but before we all drown in sick sentimentality …' he continued, uncomfortably looking at his watch without wanting to ignite the whole 'watch' debate again.

'We'd better set the fireworks up,' squealed Ellie.

'Jimmy, Dan, you do the business. Connor and I'll charge the glasses,' said Bob.

'So how ya doing mate?' said Bob putting his arm around me firmly.

'Errm, surprisingly good,' I nodded.

'No regrets about not going to America or being with a load of couples?'

'Naah,' I said with a grin, 'it's been grand,' and it had. Maybe it was the company; possibly the location; it could even have been the copious amounts of alcohol I'd consumed in the last twenty-four hours (although alcohol never usually did the trick where New Year blues were concerned). Whatever it was, everything felt good. It felt right. 'It's not quite the bright lights of Las Vegas but it'll do me,' I said. We filled seven glasses with champagne and wandered out into the brisk night air. Jimmy and Dan had just about finished setting up the fireworks. We counted down to midnight in unison and raised our glasses as the New Year became a reality. The horizon sparkled with a multitude of colours as rockets and bangers were let off in the distance.

'Go on Connor,' said Ellie, 'fire us into 1999.' I fumbled in my pocket for my lighter and carefully lit the fuses of our makeshift fireworks display. We cheered, jigged and sank the champagne as a plethora of colour flashed and twinkled over our heads. Being the soppy kind of idiot that I am I couldn't help feeling poignant. Bob was right; it wasn't very constructive to dwell on shit things that had happened in the past and to assume that more crap was to come. Yeah, sure there'd be quarrels and upset, trials and tribulations, but every life has them. I had a warm glow for those few moments in a boggy field in Northern Ireland. Everything was going to be OK. It just remained to be seen if I could keep this feeling running well into the New Year and deal with whatever the next twelve months had to throw at me.

'Good Souls' – Starsailor